They called their country the Beautiful Land, and they were right. It perched on the edge of the continent. Before the Beautiful Land stretched the broad ocean, which few dared to cross; behind it stood the steep Rising, a cliff so high and sheer that few dared to climb. And in such isolation the people, who called themselves, of course, the Beautiful People, lived splendid lives.

Not all were rich, of course. And not all were happy. But there was such a majesty in living in the Beautiful Land that the poverty could easily be missed by the undiscerning eye, and misery seemed so very fleeting.

Except to Kiren.

To Kiren, misery was the way of life. For though she lived in a rich house with servants and had, it seemed, anything she could possibly want, she was deeply miserable most of the time. For this was a land where cursing and blessing and magic worked— not always, and not always in the way the person doing it might have planned—but sometimes the cursing worked, and in her case it had.

—from "The Porcelain Salamander"

Tor books by Orson Scott Card

*

Ender's Game
The Folk of the Fringe
Future on Fire (editor)
Future on Ice (editor)*
Saints
Maps in a Mirror:
   The Short Fiction of Orson Scott Card
Songmaster
Speaker for the Dead
The Worthing Saga
Wyrms
Xenocide

THE TALES OF ALVIN MAKER

Seventh Son
Red Prophet
Prentice Alvin

*forthcoming

ORSON
SCOTT CARD
MONKEY SONATAS

A TOM DOHERTY ASSOCIATES BOOK
NEW YORK

MONKEY SONATAS

Copyright © 1992 by Orson Scott Card

Previously published as book three of *Maps in a Mirror* by Orson Scott Card (Tor, 1990)

Cover art by Peter Scanlan

A Tor Book
Published by Tom Doherty Associates, Inc.
175 Fifth Avenue
New York, N.Y. 10010

Tor ® is a registered trademark of Tom Doherty Associates, Inc.

ISBN: 0-812-52367-9

First edition: March 1993

Printed in the United States of America

0 9 8 7 6 5 4 3 2 1

To Charlie Ben,
who can fly

CONTENTS

Introduction   *1*

Unaccompanied Sonata   9
  Omni, March 1979

A Cross-Country Trip to Kill Richard Nixon   33
  Chrysalis 7, ed. Roy Torgeson (Zebra, 1979)

The Porcelain Salamander   55
  Unaccompanied Sonata and Other Stories,
  Dial Press 1981

Middle Woman   67
  Dragons of Darkness, ed. Orson Scott Card
  (Ace, 1981; as Byron Walley)

The Bully and the Beast   73
  Other Worlds 1, ed. Roy Torgeson
  (Zebra Books, 1979)

The Princess and the Bear   139
  Berkley Showcase 1, ed. Victoria Schochet
  (Berkley, 1980)

Sandmagic   177
  Swords Against Darkness 4, ed. Andrew J. Offutt
  (Zebra, 1979)

The Best Day   199
  Woman of Destiny, ed. Roy Torgeson
  (Berkley, 1984; as Dinah Kirkham)

A Plague of Butterflies   205
  Amazing, November 1981

The Monkeys Thought 'Twas All in Fun   231
  Analog, May 1979

Afterword   289

INTRODUCTION

I DON'T BELIEVE IN the "collective unconscious," not in the Jungian way I've seen it used. But I do believe that it is in large part through shared stories that communities create themselves and bind themselves together.

It begins with the way we establish our identity, which is intimately tied to our discovery of causality. All of nature relies on mechanical causation: Stimulus A causes response B. But almost as soon as we acquire language, we are taught an entirely different system: purposive causation, in which a person engaged in behavior B in order to accomplish result A. Never mind that it was X and Y, not A, that resulted. When it comes to evaluating human behavior, we quickly learn that it is the story we believe about a person's *purpose* that counts most.

You know the phrases of moral evaluation: "Why did you do that?" "I didn't mean to." "I was just trying to surprise you." "Do you want me to be humiliated in front of everybody?" "I don't work my fingers to the bone so you can go out and . . ." All of these sentences contain or invite stories; it is the stories we believe about our behavior that give them their moral value. Even the cruelest or weakest among us must find stories that excuse—or even ennoble—their own character flaws. On the day I'm writing this, the mayor of a major American city, arrested for using cocaine, actually stood before the cameras and said, in effect, "I guess I've just been working so hard serving the people that I didn't have time to take care of my own needs." What a story— smoking crack as an altruistic, selfless endeavor. The point is not whether the story is true; the point is that all human beings engage in storytelling about themselves, creating the story they want to believe about themselves, the story they actually believe about themselves, the story they want *others* to believe about them, the stories they believe about others, and the stories that they are afraid *might* be true about themselves and others.

Our very identity is a collection of the stories we have come to believe about ourselves. We are bombarded with the stories of others about us; even our memories of our own lives are filtered through the stories we have constructed to interpret those past events. We revise our identity by revising our self-story. Traditional psychotherapies rely heavily on this process: You *thought* you were trying to do *X*, but in fact your unconscious purpose was *Y*. Ah, now I understand myself! But I think not—I think that in the moment of believing the new story you simply *revised* your identity. I am no longer a person who tries to do *X*. I am a person who was being driven to do *Y*, without even realizing it. You remain the same person, who performed the same acts. Only the story has been changed.

All this deals with individual identities, and the

tragedy of the individual is that the true cause of his behavior remains forever unknowable. And if we cannot know ourselves, true understanding of any other human being is permanently out of reach. Other people's behavior must be, in that case, completely unpredictable. And yet no human community could ever exist if we had no mechanism to enable us to feel safe in trusting other people's behavior to follow certain predictable patterns. And these predictable patterns can't arise solely from personal experience—we must know, with some certainty, *before* we have observed another member of the community for any length of time, what he or she is likely to do in most situations.

There are two kinds of stories that not only give us the illusion of understanding other people's behavior, but also go a long way toward making that illusion true. Each community has its own epic: a complex of stories about what it means to be a member of that community. These stories can arise from shared experience: Have you ever heard two Catholics reminisce about catechism or being taught in Catholic school by nuns? Or they can arise from what is perceived to be a common heritage, spreading a sense of community identity across space and time. Thus it is that Americans feel there is nothing incongruous about referring to Washington as "our" first president, even though no living American was present for his administration and most Americans have precious few ancestors who lived here during that time. Thus it is that an American living in Los Angeles can hear of something that happened in Springfield, Illinois, or Springfield, Massachusetts, and say, "Only here in America . . ."

Of course, membership in communities is never absolute. The same person could just as easily say, "We sure aren't like that here in California" or "here in L.A.," thus asserting the epic of another community. But the more important a community is to us, the more power its stories have in forming our view of the world—and in shaping our own behavior. I don't think my children are the only ones who've heard prescriptive epic stories like this one: "I don't care what other people's children do. In *our* family we ..." Every community's epic includes shibboleth stories—stories that define what members do and do not do. "No good Baptist would ever ..." "... just like a true American." And the stories that define a person's individual identity are often interpreted by the role that person plays within the community. "You make us all so proud of you, son." "An outstanding role model for young ———s." "I just wish other young people would be more like you." "I hope you're proud of the example you're setting for the other kids." "Now everybody's going to think all us blacks/Rotarians/Jews/Americans are like you!" Thus we not only are defined by the epic stories of the communities we belong to, but also help revise the community's epic stories by our behavior. (If I were going into this in detail, I'd talk about the role of outsiders in shaping a community's epic, and also about negative epic. But this is an essay, not a book in itself.)

The second category of story that shapes human behavior so that we can live together is not perceived as being tied to a particular community. It is mythic; those who believe in the story believe that it defines the way *human beings* behave. These stories are not really about how this character or that character behaved in a certain situation. They are about how *people* behave in such situations.

All storytelling contains elements of the particular, the epic, and the mythic. Fiction and scripture are both uniquely suited to telling mythic tales, however, because by definition fiction is *not* tied to particular people in the real world, and by definition scripture is perceived by its believers to be the universal truth rather than being merely and particularly true, the way history is usually received. That fiction and scripture are also inevitably epic, reflecting values and assumptions of the community out of which they arose, is true but not terribly important, for their audience *believes* mythic stories to be universal and, over time, comes to behave as if they *were* universal.

But fiction is not all equally mythic. Some fiction is quite particular, tied to a time and place and even characters in the real world. Thus historical fiction or contemporary realistic fiction with a strong sense of place can lead the reader to say, "Those people certainly were/are strange," rather than the more mythic response, "People certainly are strange," or the even more mythic response, "I never knew people were like that," or the ultimate mythic response, "Yes, that's how people are."

It might seem then that fiction becomes more mythic as it is divorced from identifiable real-world patterns, but it is not really the disconnection from reality that makes fiction mythic—if that were so, our myths would all be of madmen. Rather a story becomes more mythic as it connects to things that transcend reality. Tolkien's Middle Earth is so thoroughly created in *The Lord of the Rings* that the wealth of detail makes readers feel as though they had visited in a real place; but it is a place where human behavior takes on enormous importance, so that moral issues (the goodness or evil of a person's choices and actions) and causal issues (why things happen; the way the world works) take on far greater clarity. We find in Aragorn, not just that he is noble, but Nobility. We find in Frodo, not just that he is willing to bear a difficult burden, but Acceptance. And Samwise is not just a faithful servant, but also the personification of Service.

Thus it is in fantasy that we can most easily explore, not human behaviors, but Humanity. And in exploring it, we also define it; and in defining, invent it. Those of us who have received a story and believed in its truth (even if we don't believe in its factuality) carry those memories inside us and, if we care enough about the tale, act out the script it provides us. Because I remember standing at the Cracks of Doom, and because I remember experiencing it through Sam Gamgee's eyes, I clearly remember seeing that those who reach for power are possessed by it, and if they are not utterly destroyed by it, they lose part of themselves in getting free. I doubt that in crucial situations I'll summon up the memory of *Lord of the Rings* and consciously use it as a guide to my behavior—who has time for such involved mental processes when a choice is urgent, anyway? But unconsciously I remember being a person who made certain choices, and at that unconscious level I don't believe that I—or anyone—distinguishes between personal and community memories. They are all stories, and we act out the ones we believe in and care about most, the ones that have become part of us.

While I have been speaking about what fantasy *can* be—a particularly powerful source of mythic stories—it is worth pointing out that most fantasy, like most other kinds of fiction, doesn't live up to its potential. Furthermore, because it is to be received and acted upon unconsciously, the most successful fantasy is not often that which *looks* most mythic; often the most powerful fantasies are those that seem to be very realistic and particular. I think this is part of the reason that Tolkien shunned allegory. Consciously figured storytelling is received intellectually; it is never as powerful as stories whose symbols and figures—whose mythic connections— are received unconsciously. And I've come to believe that the most successful mythic writing is that story-telling in which the author was unconscious of his or her most powerful mythic elements.

So, while the best fantasy will have a powerful mythic effect, the most successful fantasists are not those who set out to write myth. Rather, the best fantasies come, I think, from storytellers who strive to create a particular story very well—but who use settings and events that give great freedom to their imagination, so that mythic elements can arise from their unconscious and play a strong role in the story. A fantasist who works from a deliberate plan will almost never achieve as much as the fantasist who is constantly surprised by the best moments in his or her stories.

You can see, then, that I'm not defining *fantasy* the way the word is used in contemporary publishing. When publishers speak of *fantasy* they generally mean stories set in a kind of pseudo-medieval world in which some kind of magic plays a role. Certainly good mythic fantasy can still be written in that kind of setting; but since such a world has been a staple of romance since before Chaucer, one can hardly credit most authors who work in it with having allowed their imagination to play a large role in their writing. Most such "fantasists" tuck their imagination away somewhere before they enter the mythic market-place; they have come to buy, not to sell.

It's worth pointing out that works of derivative fantasists often sell very well; there is a large audience that buys fantasy in order to have their pre-existing vision of The Way Things Work reaffirmed. And some quite brilliant fantasists remain obscure, because their mythic universe is so challenging that few readers are happy to dwell in it. But when a fantasist imagines well—and writes evocatively—many people drink in the story as if it were water, and their lives till then a vast desert in which they wandered without ever realizing how much they thirsted.

The real fantasists are not content to echo other writers' myths. They must discover their own. They venture into the most dangerous, uncharted places in the human soul, where existing stories don't yet explain what people think and feel and do. In that frightening place they find a mirror that lets them glimpse a true image. Then they return and hold up the mirror, and unlike mirrors in the real world, this one holds the storyteller's image for just a fleeting moment, just long enough for us also to glimpse the long-shadowed soul that brightly lingers there. In that moment we make the mythic connection; for that moment we *are* another person; and we carry that rare and precious understanding with us until we die.

And what am I? Like most who attempt fantasy, I imagine that I am doing true Imagining; like most, I am usually echoing other people's visions. There's always the hope, though, that at least some readers will dip into the old dry well and find new water there, seeped in from an undiscovered spring.

UNACCOMPANIED SONATA

TUNING UP

WHEN CHRISTIAN HAROLDSEN was six months old, preliminary tests showed a predisposition toward rhythm and a keen awareness of pitch. There were other tests, of course, and many possible routes still open to him. But rhythm and pitch were the governing signs of his own private zodiac, and already the reinforcement began. Mr. and Mrs. Haroldsen were provided with tapes of many kinds of sound, and instructed to play them constantly, waking or sleeping.

When Christian Haroldsen was two years old, his seventh battery of tests pinpointed the future he would inevitably follow. His creativity was exceptional, his curiosity insatiable, his understanding of music so intense that the top of all the tests said "Prodigy."

Prodigy was the word that took him from his parents' home to a house in a deep deciduous forest where winter was savage and violent and summer a brief desperate eruption of green. He grew up cared for by unsinging servants, and the only music he was allowed to hear was birdsong, and windsong, and the cracking of winter wood; thunder, and the faint cry of golden leaves as they broke free and tumbled to the earth; rain on the roof and the drip of water from icicles; the chatter of squirrels and the deep silence of snow falling on a moonless night.

These sounds were Christian's only conscious music; he grew up with the symphonies of his early years only a distant and impossible-to-retrieve memory. And so he learned to hear music in unmusical things—for he had to find music, even when there was none to find.

He found that colors made sounds in his mind; sunlight in summer a blaring chord; moonlight in winter a thin mournful wail; new green in spring a low murmur in almost (but not quite) random rhythms; the flash of a red fox in the leaves a gasp of startlement.

And he learned to play all those sounds on his Instrument.

In the world were violins, trumpets, clarinets and krumhorns, as there had been for centuries. Christian knew nothing of that. Only his Instrument was available. It was enough.

One room in Christian's house, which he had alone most of the time, he lived in: a bed (not too soft), a chair and table, a silent machine that cleaned him and his clothing, and an electric light.

The other room contained only his Instrument. It was a console with many keys and strips and levers and bars, and when he touched any part of it, a sound came out. Every key made a different sound; every point on the strips made a different pitch; every lever modified the tone; every bar altered the structure of the sound.

When he first came to the house, Christian played (as children will) with the Instrument, making strange and funny noises. It was his only playmate; he learned it well, could produce any sound he wanted to. At first he delighted in loud, blaring tones. Later he began to play with soft and loud, and to play two sounds at once, and to change those two sounds together to make a new sound, and to play again a sequence of sounds he had played before.

Gradually, the sounds of the forest outside his house found their way into the music he played. He learned to make winds sing through his Instrument; he learned to make summer one of the songs he could play at will; green with its infinite variations was his most subtle harmony; the birds cried out from his Instrument with all the passion of Christian's loneliness.

And the word spread to the licensed Listeners:

"There's a new sound north of here, east of here; Christian Haroldsen, and he'll tear out your heart with his songs."

The Listeners came, a few to whom variety was everything first, then those to whom novelty and vogue mattered most, and at last those who valued beauty and passion above everything else. They came, and stayed out in Christian's woods, and listened as his music was played through perfect speakers on the roof of his house. When the music stopped, and Christian came out of his house, he could see the Listeners moving away; he asked, and was told why they came; he marveled that the things he did for love on his Instrument could be of interest to other people.

He felt, strangely, even more lonely to know that he could sing to the Listeners and yet would never be able to hear their songs.

"But they have no songs," said the woman who came to bring him food every day. "They are Listeners. You are a Maker. You have songs, and they listen."

"Why?" asked Christian, innocently.

The woman looked puzzled. "Because that's what they want most to do. They've been tested, and they are happiest as Listeners. You are happiest as a Maker. Aren't you happy?"

"Yes," Christian answered, and he was telling the truth. His life was perfect, and he wouldn't change anything, not even the sweet sadness of the backs of the Listeners as they walked away at the end of his songs.

Christian was seven years old.

FIRST MOVEMENT

For the third time the short man with glasses and a strangely inappropriate mustache dared to wait in the underbrush for Christian to come out. For the third time he was overcome by the beauty of the song that had just ended, a mournful symphony that made the short man with glasses feel the pressure of the leaves above him even though it was summer and they had months left before they would fall. The fall is still inevitable, said Christian's song; through all their life the leaves hold within them the power to die, and that must color their life. The short man with glasses wept—but when the song ended and the other Listeners moved away, he hid in the brush and waited.

This time his wait was rewarded. Christian came out of his house, and walked among the trees, and came toward where the short man with glasses waited. The short man admired the easy, unpostured way that Christian walked. The composer looked to be about thirty, yet there was something childish in the way he looked around him, the way his walk was aimless, and prone to stop just so he could touch (not break) a fallen twig with his bare toes.

"Christian," said the short man with glasses.

Christian turned, startled. In all these years, no Listener had ever spoken to him. It was forbidden. Christian knew the law.

"It's forbidden," Christian said.

"Here," the short man with glasses said, holding out a small black object.

"What is it?"

The short man grimaced. "Just take it. Push the button and it plays."

"Plays?"

"Music."

Christian's eyes went wide. "But that's forbidden. I can't have my creativity polluted by hearing other musicians' work. That would make me imitative and derivative instead of original."

"Reciting," the man said. "You're just reciting that. This is the music of Bach." There was reverence in his voice.

"I can't," Christian said.

And then the short man shook his head. "You don't know. You don't know what you're missing. But I heard it in your song when I came here years ago, Christian. You want this."

"It's forbidden," Christian answered, for to him the very fact that a man who knew an act was forbidden still wanted to perform it was astounding, and he couldn't get past the novelty of it to realize that some action was expected of him.

There were footsteps and words being spoken in the distance, and the short man's face became frightened. He ran at Christian, forced the recorder into his hands, then took off toward the gate of the preserve.

Christian took the recorder and held it in a spot of sunlight through the leaves. It gleamed dully. "Bach," Christian said. Then, "Who is Bach?"

But he didn't throw the recorder down. Nor did he give the recorder to the woman who came to ask him what the short man with glasses had stayed for. "He stayed for at least ten minutes."

"I only saw him for thirty seconds," Christian answered.

"And?"

"He wanted me to hear some other music. He had a recorder."

"Did he give it to you?"

"No," Christian said. "Doesn't he still have it?"

"He must have dropped it in the woods."

"He said it was Bach."

"It's forbidden. That's all you need to know. If you should find the recorder, Christian, you know the law."

"I'll give it to you."

She looked at him carefully. "You know what would happen if you listened to such a thing."

Christian nodded.

"Very well. We'll be looking for it, too. I'll see you tomorrow, Christian. And next time somebody stays after, don't talk to him. Just come back in the house and lock the doors."

"I'll do that," Christian said.

When she left, he played his Instrument for hours. More Listeners came, and those who had heard Christian before were surprised at the confusion in his song.

There was a summer rainstorm that night, wind and rain and thunder, and Christian found that he could not sleep. Not from the music of the weather—he'd slept through a thousand such storms. It was the recorder that lay behind the Instrument against the wall. Christian had lived for nearly thirty years surrounded only by this wild, beautiful place and the music he himself made. But now.

Now he could not stop wondering. Who was Bach? Who *is* Bach? What is his music? How it is different from mine? Has he discovered things that I don't know?

What is his music?

What is his music?

What is his music?

Until at dawn, when the storm was abating and the wind had died, Christian got out of his bed, where he had not slept but only tossed back and forth all night, and took the recorder from its hiding place and played it.

At first it sounded strange, like noise, odd sounds that had nothing to do with the sounds of Christian's life. But the patterns were clear, and by the end of the recording, which was not even a half-hour long, Christian had mastered the idea of fugue and the sound of the harpsichord preyed on his mind.

Yet he knew that if he let these things show up in his music, he would be discovered. So he did not try a fugue. He did not attempt to imitate the harpsichord's sound.

And every night he listened to the recording, for many nights, learning more and more until finally the Watcher came.

The Watcher was blind, and a dog led him. He came to the door and because he was a Watcher the door opened for him without his even knocking.

"Christian Haroldsen, where is the recorder?" the Watcher asked.

"Recorder?" Christian asked, then knew it was hopeless, and took the machine and gave it to the Watcher.

"Oh, Christian," said the Watcher, and his voice was mild and sorrowful. "Why didn't you turn it in without listening to it?"

"I meant to," Christian said. "But how did you know?"

"Because suddenly there are no fugues in your work. Suddenly your songs have lost the only Bach-like thing about them. And you've stopped experimenting with new sounds. What were you trying to avoid?"

"This," Christian said, and he sat down and on his first try duplicated the sound of the harpsichord.

"Yet you've never tried to do that until now, have you?"

"I thought you'd notice."

"Fugues and harpsichord, the two things you noticed first—and the only things you didn't absorb into your music. All your other songs for these last weeks have been tinted and colored and influenced by Bach. Except that there was no fugue, and there was no harpsichord. You have broken the law. You were put here because you were a genius, creating new things with only nature for your inspiration. Now, of course, you're derivative, and truly new creation is impossible for you. You'll have to leave."

"I know," Christian said, afraid yet not really understanding what life outside his house would be like.

"We'll train you for the kinds of jobs you can pursue now. You won't starve. You won't die of boredom. But because you broke the law, one thing is forbidden to you now."

"Music."

"Not all music. There is music of a sort, Christian, that the common people, the ones who aren't Listeners, can have. Radio and television and record music. But living music and new music—those are forbidden to you. You may not sing. You may not play an instrument. You may not tap out a rhythm."

"Why not?"

The Watcher shook his head. "The world is too perfect, too at peace, too happy for us to permit a misfit who broke the law to go about spreading discontent. The common people make casual music of a sort, knowing nothing better because they haven't the aptitude to learn it. But if you—never mind. It's the law. And if you make more music, Christian, you will be punished drastically. Drastically."

Christian nodded, and when the Watcher told him to come, he came, leaving behind the house and the woods and his Instrument. At first he took it calmly, as the inevitable punishment for his infraction; but he had little concept of punishment, or of what exile from his Instrument would mean.

Within five hours he was shouting and striking out at anyone who came near him, because his fingers craved the touch of the Instrument's keys and levers and strips and bars, and he could not have them, and now he knew that he had never been lonely before.

It took six months before he was ready for normal life. And when he left the Retraining Center (a small building, because it was so rarely used), he looked tired, and years older, and he didn't smile at anyone. He became a delivery truck driver, because the tests said that this was a job that would least grieve him, and least remind him of his loss, and most engage his few remaining aptitudes and interests.

He delivered doughnuts to grocery stores.

And at night he discovered the mysteries of alcohol, and the alcohol and the doughnuts and the truck and his dreams were enough that he was, in his way, content. He had no anger in him. He could live the rest of his life this way, without bitterness.

He delivered fresh doughnuts and took the stale ones away with him.

SECOND MOVEMENT

"With a name like Joe," Joe always said, "I had to open a bar and grill, just so I could put up a sign saying Joe's Bar and Grill." And he laughed and laughed, because after all Joe's Bar and Grill was a funny name these days.

But Joe was a good bartender, and the Watcher had put him in the right kind of place. Not in a big city, but in a smaller town; a town just off the freeway, where truck drivers often came; a town not far from a large city, so that interesting things were nearby to be talked about and worried about and bitched about and loved.

Joe's Bar and Grill was, therefore, a nice place to come, and many people came there. Not fashionable people, and not drunks, but lonely people and friendly people in just the right mixture. "My clients are like a good drink, just enough of this and that to make a new flavor that tastes better than any of the ingredients." Oh, Joe was a poet, he was a poet of alcohol and like many another person these days, he often said, "My father was a lawyer, and in the old days I would have probably ended up a lawyer, too, and I never would have known what I was missing."

Joe was right. And he was a damn good bartender, and he didn't wish he were anything else, and so he was happy.

One night, however, a new man came in, a man with a doughnut delivery truck and a doughnut brand name on his uniform. Joe noticed him because silence clung to the man like a smell—wherever he walked, people sensed it, and though they scarcely looked at him, they lowered their voices, or stopped talking at all, and they got reflective and looked at the walls and the mirror behind the bar. The doughnut delivery man sat in a corner and had a watered-down drink that meant he intended to stay a long time and didn't want his alcohol intake to be so rapid that he was forced to leave early.

Joe noticed things about people, and he noticed that this man kept looking off in the dark corner where the piano stood. It was an old, out-of-tune monstrosity from the old days (for this had been a bar for a long time) and Joe wondered why the man was fascinated by it. True, a lot of Joe's customers had been interested, but they had always walked over and plunked on the keys, trying to find a melody, failing with the out-of-tune keys, and finally giving up. This man, however, seemed almost afraid of the piano, and didn't go near it.

At closing time, the man was still there, and then, on a whim, instead of making the man leave, Joe turned off the piped-in music and turned off most of the lights, and then went over and lifted the lid and exposed the grey keys.

The doughnut delivery man came over to the piano. *Chris*, his nametag said. He sat and touched a single key. The sound was not pretty. But the man touched all the keys one by one, and then touched them in different orders, and all the time Joe watched, wondering why the man was so intense about it.

"Chris," Joe said.

Chris looked up at him.

"Do you know any songs?"

Chris's face went funny.

"I mean, some of those old-time songs, not those fancy ass-twitchers on the radio, but *songs*. 'In a Little Spanish Town.' My mother sang that one to me." And Joe began to sing, "In a little Spanish town, 'twas on a night like this. Stars were peek-a-booing down, 'twas on a night like this."

Chris began to play as Joe's weak and toneless

baritone went on with the song. But it wasn't an accompaniment, not anything Joe could call an accompaniment. It was instead an opponent to his melody, an enemy to it, and the sounds coming out of the piano were strange and unharmonious and by God beautiful. Joe stopped singing and listened. For two hours he listened, and when it was over he soberly poured the man a drink, and poured one for himself, and clinked glasses with Chris the doughnut delivery man who could take that rotten old piano and make the damn thing sing.

Three nights later Chris came back, looking harried and afraid. But this time Joe knew what would happen (had to happen) and instead of waiting until closing time, Joe turned off the piped-in music ten minutes early. Chris looked up at him pleadingly. Joe misunderstood—he went over and lifted the lid to the keyboard and smiled. Chris walked stiffly, perhaps reluctantly, to the stool and sat.

"Hey, Joe," one of the last five customers shouted, "closing early?"

Joe didn't answer. Just watched as Chris began to play. No preliminaries this time; no scales and wanderings over the keys. Just power, and the piano was played as pianos aren't meant to be played; the bad notes, the out-of-tune notes were fit into the music so that they sounded right, and Chris's fingers, ignoring the strictures of the twelve-tone scale, played, it seemed to Joe, in the cracks.

None of the customers left until Chris finished an hour and a half later. They all shared that final drink, and went home shaken by the experience.

The next night Chris came again, and the next, and the next. Whatever private battle had kept him away for the first few days after his first night of playing, he had apparently won it or lost it. None of Joe's business. What Joe cared about was the fact that when Chris played the piano, it did things to him that music had never done, and he wanted it.

The customers apparently wanted it, too. Near closing time people began showing up, apparently just to hear Chris play. Joe began starting the piano music earlier and earlier, and he had to discontinue the free drinks after the playing because there were so many people it would have put him out of business.

It went on for two long, strange months. The delivery van pulled up outside, and people stood aside for Chris to enter. No one said anything to him; no one said anything at all, but everyone waited until he began to play the piano. He drank nothing at all. Just played. And between songs the hundreds of people in Joe's Bar and Grill ate and drank.

But the merriment was gone. The laughter and the chatter and the camaraderie were missing, and after a while Joe grew tired of the music and wanted to have his bar back the way it was. He toyed with the idea of getting rid of the piano, but the customers would have been angry at him. He thought of asking Chris not to come anymore, but he could not bring himself to speak to the strange silent man.

And so finally he did what he knew he should have done in the first place. He called the Watchers.

They came in the middle of a performance, a blind Watcher with a dog on a leash, and a Watcher with no ears who walked unsteadily, holding to things for balance. They came in the middle of a song, and did not wait for it to end. They walked to the piano and closed the lid gently, and Chris withdrew his fingers and looked at the closed lid.

"Oh, Christian," said the man with the seeing-eye dog.

"I'm sorry," Christian answered. "I tried not to."

"Oh, Christian, how can I bear doing to you what must be done?"

"Do it," Christian said.

And so the man with no ears took a laser knife from his coat pocket and cut off Christian's fingers and thumbs, right where they rooted into his hands. The laser cauterized and sterilized the wound even as it cut, but still some blood spattered on Christian's uniform. And, his hands now meaningless palms and useless knuckles, Christian stood and walked out of Joe's Bar and Grill. The people made way for him again, and they listened intently as the blind Watcher said, "That was a man who broke the law and was forbidden to be a Maker. He broke the law a second time, and the law insists that he be stopped from breaking down the system that makes all of you so happy."

The people understood. It grieved them, it made them uncomfortable for a few hours, but once they had returned to their exactly-right homes and got back to their exactly-right jobs, the sheer contentment of their lives overwhelmed their momentary sorrow for Chris. After all, Chris had broken the law. And it was the law that kept them all safe and happy.

Even Joe. Even Joe soon forgot Chris and his music. He knew he had done the right thing. He couldn't figure out, though, why a man like Chris would have broken the law in the first place, or what law he would have broken. There wasn't a law in the world that wasn't designed to make people happy—and there wasn't a law Joe could think of that he was even mildly interested in breaking.

Yet. Once Joe went to the piano and lifted the lid and played every key on the piano. And when he had done that he put his head down on the piano and cried, because he knew that when Chris lost that piano, lost even his fingers so he could never play again—it was like Joe losing his bar. And if Joe ever lost his bar, his life wouldn't be worth living.

As for Chris, someone else began coming to the

bar driving the same doughnut delivery van, and no one ever knew Chris again in that part of the world.

THIRD MOVEMENT

"Oh what a beautiful mornin'!" sang the road crew man who had seen *Oklahoma!* four times in his home town.

"Rock my soul in the bosom of Abraham!" sang the road crew man who had learned to sing when his family got together with guitars.

"Lead, kindly light, amid the encircling gloom!" sang the road crew man who believed.

But the road crew man without hands, who held the signs telling the traffic to Stop or go Slow, listened but never sang.

"Whyn't you never sing?" asked the road crew man who liked Rodgers and Hammerstein; asked all of them, at one time or another.

And the man they called Sugar just shrugged. "Don't feel like singin'," he'd say, when he said anything at all.

"Why they call him Sugar?" a new guy once asked. "He don't look sweet to me."

And the man who believed said, "His initials are *C H*. Like the sugar. C&H, you know." And the new guy laughed. A stupid joke, but the kind of gag that makes life easier on the road-building crew.

Not that life was that hard. For these men, too, had been tested, and they were in the job that made them happiest. They took pride in the pain of sunburn and pulled muscles, and the road growing long and thin behind them was the most beautiful thing in the world. And so they sang all day at their work, knowing that they could not possibly be happier than they were this day.

Except Sugar.

Then Guillermo came. A short Mexican who spoke with an accent, Guillermo told everyone who asked, "I may come from Sonora, but my heart belongs in Milano!" And when anyone asked why (and often when no one asked anything) he'd explain. "I'm an Italian tenor in a Mexican body," and he proved it by singing every note that Puccini and Verdi ever wrote. "Caruso was nothing," Guillermo boasted. "Listen to this!"

Guillermo had records, and sang along with them, and at work on the road crew he'd join in with any man's song and harmonize with it, or sing an obbligato high above the melody, a soaring tenor that took the roof off his head and filled the clouds. "I can sing," Guillermo would say, and soon the other road crew men answered. "Damn right, Guillermo! Sing it again!"

But one night Guillermo was honest, and told the truth. "Ah, my friends, I'm no singer."

"What do you mean? Of course you are!" came the unanimous answer.

"Nonsense!" Guillermo cried, his voice theatrical. "If I am this great singer, why do you never see me going off to record songs? Hey? This is a great singer? Nonsense! Great singers they raise to be great singers. I'm just a man who loves to sing, but has no talent! I'm a man who loves to work on the road crew with men like you, and sing his guts out, but in the opera I could never be! Never!"

He did not say it sadly. He said it fervently, confidently. "Here is where I belong! I can sing to you who like to hear me sing! I can harmonize with you when I feel a harmony in my heart. But don't be thinking that Guillermo is a great singer, because he's not!"

It was an evening of honesty, and every man there explained why it was he was happy on the road crew, and didn't wish to be anywhere else. Everyone, that is, except Sugar.

"Come on, Sugar. Aren't you happy here?"

Sugar smiled. "I'm happy. I like it here. This is good work for me. And I love to hear you sing."

"Then why don't you sing with us?"

Sugar shook his head. "I'm not a singer."

But Guillermo looked at him knowingly. "Not a singer, ha! Not a singer. A man without hands who refuses to sing is not a man who is not a singer. Hey?"

"What the hell does that mean?" asked the man who sang folksongs.

"It means that this man you call Sugar, he's a fraud. Not a singer! Look at his hands. All his fingers gone! Who is it who cuts off men's fingers?"

The road crew didn't try to guess. There were many ways a man could lose fingers, and none of them were anyone's business.

"He loses his fingers because he breaks the law and the Watchers cut them off! That's how a man loses fingers. What was he doing with his fingers that the Watchers wanted him to stop? He was breaking the law, wasn't he?"

"Stop," Sugar said.

"If you want," Guillermo said, but for once the others would not respect Sugar's privacy.

"Tell us," they said.

Sugar left the room.

"Tell us," and Guillermo told them. That Sugar must have been a Maker who broke the law and was forbidden to make music anymore. The very thought that a Maker was working on the road crew with them—even a lawbreaker—filled the men with awe. Makers were rare, and they were the most esteemed of men and women.

"But why his fingers?"

"Because," Guillermo said, "he must have tried to make music again afterward. And when you break the law a second time, the power to break it a third time is taken away from you." Guillermo spoke seriously, and so to the road crew men Sugar's story sounded as majestic and terrible as an opera. They crowded into Sugar's room, and found the man staring at the wall.

"Sugar, is it true?" asked the man who loved Rodgers and Hammerstein.

"Were you a Maker?" asked the man who believed.

"Yes," Sugar said.

"But Sugar," the man who believed said, "God can't mean for a man to stop making music, even if he broke the law."

Sugar smiled. "No one asked God."

"Sugar," Guillermo finally said, "There are nine of us on the crew, nine of us, and we're miles from any human beings. You know us, Sugar. We swear on our mother's graves, every one of us, that we'll never tell a soul. Why should we? You're one of us. But sing, dammit man, sing!"

"I can't," Sugar said. "You don't understand."

"It isn't what God intended," said the man who believed. "We're all doing what we love best, and here you are, loving music and not able to sing a note. Sing for us! Sing with us! And only you and us and God will know!"

They all promised. They all pleaded.

And the next day as the man who loved Rodgers and Hammerstein sang "Love, Look Away," Sugar began to hum. As the man who believed sang "God of Our Fathers" Sugar sang softly along. And as the man who loved folksongs sang "Swing Low, Sweet Chariot," Sugar joined in with a strange, piping voice and all the men laughed and cheered and welcomed Sugar's voice to the songs.

Inevitably Sugar began inventing. First harmonies,

of course, strange harmonies that made Guillermo frown and then, after a while, grin as he joined in, sensing as best he could what Sugar was doing to the music.

And after harmonies, Sugar began singing his own melodies, with his own words. He made them repetitive, the word simple and the melodies simpler still. And yet he shaped them into odd shapes, and built them into songs that had never been heard of before, that sounded wrong and yet were absolutely right. It was not long before the man who loved Rodgers and Hammerstein and the man who sang folksongs and the man who believed were learning Sugar's songs and singing them joyously or mournfully or angrily or gaily as they worked along the road.

Even Guillermo learned the songs, and his strong tenor was changed by them until his voice, which had, after all, been ordinary, became something unusual and fine. Guillermo finally said to Sugar one day, "Hey, Sugar, your music is all wrong, man. But I like the way it feels in my nose! Hey, you know? I like the way it feels in my mouth!"

Some of the songs were hymns: "Keep me hungry, Lord," Sugar sang, and the road crew sang it too.

Some of the songs were love songs: "Put your hands in someone else's pockets," Sugar sang angrily; "I hear your voice in the morning," Sugar sang tenderly; "Is it summer yet?" Sugar sang sadly; and the road crew sang it, too.

Over the months the road crew changed, one man leaving on Wednesday and a new man taking his place on Thursday, as different skills were needed in different places. Sugar was silent when each newcomer came, until the man had given his word and the secret was sure to be kept.

What finally destroyed Sugar was the fact that his songs were so unforgettable. The men who left would sing the songs with their new crews, and those crews would learn them, and teach them to others. Crewmen taught the songs in bars and on the road; people learned them quickly, and loved them; and one day a blind Watcher heard the songs and knew, instantly, who had first sung them. They were Christian Haroldsen's music, because in those melodies, simple as they were, the wind of the north woods still whistled and the fall of leaves still hung oppressively over every note and—and the Watcher sighed. He took a specialized tool from his file of tools and boarded an airplane and flew to the city closest to where a certain road crew worked. And the blind Watcher took a company car with a company driver up the road and at the end of it, where the road was just beginning to pierce a strip of wilderness, the blind Watcher got out of the car and heard singing. Heard a piping voice singing a song that made even an eyeless man weep.

"Christian," the Watcher said, and the song stopped.

"You," said Christian.

"Christian, even after you lost your fingers?"

The other men didn't understand—all the other men, that is, except Guillermo.

"Watcher," said Guillermo. "Watcher, he done no harm."

The Watcher smiled wryly. "No one said he did. But he broke the law. You, Guillermo, how would you like to work as a servant in a rich man's house? How would you like to be a bank teller?"

"Don't take me from the road crew, man," Guillermo said.

"It's the law that finds where people will be happy. But Christian Haroldsen broke the law. And he's gone around ever since making people hear music they were never meant to hear."

Guillermo knew he had lost the battle before it

began, but he couldn't stop himself. "Don't hurt him, man. I was meant to hear his music. Swear to God, it's made me happier."

The Watcher shook his head sadly. "Be honest, Guillermo. You're an honest man. His music's made you miserable, hasn't it? You've got everything you could want in life, and yet his music makes you sad. All the time, sad."

Guillermo tried to argue, but he was honest, and he looked into his own heart, and he knew that the music was full of grief. Even the happy songs mourned for something; even the angry songs wept; even the love songs seemed to say that everything dies and contentment is the most fleeting thing. Guillermo looked in his own heart and all Sugar's music stared back up at him and Guillermo wept.

"Just don't hurt him, please," Guillermo murmured as he cried.

"I won't," the blind Watcher said. Then he walked to Christian, who stood passively waiting, and he held the special tool up to Christian's throat. Christian gasped.

"No," Christian said, but the word only formed with his lips and tongue. No sound came out. Just a hiss of air. "No."

The road crew watched silently as the Watcher led Christian away. They did not sing for days. But then Guillermo forgot his grief one day and sang an aria from *La Bohème*, and the songs went on from there. Now and then they sang one of Sugar's songs, because the songs could not be forgotten.

In the city, the blind Watcher furnished Christian with a pad of paper and a pen. Christian immediately gripped the pencil in the crease of his palm and wrote: "What do I do now?"

The driver read the note aloud, and the blind

Watcher laughed. "Have we got a job for you! Oh, Christian, have we got a job for you!" The dog barked loudly, to hear his master laugh.

APPLAUSE

In all the world there were only two dozen Watchers. They were secretive men, who supervised a system that needed little supervision because it actually made nearly everybody happy. It was a good system, but like even the most perfect of machines, here and there it broke down. Here and there someone acted madly, and damaged himself, and to protect everyone and the person himself, a Watcher had to notice the madness and go to fix it.

For many years the best of the Watchers was a man with no fingers, a man with no voice. He would come silently, wearing the uniform that named him with the only name he needed—Authority. And he would find the kindest, easiest, yet most thorough way of solving the problem and curing the madness and preserving the system that made the world, for the first time in history, a very good place to live. For practically everyone.

For there were still a few people—one or two each year—who were caught in a circle of their own devising, who could neither adjust to the system nor bear to harm it, people who kept breaking the law despite their knowledge that it would destroy them.

Eventually, when the gentle maimings and deprivations did not cure their madness and set them back into the system, they were given uniforms and they, too, went out. Watching.

The keys of power were placed in the hands of those who had most cause to hate the system they had to preserve. Were they sorrowful?

"I am," Christian answered in the moments when he dared to ask himself that question.

In sorrow he did his duty. In sorrow he grew old. And finally the other Watchers, who reverenced the silent man (for they knew he had once sung magnificent songs), told him he was free. "You've served your time," said the Watcher with no legs, and he smiled.

Christian raised an eyebrow, as if to say, "And?"

"So wander."

Christian wandered. He took off his uniform, but lacking neither money nor time he found few doors closed to him. He wandered where in his former lives he had once lived. A road in the mountains. A city where he had once known the loading entrance of every restaurant and coffee shop and grocery store. And at last to a place in the woods where a house was falling apart in the weather because it had not been used in forty years.

Christian was old. The thunder roared and it only made him realize that it was about to rain. All the old songs. All the old songs, he mourned inside himself, more because he couldn't remember them than because he thought his life had been particularly sad.

As he sat in a coffee shop in a nearby town to stay out of the rain, he heard four teenagers who played the guitar very badly singing a song that he knew. It was a song he had invented while the asphalt poured on a hot summer day. The teenagers were not musicians and certainly were not Makers. But they sang the song from their hearts, and even though the words were happy, the song made everyone who heard it cry.

Christian wrote on the pad he always carried, and showed his question to the boys. "Where did that song come from?"

"It's a Sugar song," the leader of the group answered. "It's a song by Sugar."

Christian raised an eyebrow, making a shrugging motion.

"Sugar was a guy who worked on a road crew and made up songs. He's dead now, though," the boy answered.

"Best damn songs in the world," another boy said, and they all nodded.

Christian smiled. Then he wrote (and the boys waited impatiently for this speechless old man to go away): "Aren't you happy? Why sing sad songs?"

The boys were at a loss for an answer. The leader spoke up, though, and said, "Sure I'm happy. I've got a good job, a girl I like, and man, I couldn't ask for more. I got my guitar. I got my songs. And my friends."

And another boy said, "These songs aren't sad, Mister. Sure, they make people cry, but they aren't sad."

"Yeah," said another. "It's just that they were written by a man who knows."

Christian scribbled on his paper. "Knows what?"

"He just knows. Just knows, that's all. Knows it all."

And then the teenagers turned back to their clumsy guitars and their young, untrained voices, and Christian walked to the door to leave because the rain had stopped and because he knew when to leave the stage. He turned and bowed just a little toward the singers. They didn't notice him, but their voices were all the applause he needed. He left the ovation and went outside where the leaves were just turning color and would soon, with a slight inaudible sound, break free and fall to the earth.

For a moment he thought he heard himself singing. But it was just the last of the wind, coasting madly through the wires over the street. It was a frenzied song, and Christian thought he recognized his voice.

A Cross-Country Trip to Kill Richard Nixon

SIGGY WASN'T THE killer type. Nor did he have
delusions of grandeur. In fact, if he had any delusions, they were delusions of happiness. When he
was thirty, he gave up a good job as a commercial
artist and went down in the world, deliberately
downward in income, prestige, and tension. He
bought a cab.

"Who is going to drive this cab, Siggy?" his mother
asked. She was a German of the old school, well-bred
with contempt for the servant class.

"I am," Siggy answered mildly. He endured the
tirade that followed, but from then on his sole source
of income was the cab. He didn't work every day.
But whenever he felt like working or getting out of
the apartment or picking up some money, he would
take his cab out in Manhattan. His cab was spotless.
He gave excellent service. He enjoyed himself immensely. And when he came home, he sat down at

the easel or with a sketchpad on his knees, and did art. He wasn't very good. His talents had been best suited for commercial art. Anything more difficult than the back of a Cheerios box, and Siggy was out of his element. He never sold any of his paintings. But he didn't really care. He loved everything he did and everything he was.

So did his wife, Marie. She was French, he was German; they married and moved to America on the eve of World War II, bringing their families with them, and they were exquisitely well matched and happy through both of Siggy's careers. In 1978, at the age of fifty-seven, she died of a heart attack, and Siggy took the cab out and drove for eleven hours without picking up a single fare. At four o'clock in the morning, he finally made his decision and drove home. He would go on living. And sooner than he expected, he was happy again.

He had never dreamed of conquering the world or of getting rich or even of getting into bed with a movie star or a high-class prostitute. So it was not in his nature to imagine himself doing impossible things. It took him rather by surprise when he was chosen to save America.

She was a Disney fairy godmother, and she came in the craziest dream he had ever had. "You, Siegfried Reinhardt, are the lucky winner of exactly one wish," she said, sounding like the lady from Magic Carpet Land the last time she called to offer a free carpet cleaning.

"One?" Siggy answered in his dream, thinking this was rather below standard for godmothers.

"And you have a choice," the fairy godmother answered. "You may either use the wish on your own behalf, or you may use it to save America."

"America's going to hell and needs all the wishes it can get." Siggy said. "On the other hand, I don't really need anything I haven't got already. So it's America."

"Very well," she answered, and turned to go.

"Wait a minute," he said in his dream. "Is that all?"

"You asked for a wish for America, you get a wish for America. Which is a waste of a perfectly good wish, if you ask me, for thirty years America hasn't been worth *scheisse*. Try not to mess things up too badly, Siggy. This wish business is pretty complicated, and you're a simple type fellow." And then she was gone, and Siggy woke up, the dream impressed on his memory as dreams so rarely were.

Crazy, crazy, he thought, laughing it off. I'm getting old, Marie dragged me to too many Disney movies, I'm too lonely. But for all that he knew the dream was nonsense, he could not forget it.

I mean, what *if*, he told himself. What *if* I had a wish. Just one thing I could change, to make everybody in America happier. What would it be?

"What's wrong with America?" his mother asked, rolling her eyes and rocking back and forth in her wheelchair. To Siggy's knowledge she had never had a rocking chair in her life, and compensated by moving in every other kind of chair as if it were a rocker. "Everything's wrong with America," she said.

"But one thing, Mother. Just the worst thing to fix."

"It's too late, nothing can fix it. It all started with *him*. If there is such a thing as reincarnation, may he be reincarnated as a fly that I can swat. May he come back as a fire hydrant for all the dogs to pee against." Siggy's mother was impeccably polite in German, but in English she was crude, and, as so often before, Siggy wondered why she still lingered on at a ridiculous ninety-two when Marie, who was delicate and sensitive, was dead. "Don't be crude, Mother."

"I'm an American, I have the papers, I can be crude. Nineteen sixty-eight, that's when everything went to Hell."

"You can't blame everything on one man."

"What do you know? You drive a cab."

"One man doesn't make that big a difference."

"What about Adolf Hitler!" his mother said triumphantly, slapping the arms of the wheelchair and rocking back and forth. "Adolf Hitler! One man! Just like Richard Nixon, may his electric razor short-circuit and fry his face."

She was still laughing and cursing Nixon when Siggy finally left. Fairy godmother, he said to himself. What do I need a fairy godmother for? I have Mom.

But the dream wouldn't go away. The fairy godmother kept flitting in and out, hovering on the edges of all his dreams, wordlessly saying, "Hurry and make up your mind, Siggy. Fairy godmothers are busy, you're wasting my time."

"Don't push me," he said. "I'm being careful."

"I've got other clients, give me a break."

"I resent being pushed around by figments of my imagination," he said. "I get one wish, I want to use it right." When he woke up, he was vaguely embarrassed that he was taking the fairy godmother so seriously in his dreams. "Just a dream," he said to himself. But dream or not, he started doing research.

He took a poll. He kept a notebook beside him in the cab, and asked people, "Just out of curiosity what's the worst thing wrong with America? What's the one thing you'd change if you could?"

There were quite a few suggestions, but they always came back to Richard Nixon. "It all started with Nixon," they'd say. Or, "It's Carter. But if it hadn't been for Nixon, Carter would never have been elected."

"It's the unions, driving up prices," said a woman.

And then, after a little thought, "If Nixon hadn't screwed up we might have kept some *control* in this country."

It wasn't just that his name kept coming up. It was the way people *said* it. With loathing, with contempt, with fear. It was an emotional word. It sounded evil. They said *Nixon* the way they might say *slime*. Or *spider*.

Siggy sat one night staring at the results of his poll, unable to get out of his cab because of the thoughts that had taken over his head. I'm crazy, he thought to himself, but his thoughts ignored him and went right on, the fairy godmother giggling in the background. Richard Nixon, said the thoughts. If there could be one wish, it must be used to eliminate Richard Nixon.

But I voted for him, dammit, Siggy said silently. He *thought* it would be silent, but the words echoed inside the cab after all. "I voted for him. And I thought he did a damn good job sometimes." He was almost embarrassed saying the words—they weren't the kind of sentiment that made a cabby popular with his paying passengers. But thinking of Nixon made him remember the triumphant moment when Nixon said Up Yours to the North Vietnamese and bombed the hell out of them and got them to the negotiating table that one last time. And the wonderful landslide election that kept the crazy man from South Dakota out of the White House. And the trip to China, and the trip to Russia, and the feeling that America was maybe strong like it had been under Roosevelt when Hitler got his ass kicked up into his throat. Siggy remembered that, remembered that it felt good, remembered being angry as the press attacked and attacked and attacked and finally Nixon fell apart and turned out to be exactly as rotten a person as the papers said he was.

And the feeling of betrayal that he had felt all

through 1973 came back, and Siggy said, "Nixon," and inside the cab his voice sounded even more poisonous than the passengers'.

If there was something wrong with America, Siggy knew then, it was Richard Nixon. Whether a person had ever liked him or not. Because those who liked him had been betrayed, and those who hated him had not been appeased, and there he was out in California breeding the hatred that surpassed even the hatred for the phone company and the unions and the oil companies and the Congress.

I will wish him dead, Siggy thought. And inside his mind he could hear the fairy godmother cheering. "Make the wish," she said.

"Not yet," Siggy said. "I've got to be fair."

"Fair, schmair. Make the wish, I've got work to do."

"I've got to talk to him first," Siggy said. "I can't wish him dead without he has a chance to say his piece."

Siggy had planned to travel alone. Who would understand his purpose, when he didn't really understand it himself? He told no one he was going, just pulled five hundred dollars out of the bank and got in his cab and started driving. New Jersey, Pennsylvania; found himself on I-70 and decided what the hell, I-70 goes most of the way, that's my highway. He stopped at Richmond, Indiana, to go to the bathroom and get something to eat, then decided to spend the night in a cheap motel.

It was his first night in unfamiliar surroundings in years. It bothered him; things were out of place, and the sheets were rough and harsh, and there weren't a hundred reminders of Marie and happiness. He slept badly (but, thank heaven, without the fairy godmother), and when he left in the morning he realized that he was lonelier then he thought possible. He wasn't used to driving without conversation. He wasn't used to driving without a fare.

So he picked up a hitchhiker waiting by the on-ramp to the freeway. It was a boy—no, in his own eyes doubtless a man—in his early twenties. Hair fairly long, but cleaner than the usual scruffy road-side bum, and he'd be somebody to talk to, and if there was any trouble, well, Siggy had always carried a tire iron beside the seat, though he was not quite sure what he would ever do with it, or when. It made him feel safe. Safe enough to pull over and pick up the boy.

Siggy reached over and opened the car door as the boy ran up.

"Hey, uh," the boy said, leaning into the car. "I don't need a cab, I need a free ride."

"Don't we all," Siggy said, smiling. "I'm from New York City. In Indiana, I give free rides. I'm on vacation."

The boy nodded and got in beside him. Siggy moved out and was on the freeway in moments, going at a steady fifty-five. He put on the cruise con-trol and glanced at the boy. He was looking out the front window, his face glum.

"Where are you going?" Siggy asked.

"West."

"There's lots of west in the world. Wherever you go, there's still more west on ahead."

"They put an ocean at the end, I stop before I get wet, OK?"

"I'm going to Los Angeles," Siggy offered.

The boy said nothing. Obviously didn't want to talk. That was all right. Lots of customers liked si-lence, and Siggy had no objection to giving it to them. Enough that there was someone breathing in the car. It gave Siggy a feeling of legitimacy. It was all right to drive as long as someone else was in the car.

But this couldn't go on all the way, of course, Siggy

realized. When he picked the boy up, he figured on St. Louis, maybe Kansas City, then the boy gets out and Siggy's alone again. He'd have to stop for the night, Denver, maybe. Did the boy think a motel room went along with the ride?

"Where you from?"

The boy seemed to wake up, as if he had dozed off with his eyes wide open. Looking out on Indiana as it went by.

"What do you mean, from?" the boy asked.

"I mean *from*, the opposite of *to*. I mean, where were you born, where do you live?"

"I was born in Rochester. I don't think I live anywhere."

"Rochester. What's it like in Rochester?"

"I lived in a Mafia neighborhood. Everybody kept their yards neat and nobody ever broke into the houses."

"A lot of factories?"

"Eastman Kodak and Xerox Corporation. There's a lot of shit in the world, and Rochester exists by making copies of it." The boy said it bitterly, but Siggy laughed. It was funny, after all. The boy finally smiled, too.

"What are you going to do in California?" Siggy asked.

"Find a place to sleep and maybe a job."

"Want to be an actor?"

The boy looked at Siggy with contempt. "An *actor?* Like Jane Fonda?" He said the name like poison. The tone of voice was familiar. Siggy decided to try him out on the Name.

"What do you think of Richard Nixon?" Siggy asked.

"I don't," said the boy.

And then, madly, knowing it could ruin everything, Siggy blurted, "I'm going to get him."

"What?" the boy asked.

Siggy recovered his senses. Some of them, anyway. "I'm going to meet him. At San Clemente."

The boy laughed. "What do you want to meet him for?"

Siggy shrugged.

"They won't let you near him anyway. You think he wants to see people like us? Nixon." And there it was. The tone of voice. The contempt. Siggy was reassured. He was doing the right thing.

The hours passed and so did the states. Illinois came and went, and they crossed the Mississippi at St. Louis. Not as big as Siggy had expected, but still a hell of a lot of water, when you thought about it. Then Missouri, which was too wide and too dull. And because it was dull, they kept talking. The boy had a bitter streak a mile wide—everything seemed to lead to it. Siggy found it more comfortable to do the talking himself, and since the boy kept listening and saying something now and then, it seemed OK. They were beginning to pass signs that promised Kansas City as if it were a prize when Siggy got on the subject of Marie. Remembered things about her. How she loved wine—a French vice that Siggy loved in her.

"When she was a little drunk," he told the boy, "her eyes would get big. Sometimes full of tears, but she'd still smile. And she'd lift up her chin and stretch her neck. Like a deer."

Maybe the boy was getting tired of the conversation. Maybe he just resented hearing about a love that actually worked. He answered snappishly. "When you ever seen a deer, Manhattan cabdriver? The zoo?"

Siggy refused to be offended. "She was like a deer."

"I think she sounds like a giraffe." The boy smirked a little, as if saying this were somehow a victory over Siggy. Well, it was. It had worn down his patience.

"It's my wife we're talking about. She died two years ago."

"What do I care? I mean what makes you think I give a pink shit about it? You want to cry? You want to get all weepy about it? Then do it quiet. Jesus, give a guy a break, will you?"

Siggy kept his eyes on the road. There was a bitter feeling in his stomach. For a moment his hands felt violent, and he gripped the wheel. Then the feeling passed, and he got his curiosity back again.

"Hey, what're you so mad about?"

"Mad? What says I'm mad?"

"You sounded mad."

"I sounded mad!"

"Yeah, I wondered if maybe you wanted to talk about it."

The boy laughed acidly. "What, the seat reclines? It becomes maybe a couch? I stuck my thumb out because I wanted a ride. I want psychoanalysis, I stick out a different finger, you understand?"

"Hey, fine, relax."

"I'm not tense, shithead." He gripped the door handle so tightly that Siggy was afraid the door would crumple like tinfoil and fall away from the car.

"I'm sorry," the boy said finally, still looking forward. He didn't let go of the door.

"It's OK," Siggy answered.

"About your wife, I mean. I'm not like that. I don't just go around making fun of people's dead wives."

"Yeah."

"And you're right. I'm mad."

"At me?"

"You? What're you? A piss-ant. One of twelve million piss-ants in New York City. We're all piss-ants."

"What're you mad at?" Siggy could not resist adding the figures to his checklist. "Inflation? Oil companies? Nuclear plants?"

"What is this, the Gallup poll?"

"Maybe yeah. People get mad at a lot of the same things. Nuclear plants then?"

"I'm mad at nuclear plants, yeah."

"You want 'em all shut down, right?"

"Wrong, turkey. I want 'em to build a million of 'em. I want 'em to build 'em everywhere, and then on the count of three they all blow up, they wipe out this whole country."

"America?"

"From sea to shitting sea."

Then silence again. Siggy thought he could feel the whole car trembling with the young man's anger. It made Siggy sad. He kept glancing at the boy's face. It wasn't old. There were some acne scars; the beard was thin in quite a few places. Siggy tried to imagine the face without the beard. Without the anger. Without the too many drugs and too many bottles. The face when it was childish and innocent.

"You know," Siggy said, "I can't believe—I look at you, I can't believe that somebody loved you once."

"Nobody asked you to believe it."

"But they must have, right? Somebody taught you to walk. And talk. And ride a bicycle. You had a father, right?"

Suddenly the boy's fist shot out and slammed into the glove compartment door, which popped open with a crash. Siggy was startled, afraid. The boy showed no sign of pain, though it seemed he had hit hard enough to break a finger.

"Hey, careful," Siggy said.

"You want me to be careful? You tell me to be careful, asshole?" The boy grabbed the steering wheel, jerked on it. The taxi swung into another lane; a car behind them squealed on its brakes and honked.

"Are you crazy? Do you want to get us killed? Get mad, wreck the car, but don't kill us!" Siggy was screaming in anger, and the boy sat there, trembling, his eyes not quite focused. Then the car that had honked at them pulled up beside them on the right. The driver was yelling something with his window down. His face looked ugly with anger. The boy held up his middle finger. The man made the same gesture back again.

And suddenly the boy rolled down the window. "Hey, don't get us in trouble," Siggy said. The boy ignored him. He yelled a string of obscenities out the window. Siggy sped up, trying to pull away from the other car. The driver of the other car kept pace with him, yelled back his own curses.

And then the boy pulled a revolver out of his pocket, a big, mean-looking black pistol, and aimed it out the window at the driver of the other car. The man suddenly looked terrified. Siggy slammed on the brakes, but so did the other driver, and they stayed nearly parallel.

"Don't!" Siggy screamed, and he sped up, leaving the other car in the distance. The boy pulled the gun back into the car and laid it on his lap, the cock still back, his finger still on the trigger.

"It isn't loaded, right?" Siggy asked. "It was just a joke, right? Would you take your finger off the trigger?"

But it was as if the boy didn't hear him. As if he didn't even remember the last few minutes. "You wanted to know if I had a father, right? I have a father."

At the moment Siggy didn't much care whether the boy had been born in a test tube. But better he should talk about his father than wave the gun around.

"My father," said the boy, "spends his life making sure enough Xerox machines are getting sold and putting more ads in the magazines when they aren't."

They crossed the border into Kansas, and Siggy

hoped the incident with the pistol wouldn't get reported across state lines.

"My father never taught me to ride a bike. My brother did. My brother was killed in Mr. President Nixon's war. You know?"

"That was a long time ago," Siggy said.

The boy looked at him coldly. "It was yesterday, asshole. You don't believe those calendars, do you? All lies, so we'll think it's OK to forget about it. Maybe your wife died years ago, Mr. Cabdriver, but I thought you loved her better than that."

Then the boy looked down at the pistol in his lap, still cocked, still ready to fire.

"I thought I left this home," he said in surprise. "What's it doing here?"

"I should know?" Siggy asked. "Do me a favor, uncock the thing and put it away."

"OK," the boy said. But he didn't do anything.

"Hey, please," Siggy said. "You scare me, that thing sitting there ready to shoot."

The boy bowed his head over the pistol for a few moments. "Let me out," he said. "Let me get out."

"Hey, come on, just put the gun away, you don't have to get out, I won't be mad, just put the gun away."

The boy looked up at him and there were tears in his eyes, spilling out onto his cheeks. "You think I brought this gun by accident? I don't want to kill you."

"Then why'd you bring it?"

"I don't know. Jesus, man, let me out."

"You want to go to California, I'm going to California."

"I'm dangerous," the boy said.

Damn right you're dangerous, Siggy thought. Damn right. And I'm a doubledamned fool not to let you out of here right this second, right this minute, very next off-ramp I'll pull over and let him off.

"Not to me," Siggy said, wondering why he wasn't more afraid.

"To you. I'm dangerous to you."

"Not to me." And Siggy realized why he was so confident. It was the fairy godmother, sitting inside the back of his head. "You think I'm going to let anything happen to you, *dummkopf?*" she asked him silently. "If you knock off before you make your wish, it ruins my life. The clerical work alone would take years." I'm crazy, thought Siggy. This boy is nuts, but I'm crazy.

"Yeah," the boy said finally, gently letting down the hammer and putting the gun back into the pocket of his jacket. "Not to you."

They drove in silence for a while, as the plains flattened out and the sky went even flatter and the sun went dim behind the gray overcast. "Richard Nixon, huh?" the boy asked.

"Yeah."

"You really think they'll let us get near him?"

"I'll see to it," Siggy said. And it occurred to him for the first time that fairy godmothers might fulfill wishes in unpleasant ways. Wish him dead? I should wish Nixon dead, and this boy goes to prison forever for killing him? Watch it, fairy godmother, he warned. I won't let you trick me. I have a plan, and I won't let you trick me into hurting this boy.

"Hungry, Son?" Siggy asked. "Or can you hold out till Denver?"

"Denver's fine," said the boy. "But don't call me Son."

It was hot in Los Angeles, but as Siggy neared the sea the breezes became steadily cooler. He was tired. He was used to driving, but not so long a stretch, not so far. In a way the freeways were restful—no traffic, no guesswork about where the car to the right would be a few minutes later. People actually paid attention to the lines between lanes. But the freeways went on, relentlessly, mile after mile, until he felt like he was standing still and the road and the scenery played swiftly past him and under him. At last they had brought Los Angeles to him, and here the scenery would stop for him and wait for him to act. San Clemente. Richard Nixon's house. He found them easily, as if he had always known the way. The boy, asleep beside him for the last few hundred miles, woke up when Siggy brought the cab to a halt.

"What?" asked the boy, sleepily.

"Go back to sleep," Siggy said, getting out of the car. The boy got out, too.

"This is it?"

"Yes," Siggy said, already walking toward the entrance.

"I gotta pee," the boy said. But Siggy ignored him, and kept on walking. The boy followed, ran a little, caught up, saying softly, "Shit can't you even wait a minute?"

Secret Service men were everywhere, of course, but by now Siggy's madness was complete. He knew that they could not stop him. He had to meet Richard Nixon, and so he would. He had parked a long way from the mansion, and he just walked in, the boy at his heels. He didn't climb fences or do anything extraordinary. Just walked up the drive, around the house, and out onto the beach. No one saw him. No one called out to him. Secret Servicemen seemed always to have their backs to him, or to be on an urgent errand somewhere else. He would have his meeting with Richard Nixon. He would use his wish.

And he was standing where the water charged up the sand, always falling short of its last achievement as the tide ebbed. The boy stood beside him. Siggy watched the house, but the boy watched Siggy. "I thought they had us," the boy said. "I can't believe we got in here."

"Sh," Siggy answered softly. "Sh."

Siggy felt as nervous as a virgin at her wedding, more dreading than longing for what was to come. What if Nixon thinks I'm a fool? he thought. He needn't have worried. As he stood in the sand, Nixon emerged from the house, came down to the beach, and stopped at the waterline, staring out to sea. He was alone.

Taking a deep breath, Siggy walked to him. The sand kept slipping under his feet, so that every step forward tried to turn him out of his path. He persevered, and stood beside Richard Nixon. It was the face, the nose, at once the heavily shadowed evil face of the Herblock cartoons and the hopeful, strong face of the man Siggy had voted for three times.

"Mr. Nixon," Siggy said.

Nixon did not turn at first. He just said, "How did you get here?"

Siggy shrugged. "I had to see you."

Then Nixon turned to him, his face set to smile. Siggy watched as Nixon's eyes met his, then glanced over his shoulder at the boy, who was walking up, who stopped just behind Siggy.

The boy spoke. "We've come to kill you," he said.

And the boy had his hand in his pocket, where the gun was, and Siggy felt a moment of panic. But the voice of the fairy godmother sounded gently in his ear. "Don't worry," she said. "Take your time."

So Siggy shook his head at the boy, who frowned but did not shoot, and then Siggy turned back to Nixon. The former president was still smiling, his eyes narrowed a bit, but not showing any fear. Siggy felt a moment of satisfaction. This was the Nixon he had admired, the man with such great physical courage, who had faced mobs of Communists in Venezuela and Peru without flinching.

"You wouldn't be the first to want to," Nixon said.

"Oh, but I don't want to," Siggy said. "I have to. For America."

"Ah." Nixon nodded, knowingly. "We all do the most unpleasant things, don't we, for America."

Siggy felt a stab of relief. He understood, which would make it all so much easier.

"You're lucky," Nixon said. "I came out here alone, this once. To say good-bye. I'm leaving here. Tomorrow I would have been gone." He shook his head slightly, slowly, from side to side. "Well, get on with it. I can't stop you."

"Oh," Siggy said. "I'm not going to shoot you. All I have to do is *wish* you dead." Behind him Siggy heard the boy gasp a little. And Nixon sighed slightly. For a moment it sounded to Siggy like disappointment. Then he realized it was relief. And the smile returned to Nixon's face.

"But not today," Siggy went on. "I can't just wish for you to be assassinated now, Mr. Nixon. Or for you to die in bed or in an accident. The damage is done. So I'll have to have you die in the past."

The boy made a soft noise behind him.

Nixon nodded wisely. "That will be much better, I think."

"So I've decided that the best time will be right after you're sworn into office the second time. In 1972, before the Watergate thing got out of hand, right after you got a peace treaty from the Vietnamese and right after your landslide victory. Then an assassin picks you off, and you're a bigger hero and a greater legend than Kennedy."

"And everything since then?" Nixon asked.

"Changed. They won't keep after you, you see, after you're dead. You'll be a pleasant memory to almost everybody. Their hate will be gone, mostly."

Nixon shook his head. "You said your wish was supposed to be for the good of America, didn't you?"

Siggy nodded.

"Well, if I had been assassinated then, Spiro Agnew would have become president."

Siggy had forgotten. Spiro Agnew. What a bum. There was no way that could be good for the country. "You're right," Siggy said. "So it'll have to be before. Right before the election. It'll be almost as good then, you were leading in the polls."

"But then," Nixon said, "George McGovern would have been president."

Worse and worse. Siggy began to realize the difficulties involved in carrying out his responsibility. Everything he changed would have consequences. How could he fix the country's woes, if he kept increasing them with the changes he made?

"And if you have me killed in 1968, it's either Spiro Agnew or Hubert Humphrey," Nixon added. "Maybe you'll just have to wish for me to win in 1960."

Siggy thought of that. Thought very carefully. "No," he said. "That would be good for *you*. It would have made you a better president, not to have those bad experiences first. But would you have taken us to the moon? Would you have kept the Vietnam War as small as it was?"

"Smaller," Nixon said. "I would have won it by 1964."

Siggy shook his head. "And been at war with Red China, and the world might have been destroyed, and millions of people killed. I don't think the wrong man won in 1960."

Nixon's face went kind of sad. "Then maybe it would be kindest of all if you simply wished for me to lose every election I ever tried. Keep me out of Congress, out of the vice-presidency. Let me be a used car salesman." And he smiled a twisted, sad smile.

Siggy reached out and touched the man's shoulder.

"Maybe I should," he said, and the boy behind him made another soft sound.

"But no," Nixon said. "You wanted to save America. And it wouldn't make any difference to keep me out of government. If it hadn't been me, it would have been someone else. There would have been a Richard Nixon anyway. If they hadn't wanted me, I wouldn't have been there. If Richard Nixon hadn't existed, they would have made one."

Siggy sighed. "Then I don't know what to do," he said.

Nixon turned and looked out over the water. "I only did what they wanted me to do. And when they changed their minds, they were surprised at what I was." The beach was cold and damp between waves. The breeze from the land carried the air of Los Angeles with it, and it made the beach smell slimy and old. "Maybe," Nixon said, "there's nothing you can wish for that will save America. Maybe there's nothing you can do at all."

And the noise the boy made was loud enough that Siggy at last turned to look at him. To his surprise, the boy was no longer standing up. He was sitting cross-legged in the sand, bowed over, his hands gripping each other behind his neck. His body shook.

"What's wrong, Son?" Nixon asked. He sounded concerned.

The boy looked up, anger and grief in his face. "You," he said, and his voice shook. "*You* can call me Son."

Nixon knelt in the sand, painfully as if his leg hurt, and touched the boy's shoulder. "What's wrong, Son?"

"His brother was killed in Vietnam," Siggy said, as if that explained anything.

"I'm sorry," Nixon said. "I'm really sorry."

The boy threw off Nixon's hand. "Do you think that matters? Do you think it makes any difference how *sorry* you are?" The words stung Nixon, clearly. He shuddered as if his face had been slapped.

"I don't know what else I can do," Nixon said softly.

The boy's hand shot out and grabbed him by the lapels of his suit, pulling him down until they were face to face, and the boy screamed, "You can pay for it! You can pay and pay and pay—" and the boy's lips and teeth were almost touching Nixon's face, and Nixon looked pathetic and helpless in the boy's grip, flecks of the boy's spit beginning to dot his cheeks and lips. Siggy watched, and realized there was nothing that Nixon could do that would pay it all, that would give the boy back what he had lost, realized that Nixon had not really taken it from the boy. Had not taken it, could not return it, was as much a victim as anyone else. How could Siggy, with a single wish, set it all right? How could he even up all the scales?

"Think, idiot," said the fairy godmother. "I'm losing patience."

"I don't know what to do," he said to her.

"And you're the one with the plan," she answered contemptuously.

The boy was still screaming, again and again, and Nixon was weeping now, silently letting the tears flow to join the spittle on his face, as if to agree, as if to make it unanimous.

"I wish," said Siggy, "for everyone to forgive you, Mr. Nixon. For everyone in America to stop hating you, little by little, until all the hate is gone."

The fairy godmother danced in his mind, waving her wand around and turning everything pink.

And the boy stopped screaming and let go of Nixon, gazed wonderingly into the old man's eyes at the tears there, and said, "I'm sorry for you," and meant it with all his heart. Then Siggy helped the boy to his feet and they turned away, leaving Nixon on the beach. The world was tinged with pink and Siggy put his arm around the boy and they smiled at each other. And they headed back to the cab. Siggy saw the fairy godmother flying away ahead of them, north and east from San Clemente, trailing stars behind her as she flew.

"Bibbity bobbity boo," she cried, and she was gone.

THE PORCELAIN SALAMANDER

THEY CALLED THEIR country the Beautiful Land, and they were right. It perched on the edge of the continent. Before the Beautiful Land stretched the broad ocean, which few dared to cross; behind it stood the steep Rising, a cliff so high and sheer that few dared to climb. And in such isolation the people, who called themselves, of course, the Beautiful People, lived splendid lives.

Not all were rich, of course. And not all were happy. But there was such a majesty to living in the Beautiful Land that the poverty could easily be missed by the undiscerning eye, and misery seemed so very fleeting.

Except to Kiren.

To Kiren, misery was the way of life. For though she lived in a rich house with servants and had, it seemed, anything she could possibly want, she was deeply miserable most of the time. For this was a land where cursing and blessing and magic worked—

not always, and not always in the way the person doing it might have planned—but sometimes the cursing worked, and in her case it had.

Not that she had done anything to deserve it; she had been as innocent as any other child in her cradle. But her mother had been a weak woman, and the pain and terror of giving birth had killed her. And Kiren's father loved his wife so much that when he learned of the news, and saw the baby that had been born even as her mother died, he cried out, "You killed her! You killed her! May you never move a muscle in your life, until you lose someone you love as much as I loved her!" It was a terrible curse, and the nurse wept when she heard it, and the doctors stopped Kiren's father's mouth so that he could say no more in his madness.

But his curse took hold, and though he regretted it a million times during Kiren's infancy and childhood, there was nothing he could do. Oh, the curse was not all *that* strong. Kiren did learn to walk, after a fashion. And she could stand for as much as two minutes at a time. But most of the times she sat or lay down, because she grew so weary, and her muscles only weakly did what she told them to. She could lift a spoon to her mouth, but soon became tired, and had to be fed. She scarcely had the energy to chew.

And every time her father saw her, he wanted to weep, and often did weep. And sometimes he even thought of killing himself to finally wipe away his guilt. But he knew that this would only injure poor Kiren even more, and she had done nothing to deserve injury.

When his guilt grew too much for him to bear, however, he did escape. He put a bag of fine fruits and clever handwork from the Beautiful Land on his back, and set out for the Rising. He would be gone for months, and no one knew when he would return, or whether the Rising would this time prove too much for him and send him plunging to his death. But when he returned, he always brought something for Kiren. And for a while she would smile, and she would say, "Father, thank you." And things would go well, for a time, until she again became despondent and her father again suffered from watching the results of his ill-thought curse.

It was late spring in the year Kiren turned eleven when her father came home even happier than he usually was after a trip up the Rising. He rushed to his daughter where she lay wanly on the porch listening to the birds.

"Kiren!" he cried. "Kiren! I've brought you a gift!"

And she smiled, though even the muscles for smiling were weak, which made her smile sad. Her father reached into his bag (which was full of all kinds of wonders, which he would, being a careful man, sell to those with money to pay, not just for goods, but for rarity) and he pulled out his gift and handed it to Kiren.

It was a box, and the box lurched violently this way and that.

"There's something alive in there," Kiren said.

"No, my dear Kiren, there is not. But there's something moving, and it's yours. And before I help you open it, I'll tell you the story. I came one day in my wanderings to a town I had never visited before, and in the town were many merchants. And I asked a man, 'Who has the rarest and best merchandise in town?' He told me that I had to see Irvass. So I found the man in a humble and poor-looking shop. But inside were wonders such as you've never seen. I tell you, the man understands the bright magic from over the sky. And he asked, 'What do you want most in the world?' and of course I said to him, 'I want my daughter to be healed.' "

"Oh, Father," said Kiren. "You don't mean—"

"I do mean. I mean it very much. I told him exactly how you are and exactly how you got that way, and he said, 'Here is the cure,' and now let's open the box so you can see."

So Kiren opened the box, with more than a little help from her father, but she dared not reach inside. "You get it out, Father," she suggested, and he reached inside and pulled out a porcelain salamander. It was shiny yet deep with fine enameling, and though it was white—not at all the normal color for salamanders—the shape was unmistakable.

It was, in fact, a perfect model of a salamander. And it moved.

The legs raced madly in the air; the tongue darted in and out of the lips; the head turned; the eyes rolled. And Kiren cried out and laughed and said, "Oh, Father, what did he do to make it move so wonderfully!"

"Well," said her father, "he told me that he had given it the gift of movement—but not the gift of life. And if it ever *stops* moving, it will immediately become like any other porcelain. Stiff and hard and cold."

"How it races," she said, and it became the delight of her life.

When she awoke in the morning the salamander danced on her bed. At mealtimes it raced around the table. Wherever she lay or sat, the salamander was forever chasing after something or exploring something or trying to get away from something. She watched him constantly, and he in turn never got out of sight. And then at night, while she slept, he raced around and around in her room, the porcelain feet hitting the carpet silently, only occasionally making a slight tinkling sound as it ran lightly across the brick of the hearth.

Her father watched for a cure, and slowly but

surely it began to come. For one thing, Kiren was no longer miserable. The salamander was too funny not to laugh at. It never went away. And so she felt better. Feeling better was not all of it, though. She began to walk a bit more often, and stay standing more, and sit when ordinarily she would have lain. She began to go from one room to another by her own choice.

By the end of the summer she even took walks into the woods. Though she often had to stop and rest, she enjoyed the journey, and grew a little stronger.

What she never told anyone (partly because she was afraid that it might be her imagination) was that the salamander could also speak.

"You can speak," she said in surprise one day, when the salamander ran across her foot and said, "Excuse me."

"Of course," he said. "To *you*."

"Why not anyone else?"

"Because I'm here for *you*," he answered, as he ran along the top of the garden wall, then leaped down near her. "It's the way I am. Movement and speech. Best I can do, you know. Can't have life. Doesn't work that way."

And so on their long walks in the forest they also talked, and Kiren fancied that the salamander had grown as fond of her as she had grown of him. In fact, she told the salamander one day, "I love you."

"Love love love love love love love," he answered, scampering up and down a tree.

"Yes," Kiren said. "More than life. More than anything at all."

"More than your father?" asked the salamander.

It was hard. Kiren was not a disloyal child, and really had forgiven her father for the curse years before. Yet she had to be honest to her salamander.

"Yes," she said. "More than Father. More than—more than my dream of my mother. For you love me and can play with me and talk to me all the time."

"Love love love," said the salamander. "Unfortunately, I'm porcelain. Love love love love love. It's a word. Two consonants and a vowel. Like sap sap sap sap sap. Lovely sound." And he leaped across a small brook in the way.

"Don't—don't you love me?"

"I can't. It's an emotion, you know. I'm porcelain. Beg your pardon," and he clambered down her back as she leaned her shoulder on a tree. "Can't love. So sorry."

She was terribly, terribly hurt. "Don't you feel anything toward me at all?"

"Feel? Feel? Don't confuse things. Emotions come and go. Who can trust them? Isn't it enough that I spend every moment with you? Isn't it enough that I talk only to you? Isn't it enough that I would—that I would—"

"Would what?"

"I was about to start making foolish predictions. I was about to say, isn't it enough that I would die for you? But of course that's nonsense, because I'm not I'm not alive. Just porcelain. Watch out for the spider."

She stepped out of the path of a little green hunting spider that could fell a horse with one bite. "Thank you," she said. "And thank you." The first was for saving her life, but that was his job. The second was for telling her that, in his own way, he loved her after all. "So I'm not foolish for loving you, am I?"

"Foolish you are. Foolish indeed. Foolish as the moons are foolish, to dance endlessly in the sky and never never never go home together."

"I love you," said Kiren, "better than I love the hope of being whole."

And, you see, it was because she said that that the

odd man came to the door of her father's house the very next day.

"I'm sorry," said the servant. "You haven't an appointment."

"Just tell him," said the odd man, "that Irvass has come."

Kiren's father came running down the stairs. "Oh, you can't take the salamander back!" he cried. "The cure has only begun!"

"Which I know much better than you do," said Irvass. "The girl is in the woods?"

"With the salamander. What marvelous changes— but why are you here?"

"To finish the cure," said Irvass.

"What?" asked Kiren's father. "Isn't the salamander itself the cure?"

"What were the words of your curse?" Irvass asked, instead of answering.

Kiren's father's face grew dour, but he forced himself to quietly say the very words. "May you never move a muscle in your life, until you lose someone you love as much as I loved her."

"Well then," said Irvass. "She now loves the salamander exactly as much as you loved your wife."

It took only a moment for Kiren's father to realize. "No!" he cried out. "I can't let her suffer what I suffered!"

"It's the only cure. Isn't it better with a little piece of porcelain than if she had come to love *you* that much?"

And Kiren's father shuddered, and then wept, for he alone knew exactly how much pain she would suffer.

Irvass said nothing more, though the look he gave to Kiren's father might have been a pitying one. All he did was draw a rectangle in the soil of the garden, and place two stones within it, and mumble a few words.

And at that moment, out in the wood, the salamander said, "Very odd. Wasn't a wall here ever before. Never before. Here's a wall." And it was a wall. It was just high enough that when Kiren reached as high as she could, her fingers were one inch short of touching the top.

The salamander tried to climb it, but found it slippery—though he had always been able to climb every other wall he found. "Magic. Must be magic," The porcelain salamander mumbled.

So they circled the wall, hunting for a gate. There was none. It was all around them, though they had never entered it. And at no point did a tree limb cross the wall. They were trapped.

"I'm afraid," said Kiren. "There's good magic and bad magic, but how could such a thing as this be a blessing? It must be a curse." And the thought of a curse caused too much of the old misery to return, and she fought back the tears.

Fought back the tears until night, and then in the darkness, as the salamander scampered here and there, she could fight no longer.

"No," wailed the salamander.

"I can't help crying," she answered.

"I can't bear it," he said. "It makes me cold."

"I'll try to stop," she said, and she tried, and she pretty much stopped except for a few whimpers and sniffles until morning brought the light, and she saw that the wall was exactly where it had been.

No, not exactly. For behind her the wall had crept up in the night, and was only a few feet away. Her prison was now not even a quarter the size it had been the day before.

"Not good," said the salamander. "Oh, it could be dangerous."

"I know," she answered.

"You must get out," said the salamander.

"And you," she answered. "But how?"

And throughout the morning the wall played vicious taunting games with them, for whichever way neither of them was looking, the wall would creep up a foot or two. Since the salamander was faster, and moved constantly, he watched three sides. "And you hold the other in place." But Kiren couldn't help blinking, and anytime the salamander looked away the wall twitched, and by noon their prison was only ten feet square.

"Getting pretty tight here," said the salamander.

"Oh, salamander, can't I throw you over the wall?"

"We could try that, and I could run and get help—"

And so they tried. But though she used every ounce of strength she had, the wall seemed to leap up and catch him and send him sliding back down to the ground. Inside.

Soon she was exhausted, and the salamander said, "No more." Even as they had been trying, the walls had shrunk, and now the space was only five feet square. "Getting cramped," said the salamander as he raced around the tiny space remaining. "But I know the only solution."

"Tell me!" Kiren cried.

"I think," said the salamander, "that if you had something you could stand on, you could climb out."

"How could I?" she asked. "The wall won't let anything out!"

"I think," said the salamander, "that the wall only won't let *me* out. Because the birds are flying back and forth, and the wall doesn't catch them." It was true. A bird was singing in a nearby tree; it flew across just afterward, as if to prove the salamander's point. "I'm not alive, you see," said the salamander. "I'm moving only by magic. So you *could* get out."

"But what would I stand on?"

"Me," said the salamander.

"You?" she asked. "But you move so quickly—"

"For you," he said, "I'll hold still."

"No!" she cried. "No, no!" she screamed.

But the salamander stood at the edge of the wall, and he was only a statue in porcelain, hard and stiff and cold.

Kiren only wept for a moment, for then the wall behind her began to push at her, and her prison was only three feet square. The salamander had given his life so she could climb out. She ought at least to try.

So she tried. Standing on the salamander, she could reach the top of the wall. By standing tiptoe, she could get a grip on the top. And by using every bit of strength she had in her, she was able to force her body to the top and gradually heave herself over.

She fell in a heap on the ground. And in that moment, that very moment, two things happened. The walls shrank quickly until they were only a pillar, and then they disappeared completely, taking the salamander with them. And all the normal, natural strength of an eleven-year-old child came to Kiren, and she was able to run. She was able to leap. She was able to swing from the tree branches.

The strength was in her as suddenly as strong wine, and she could not lie on the ground. She jumped to her feet, and the movement was so strong she nearly fell over. She ran, leaped over brooks, clambered up into the trees as high as she could climb. The curse had ended. She was free.

But even normal children grow tired. And as she slowed down, she was no longer caught up in her own strength. And she remembered the porcelain salamander, and what he had done for her.

They found her that afternoon, weeping miserably into a pile of last year's leaves.

"You see," said Irvass, who had insisted on leading the way in the search—which is why they found her immediately—"You see, she has her strength, and the curse is ended."

"But her heart is broken," said her father as he gathered his little girl into his arms.

"Broken?" asked Irvass. "It should not be. For the porcelain salamander was never alive."

"Yes he was!" she shouted. "He spoke to me! He gave his life for me!"

"He did all that," said Irvass. "But think. For all the time the magic was on him, he could never, never rest. Do you think he never got tired?"

"Of course he didn't."

"Yes he did," said Irvass. "Now he can rest. But more than rest. For when he stopped moving and froze forever in one position, what was going through his mind?"

Irvass stood up and turned to leave. But only a few steps away, he turned back. "Kiren," he said.

"I want my salamander," she answered, her voice an agony of sobs.

"Oh, he would have become boring by and by," said Irvass. "He would have ceased to amuse you, and you would have avoided him. But now he is a memory. And, speaking of memory, remember that he also has memory, frozen as he is."

It was scant comfort then, for eleven-year-olds are not very philosophical. But when she grew older, Kiren remembered. And she knew that wherever the porcelain salamander was, he lived in one frozen, perfect moment—the moment when his heart was so full of love—

No, not love. The moment when he decided, without love, that it would be better for his life, such as it was, to end than to have to watch Kiren's life end.

It is a moment that can be lived with for eternity. And as Kiren grew older, she knew that such moments come rarely to people, and last only a moment, while the porcelain salamander would never lose it.

And as for Kiren—she became known, though she

never sought fame, as the most Beautiful of the Beautiful People, and more than one of the rare wanderers from across the sea or from beyond Rising came only to see her, and talk to her, and draw her face in their minds to keep it with them forever.

And when she talked, her hands always moved, always danced in the air. Never stopped moving at all, it seemed, and they were white and lustrous as deep-enameled porcelain, and her smile was as bright as the moons, and came back to her face as constantly as the sea, and those who knew her well could almost see her gaze keep flickering about the room or about the garden, as if she watched a bright, quick animal scamper by.

MIDDLE WOMAN

AH-CHEU WAS A woman of the great kingdom of Ch'in, a land of hills and valleys, a land of great wealth and dire poverty. But Ah-Cheu was a middle person, neither rich nor poor, neither old nor young, and her husband's farm was half in the valley and half on the hill. Ah-Cheu had a sister older than her, and a sister younger than her, and one lived thirty leagues to the north, and the other thirty leagues to the south. "I am a middle woman," Ah-Cheu boasted once, but her husband's mother rebuked her, saying, "Evil comes to the middle, and good goes out to the edges."

Every year Ah-Cheu put a pack on her back and journeyed for a visit either to the sister to the north or to the sister to the south. It took her three days to make the journey, for she did not hurry. But one year she did not make the journey, for she met a dragon on the road.

The dragon was long and fine and terrible, and Ah-

Cheu immediately knelt and touched her forehead to the road and said, "Oh, dragon, spare my life!"

The dragon only chuckled deep in his throat and said, "Woman, what do they call you?"

Not wishing to tell her true name to the dragon, she said, "I am called Middle Woman."

"Well, Middle Woman, I will give you a choice. The first choice is to have me eat you here in the road. The second choice is to have me grant you three wishes."

Surprised, Ah-Cheu raised her head. "But of course I take the second choice. Why do you set me a problem with such an easy solution?"

"It is more amusing," said the dragon, "to watch human beings destroy themselves than to overpower them quickly."

"But how can three wishes destroy me?"

"Make a wish, and see."

Ah-Cheu thought of many things she might wish for, but was soon ashamed of her greed. "I wish," she finally said, having decided to ask for only what she truly needed, "for my husband's farm to always produce plenty for all my family to eat."

"It shall be done," said the dragon, and he vanished, only to reappear a moment later, smiling and licking his lips. "I have done," he said, "exactly what you asked—I have eaten all your family, and so your husband's farm, even if it produces nothing, will always produce plenty for *them* to eat."

Ah-Cheu wept and mourned and cursed herself for being a fool, for now she saw the dragon's plan. Any wish, however innocent, would be turned against her.

"Think all you like," said the dragon, "but it will do you no good. I have had lawyers draw up legal documents eight feet long, but I have found the loopholes."

Then Ah-Cheu knew what she had to ask for. "I wish for all the world to be exactly as it was one minute before I left my home to come on this journey."

The dragon looked at her in surprise. "That's all? That's all you want to wish for?"

"Yes," said Ah-Cheu. "And you must do it now."

And suddenly she found herself in her husband's house, putting on her pack and bidding good-bye to her family. Immediately she set down the pack.

"I have changed my mind," she said. "I am not going."

Everyone was shocked. Everyone was surprised. Her husband berated her for being a changeable woman. Her mother-in-law denounced her for having forgotten her duty to her sisters. Her children pouted because she had always brought them each a present from her journeys to the north and south. But Ah-Cheu was firm. She would not risk meeting the dragon again.

And when the furor died down, Ah-Cheu was far more cheerful than she had ever been before, for she knew that she had one wish left, the third wish, the unused wish. And if there were ever a time of great need, she could use it to save herself and her family.

One year there was a fire, and Ah-Cheu was outside the house, with her youngest child trapped within. Almost she used her wish, but then thought, Why use the wish, when I can use my arms? And she ducked low, and ran into the house, and saved the boy, though it singed off all her hair. And she still had her son, and she still had her wish.

One year there was a famine, and it looked like all the world would starve. Ah-Cheu almost used her wish, but then thought, Why use the wish, when I can use my feet? And she wandered up into the hills, and came back with a basket of roots and leaves, and with such food she kept her family alive until the Emperor's men came with wagons full of rice. And she still had her family, and she still had her wish.

And in another year there was a great flood, and all the homes were swept away, and as Ah-Cheu and her son's baby sat upon the roof, watching the water eat away the walls of the house, she almost used her wish to get a boat so she could escape. But then she thought, Why use the wish, when I can use my head? And she took up the boards from the roof and walls, and with her skirts she tied them into a raft large enough for the baby, and setting the child upon it she swam away, pushing the raft until they reached high ground and safety. And when her son found her alive, he wept with joy, and said, "Mother Ah-Cheu, never has a son loved his mother more!"

And Ah-Cheu had her posterity, and yet still she had her wish.

And then it was time for Ah-Cheu to die, and she lay sick and frail upon a bed of honor in her son's house, and the women and children and old men of the village came to keen for her and honor her as she lay dying. "Never has there been a more fortunate woman than Ah-Cheu," they said. "Never has there been a kinder, a more generous, a more godfavored woman!" And she was content to leave the world, because she had been so happy in it.

And on her last night, as she lay alone in darkness, she heard a voice call her name.

"Middle Woman," said the voice, and she opened her eyes, and there was the dragon.

"What do you want with me?" she asked. "I'm not much of a morsel to eat now, I'm afraid."

But then she saw the dragon looked terrified, and she listened to what he had to say.

"Middle Woman," said the dragon, "you have not used your third wish."

"I never needed it."

"Oh, cruel woman! What a vengeance you take! In the long run, I never did you any harm! How can you do this to me?"

"But what am I doing?" she asked.

"If you die, with your third wish unused, then I, too, will die!" he cried. "Maybe that doesn't seem so bad to you, but dragons are usually immortal, and so you can believe me when I say my death would cut me off with most of my life unlived."

"Poor dragon," she said. "But what have I to wish for?"

"Immortality," he said. "No tricks. I'll let you live forever."

"I don't want to live forever," she said. "It would make the neighbors envious."

"Great wealth, then, for your family."

"But they have all they need right now."

"Any wish!" he cried. "Any wish, or I will die!"

And so she smiled, and reached out a frail old hand and touched his supplicating claw, and said, "Then I wish a wish, dragon. I wish that all the rest of your life should be nothing but happiness for you and everyone you meet."

The dragon looked at her in surprise, and then in relief, and then he smiled and wept for joy. He thanked her many times, and left her home rejoicing.

And that night Ah-Cheu also left her home, more subtly than the dragon, and far less likely to return, but no less merrily for all that.

THE BULLY AND THE BEAST

T HE PAGE ENTERED the Count's chamber at a dead run. He had long ago given up sauntering—when the Count called, he expected a page to appear immediately, and any delay at all made the Count irritable and likely to assign a page to stable duty.

"My lord," said the page.

"My lord indeed," said the Count. "What kept you?" The Count stood at the window, his back to the boy. In his arms he held a velvet gown, incredibly embroidered with gold and silver thread. "I think I need to call a council," said the Count. "On the other hand, I haven't the slightest desire to submit myself to a gaggle of jabbering knights. They'll be quite angry. What do you think?"

No one had ever asked the page for advice before, and he wasn't quite sure what was expected of him. "Why should they be angry, my lord?"

"Do you see this gown?" the Count asked, turning around and holding it up.

"Yes, my lord."

"What do you think of it?"

"Depends, doesn't it, my lord, on who wears it."

"It cost eleven pounds of silver."

The page smiled sickly. Eleven pounds of silver would keep the average knight in arms, food, women, clothing, and shelter for a year with six pounds left over for spending money.

"There are more," said the Count. "Many more."

"But who are they for? Are you going to marry?"

"None of your business!" roared the Count. "If there's anything I hate, it's a meddler!" The Count turned again to the window and looked out. He was shaded by a huge oak tree that grew forty feet from the castle walls. "What's today?" asked the Count.

"Thursday, my lord."

"The day, the day!"

"Eleventh past Easter Feast."

"The tribute's due today," said the Count. "Due on Easter, in fact, but today the Duke will be certain I'm not paying."

"Not paying the tribute, my lord?"

"How? Turn me upside down and shake me, but I haven't a farthing. The tribute money's gone. The money for new arms is gone. The travel money is gone. The money for new horses is gone. Haven't got any money at all. But gad, boy, what a wardrobe." The Count sat on the sill of the window. "The Duke will be here very quickly, I'm afraid. And he has the latest in debt collection equipment."

"What's that?"

"An army." The Count sighed. "Call a council, boy. My knights may jabber and scream, but they'll fight. I know they will."

The page wasn't sure. "They'll be very angry, my lord. Are you sure they'll fight?"

"Oh, yes," said the Count. "If they don't, the Duke will kill them."

"Why?"

"For not honoring their oath to me. Do go now, boy, and call a council."

The page nodded. Kind of felt sorry for the old boy. Not much of a Count, as things went, but he could have been worse, and it was pretty plain the castle would be sacked and the Count imprisoned and the women raped and the page sent off home to his parents. "A council!" he cried as he left the Count's chamber. "A council!"

In the cold cavern of the pantry under the kitchen, Bork pulled a huge keg of ale from its resting place and lifted it, not easily, but without much strain, and rested it on his shoulders. Head bowed, he walked slowly up the stairs. Before Bork worked in the kitchen, it used to take two men most of an afternoon to move the huge kegs. But Bork was a giant, or what passed for a giant in those days. The Count himself was of average height, barely past five feet. Bork was nearly seven feet tall, with muscles like an ox. People stepped aside for him.

"Put it there," said the cook, hardly looking up. "And don't drop it."

Bork didn't drop the keg. Nor did he resent the cook's expecting him to be clumsy. He had been told he was clumsy all his life, ever since it became plain at the age of three that he was going to be immense. Everyone knew that big people were clumsy. And it was true enough. Bork was so strong he kept doing things he never meant to do, accidentally. Like the time the swordmaster, admiring his strength, had invited him to learn to use the heavy battleswords. Bork hefted them easily, of course, though at the time he was only twelve and hadn't reached his full strength.

"Hit me," the swordmaster said.

"But the blade's sharp," Bork told him.

"Don't worry. You won't come near me." The swordmaster had taught a hundred knights to fight. None of them had come near him. And, in fact, when Bork swung the heavy sword the swordmaster had his shield up in plenty of time. He just hadn't counted on the terrible force of the blow. The shield was battered aside easily, and the blow threw the sword upward, so it cut off the swordmaster's left arm just below the shoulder, and only narrowly missed slicing deeply into his chest.

Clumsy, that was all Bork was. But it was the end of any hope of his becoming a knight. When the swordmaster finally recovered, he consigned Bork to the kitchen and the blacksmith's shop, where they needed someone with enough strength to skewer a cow end to end and carry it to the fire, where it was convenient to have a man who, with a double-sized ax, could chop down a large tree in half an hour, cut it into logs, and carry a month's supply of firewood into the castle in an afternoon.

A page came into the kitchen. "There's a council, cook. The Count wants ale, and plenty of it."

The cook swore profusely and threw a carrot at the page. "Always changing the schedule! Always making me do extra work." As soon as the page had escaped, the cook turned on Bork. "All right, carry the ale out there, and be quick about it. Try not to drop it."

"I won't," Bork said.

"He won't," the cook muttered. "Clever as an ox, he is."

Bork manhandled the cask into the great hall. It was cold, though outside the sun was shining. Little light and little warmth reached the inside of the castle. And since it was spring, the huge logpile in the pit in the middle of the room lay cold and damp. The knights were beginning to wander into the great hall and sit on the benches that lined the long,

pock-marked slab of a table. They knew enough to
carry their mugs—councils were always well-oiled
with ale. Bork had spent years as a child watching
the knights practice the arts of war, but the knights
seemed more natural carrying their cups than holding their swords at the ready. They were more dedicated to their drinking than to war.

"Ho, Bork the Bully," one of the knights greeted
him. Bork managed a half-smile. He had learned long
since not to take offense.

"How's Sam the stableman?" asked another,
tauntingly.

Bork blushed and turned away, heading for the
door to the kitchen.

The knights were laughing at their cleverness.
"Twice the body, half the brain," one of them said
to the others. "Probably hung like a horse," another
speculated, then quipped, "Which probably accounts
for those mysterious deaths among the sheep this
winter." A roar of laughter, and cups beating on the
table. Bork stood in the kitchen trembling. He could
not escape the sound—the stones carried it echoing
to him wherever he went.

The cook turned and looked at him. "Don't be
angry, boy," he said. "It's all in fun."

Bork nodded and smiled at the cook. That's what
it was. All in fun. And besides, Bork deserved it, he
knew. It was only fair that he be treated cruelly. For
he had earned the title Bork the Bully, hadn't he?
When he was three, and already massive as a ram,
his only friend, a beautiful young village boy named
Winkle, had hit upon the idea of becoming a knight.
Winkle had dressed himself in odds and ends of
leather and tin, and made a makeshift lance from a
hog prod.

"You're my destrier," Winkle cried as he mounted
Bork and rode him for hours. Bork thought it was a
fine thing to be a knight's horse. It became the height

of his ambition, and he wondered how one got started in the trade. But one day Sam, the stableman's son, had taunted Winkle for his make-believe armor, and it had turned into a fist fight, and Sam had thoroughly bloodied Winkle's nose. Winkle screamed as if he were dying, and Bork sprang to his friend's defense, walloping Sam, who was three years older, along the side of his head.

Ever since then Sam spoke with a thickness in his voice, and often lost his balance; his jaw, broken in several places, never healed properly, and he had problems with his ear.

It horrified Bork to have caused so much pain, but Winkle assured him that Sam deserved it. "After all, Bork, he was twice my size, and he was picking on me. He's a bully. He had it coming."

For several years Winkle and Bork were the terror of the village. Winkle would constantly get into fights, and soon the village children learned not to resist him. If Winkle lost a fight, he would scream for Bork, and though Bork was never again so harsh as he was with Sam, his blows still hurt terribly. Winkle loved it. Then one day he tired of being a knight, dismissed his destrier, and became fast friends with the other children. It was only then that Bork began to hear himself called Bork the Bully; it was Winkle who convinced the other children that the only villain in the fighting had been Bork. "After all," Bork overheard Winkle say one day, "he's twice as strong as anyone else. Isn't fair for him to fight. It's a cowardly thing for him to do, and we mustn't have anything to do with him. Bullies must be punished."

Bork knew Winkle was right, and ever after that he bore the burden of shame. He remembered the frightened looks in the other children's eyes when he approached them, the way they pleaded for mercy. But Winkle was always screaming and writhing in agony, and Bork always hit the child despite his terror, and for that bullying Bork was still paying. He paid in the ridicule he accepted from the knights; he paid in the solitude of all his days and nights; he paid by working as hard as he could, using his strength to serve instead of hurt.

But just because he knew he deserved the punishment did not mean he enjoyed it. There were tears in his eyes as he went about his work in the kitchen. He tried to hide them from the cook, but to no avail. "Oh, no, you're not going to cry, are you?" the cook said. "You'll only make your nose run and then you'll get snot in the soup. Get out of the kitchen for awhile!"

Which is why Bork was standing in the doorway of the great hall watching the council that would completely change his life.

"Well, where's the tribute money gone to?" demanded one of the knights. "The harvest was large enough last year!"

It was an ugly thing, to see the knights so angry. But the Count knew they had a right to be upset—it was they who would have to fight the Duke's men, and they had a right to know why.

"My friends," the Count said. "My friends, some things are more important than money. I invested the money in something more important than tribute, more important than peace, more important than long life. I invested the money in beauty. Not to create beauty, but to perfect it." The knights were listening now. For all their violent preoccupations, they all had a soft spot in their hearts for true beauty. It was one of the requirements for knighthood. "I have been entrusted with a jewel, more perfect than any diamond. It was my duty to place that jewel in the best setting money could buy. I can't explain. I can only show you." He rang a small bell, and behind him one of the better-known secret doors in the castle opened, and a wizened old woman emerged. The Count whispered in her ear, and the woman scurried back into the secret passage.

"Who's she?" asked one of the knights.

"She is the woman who nursed my children after my wife died. My wife died in childbirth, you remember. But what you don't know is that the child lived. My two sons you know well. But I have a third child, my last child, whom you know not at all, and this one is not a son."

The Count was not surprised that several of the knights seemed to puzzle over this riddle. Too many jousts, too much practice in full armor in the heat of the afternoon.

"My child is a daughter."

"Ah," said the knights.

"At first, I kept her hidden away because I could not bear to see her—after all, my most beloved wife had died in bearing her. But after a few years I overcame my grief, and went to see the child in the room where she was hidden, and lo! She was the most beautiful child I had ever seen. I named her Brunhilda, and from that moment on I loved her. I was the most devoted father you could imagine. But I did not let her leave the secret room. Why, you may ask?"

"Yes, why!" demanded several of the knights.

"Because she was so beautiful I was afraid she would be stolen from me. I was terrified that I would lose her. Yet I saw her every day, and talked to her, and the older she got, the more beautiful she became, and for the last several years I could no longer bear to see her in her mother's cast-off clothing. Her beauty is such that only the finest cloths and gowns and jewels of Flanders, of Venice, of Florence would do for her. You'll see! The money was not ill spent."

And the door opened again, and the old woman emerged, leading forth Brunhilda.

In the doorway, Bork gasped. But no one heard him, for all the knights gasped, too.

She was the most perfect woman in the world. Her hair was a dark red, flowing behind her like an auburn stream as she walked. Her face was white from being indoors all her life, and when she smiled it was like the sun breaking out on a stormy day. And none of the knights dared look at her body for very long, because the longer they looked the more they wanted to touch her, and the Count said, "I warn you. Any man who lays a hand on her will have to answer to me. She is a virgin, and when she marries she shall be a virgin, and a king will pay half his kingdom to have her, and still I'll feel cheated to have to give her up."

"Good morning, my lords," she said, smiling. Her voice was like the song of leaves dancing in the summer wind, and the knights fell to their knees before her.

None of them was more moved by her beauty than Bork, however. When she entered the room he forgot himself; there was no room in his mind for anything but the great beauty he had seen for the first time in his life. Bork knew nothing of courtesy. He only knew that, for the first time in his life, he had seen something so perfect that he could not rest until it was his. Not his to own, but his to be owned by. He longed to serve her in the most degrading ways he could think of, if only she would smile upon him; longed to die for her, if only the last moment of his life were filled with her voice saying, "You may love me."

If he had been a knight, he might have thought of a poetic way to say such things. But he was not a knight, and so his words came out of his heart before his mind could find a way to make them clever. He strode blindly from the kitchen door, his huge body casting a shadow that seemed to the knights like the shadow of death passing over them. They watched with uneasiness that soon turned to outrage as he came to the girl, reached out, and took her small white hands in his.

"I love you," Bork said to her, and tears came unbidden to his eyes. "Let me marry you."

At that moment several of the knights found their courage. They seized Bork roughly by the arms, meaning to pull him away and punish him for his effrontery. But Bork effortlessly tossed them away. They fell to the ground yards from him. He never saw them fall; his gaze never left the lady's face.

She looked wonderingly into his eyes. Not because she thought him attractive, because he was ugly and she knew it. Not because of the words he had said, because she had been taught that many men would say those words, and she was to pay no attention to them. What startled her, what amazed her, was the deep truth in Bork's face. That was something she had never seen, and though she did not recognize it for what it was, it fascinated her.

The Count was furious. Seeing the clumsy giant holding his daughter's small white hands in his was outrageous. He would not endure it. But the giant had such great strength that to tear him away would mean a full-scale battle, and in such a battle Brunhilda might be injured. No, the giant had to be handled delicately, for the moment.

"My dear fellow," said the Count, affecting a joviality he did not feel. "You've only just met."

Bork ignored him. "I will never let you come to harm," he said to the girl.

"What's his name?" the Count whispered to a knight. "I can't remember his name."

"Bork," the knight answered.

"My dear Bork," said the Count. "All due respect and everything, but my daughter has noble blood, and you're not even a knight."

"Then I'll become one," Bork said.

"It's not that easy, Bork, old fellow. You must do something exceptionally brave, and then I can knight you and we can talk about this other matter. But in the meantime, it isn't proper for you to be holding my daughter's hands. Why don't you go back to the kitchen like a good fellow?"

Bork gave no sign that he heard. He only continued looking into the lady's eyes. And finally it was she who was able to end the dilemma.

"Bork," she said, "I will count on you. But in the meantime, my father will be angry with you if you don't return to the kitchen.

Of course, Bork thought. Of course, she is truly concerned for me, doesn't want me to come to harm on her account. "For your sake," he said, the madness of love still on him. The he turned and left the room.

The Count sat down, sighing audibly. "Should have got rid of him years ago. Gentle as a lamb, and then all of a sudden goes crazy. Get rid of him—somebody take care of that tonight, would you? Best to do it in his sleep. Don't want any casualties when we're likely to have a battle at any moment."

The reminder of the battle was enough to sober even those who were on their fifth mug of ale. The wizened old woman led Brunhilda away again. "But not to the secret room, now. To the chamber next to mine. And post a double guard outside her door, and keep the key yourself," said the Count.

When she was gone, the Count looked around at the knights. "The treasury has been emptied in a vain attempt to find clothing to do her justice. I had no other choice."

And there was not a knight who would say the money had been badly spent.

* * *

The Duke came late that afternoon, much sooner than he was expected. He demanded the tribute. The Count refused, of course. There was the usual challenge to come out of the castle and fight, but the Count, outnumbered ten to one, merely replied, rather saucily, that the Duke should come in and get him. The messenger who delivered the sarcastic message came back with his tongue in a bag around his neck. The battle was thus begun grimly: and grimly it continued.

The guard watching on the south side of the castle was slacking. He paid for it. The Duke's archers managed to creep up to the huge oak tree and climb it without any alarm being given, and the first notice any of them had was when the guard fell from the battlements with an arrow in his throat.

The archers—there must have been a dozen of them—kept up a deadly rain of arrows. They wasted no shots. The squires dropped dead in alarming numbers until the Count gave orders for them to come inside. And when the human targets were all under cover, the archers set to work on the cattle and sheep milling in the open pens. There was no way to protect the animals. By sunset, all of them were dead.

"Dammit," said the cook. "How can I cook all this before it spoils?"

"Find a way," said the Count. "That's our food supply. I refuse to let them starve us out."

So all night Bork worked, carrying the cattle and sheep inside, one by one. At first the villagers who had taken refuge in the castle tried to help him, but he could carry three animals inside the kitchen in the time it took them to drag one, and they soon gave it up.

The Count saw who was saving the meat. "Don't get rid of him tonight," he told the knights. "We'll punish him for his effrontery in the morning."

Bork only rested twice in the night, taking naps for an hour before the cook woke him again. And when dawn came, and the arrows began coming again, all the cattle were inside, and all but twenty sheep.

"That's all we can save," the cook told the Count.

"Save them all."

"But if Bork tries to go out there, he'll be killed!"

The Count looked the cook in the eyes. "Bring in the sheep or have him die trying."

The cook was not aware of the fact that Bork was under sentence of death. So he did his best to save Bork. A kettle lined with cloth and strapped onto the giant's head; a huge kettle lid for a shield. "It's the best we can do," the cook said.

"But I can't carry sheep if I'm holding a shield," Bork said.

"What can I do? The Count commanded it. It's worth your life to refuse."

Bork stood and thought for a few moments, trying to find a way out of his dilemma. He saw only one possibility. "If I can't stop them from hitting me, I'll have to stop them from shooting at all."

"How!" the cook demanded, and then followed Bork to the blacksmith's shop, where Bork found his huge ax leaning against the wall.

"Now's not the time to cut firewood," said the blacksmith.

"Yes it is," Bork answered.

Carrying the ax and holding the kettle lid between his body and the archers, Bork made his way across the courtyard. The arrows pinged harmlessly off the metal. Bork got to the drawbridge. "Open up!" he shouted, and the drawbridge fell away and dropped across the moat. Bork walked across, then made his way along the moat toward the oak tree.

In the distance the Duke, standing in front of his dazzling white tent with his emblem of yellow on

it, saw Bork emerge from the castle. "Is that a man
or a bear?" he asked. No one was sure.

The archers shot at Bork steadily, but the closer
he got to the tree, the worse their angle of fire and
the larger the shadow of safety the kettle lid cast
over his body. Finally, holding the lid high over his
head, Bork began hacking one-handed at the trunk.
Chips of wood flew with each blow; with his right
hand alone he could cut deeper and faster than a
normal man with both hands free.

But he was concentrating on cutting wood, and his
left arm grew tired holding his makeshift shield, and
an archer was able to get off a shot that slipped past
the shield and plunged into his left arm, in the thick
muscle at the back.

He nearly dropped the shield. Instead, he had the
presence of mind to let go of the ax and drop to his
knees, quickly balancing the kettle lid between the
tree trunk, his head, and the top of the ax handle.
Gently he pulled at the arrow shaft. It would not
come backward. So he broke the arrow and pushed
the stub the rest of the way through his arm until it
was out the other side. It was excruciatingly painful,
but he knew he could not quit now. He took hold of
the shield with his left arm again, and despite the
pain held it high as he began to cut again, girdling
the tree with a deep white gouge. The blood dripped
steadily down his arm, but he ignored it, and soon
enough the bleeding stopped and slowed.

On the castle battlements, the Count's men began
to realize that there was a hope of Bork's succeeding.
To protect him, they began to shoot their arrows into
the tree. The archers were well hidden, but the rain
of arrows, however badly aimed, began to have its
effect. A few of them dropped to the ground, where
the castle archers could easily finish them off; the
others were forced to concentrate on finding cover.

The tree trembled more and more with each blow,

until finally Bork stepped back and the tree creaked and swayed. He had learned from his lumbering work in the forest how to make the tree fall where he wanted it; the oak fell parallel to the castle walls, so it neither bridged the moat nor let the Duke's archers scramble from the tree too far from the castle. So when the archers tried to flee to the safety of the Duke's lines, the castle bowmen were able to kill them all.

One of them, however, despaired of escape. Instead, though he already had an arrow in him, he drew a knife and charged at Bork, in a mad attempt to avenge his own death on the man who had caused it. Bork had no choice. He swung his ax through the air and discovered that men are nowhere near as sturdy as a tree.

In the distance, the Duke watched with horror as the giant cut a man in half with a single blow. "What have they got!" he said. "What is this monster?"

Covered with the blood that had spurted from the dying man, Bork walked back toward the drawbridge, which opened again as he approached. But he did not get to enter. Instead the Count and fifty mounted knights came from the gate on horseback, their armor shining in the sunlight.

"I've decided to fight them in the open," the Count said. "And you, Bork, must fight with us. If you live through this, I'll make you a knight!"

Bork knelt. "Thank you, my Lord Count," he said.

The Count glanced around in embarrassment. "Well, then. Let's get to it. Charge!" he bellowed.

Bork did not realize that the knights were not even formed in a line yet. He simply followed the command and charged, alone, toward the Duke's lines. The Count watched him go, and smiled.

"My Lord Count," said the nearest knight. "Aren't we going to attack with him?"

"Let the Duke take care of him," the Count said.

"But he cut down the oak and saved the castle, my lord."

"Yes," said the Count. "An exceptionally brave act. Do you want him to try to claim my daughter's hand?"

"But my lord," said the knight, "if he fights beside us, we might have a chance of winning. But if he's gone, the Duke will destroy us."

"Some things," said the Count, with finality, "are more important than victory. Would you want to go on living in a world where perfection like Brunhilda's was possessed by such a man as that?"

The knights were silent, then, as they watched Bork approach the Duke's army, alone.

Bork did not realize he was alone until he stood a few feet away from the Duke's lines. He had felt strange as he walked across the fields, believing he was marching into battle with the knights he had long admired in their bright armor and deft instruments of war. Now the exhilaration was gone. Where were the others? Bork was afraid.

He could not understand why the Duke's men had not shot any arrows at him. Actually, it was a misunderstanding. If the Duke had known Bork was a commoner and not a knight at all, Bork would have had a hundred arrows bristling from his corpse. As it was, however, one of the Duke's men called out, "You, sir! Do you challenge us to single combat?"

Of course. That was it—the Count did not intend Bork to face an army, he intended him to face a single warrior. The whole outcome of the battle would depend on him alone! It was a tremendous honor, and Bork wondered if he could carry it off.

"Yes! Single combat!" he answered. "Your strongest, bravest man!"

"But you're a giant!" cried the Duke's man.

"But I'm wearing no armor." And to prove his sincerity, Bork took off his helmet, which was uncomfortable anyway, and stepped forward. The Duke's knights backed away, making an opening for him, with men in armor watching him pass from both sides. Bork walked steadily on, until he came to a cleared circle where he faced the Duke himself.

"Are you the champion?" asked Bork.

"I'm the Duke," he answered. "But I don't see any of my knights stepping forward to fight you."

"Do you refuse the challenge, then?" Bork asked, trying to sound as brave and scornful as he imagined a true knight would sound.

The Duke looked around at his men, who, if the armor had allowed, would have been shuffling uncomfortably in the morning sunlight. As it was, none of them looked at him.

"No," said the Duke. "I accept your challenge myself." The thought of fighting the giant terrified him. But he was a knight, and known to be a brave man; he had become Duke in the prime of his youth, and if he backed down before a giant now, his duchy would be taken from him in only a few years; his honor would be lost long before. So he drew his sword and advanced upon the giant.

Bork saw the determination in the Duke's eyes, and marvelled at a man who would go himself into a most dangerous battle instead of sending his men. Briefly Bork wondered why the Count had not shown such courage; he determined at that moment that if he could help it the Duke would not die. The blood of the archer was more than he had ever wanted to shed. Nobility was in every movement of the Duke, and Bork wondered at the ill chance that had made them enemies.

The Duke lunged at Bork with his sword flashing. Bork hit him with the flat of the ax, knocking him to the ground. The Duke cried out in pain. His armor was dented deeply; there had to be ribs broken under the dent.

"Why don't you surrender?" asked Bork.

"Kill me now!"

"If you surrender, I won't kill you at all."

The Duke was surprised. There was a murmur from his men.

"I have your word?"

"Of course. I swear it."

It was too startling an idea.

"What do you plan to do, hold me for ransom?"

Bork thought about it. "I don't think so."

"Well, what then? Why not kill me and have done with it?" The pain in his chest now dominated the Duke's voice, but he did not spit blood, and so he began to have some hope.

"All the Count wants you to do is go away and stop collecting tribute. If you promise to do that, I'll promise that not one of you will be harmed."

The Duke and his men considered in silence. It was too good to believe. So good it was almost dishonorable even to consider it. Still—there was Bork, who had broken the Duke's body with one blow, right through the armor. If he chose to let them walk away from the battle, why argue?

"I give my word that I'll cease collecting tribute from the Count, and my men and I will go in peace."

"Well, then, that's good news," Bork said. "I've got to tell the Count." And Bork turned away and walked into the fields, heading for where the Count's tiny army waited.

"I can't believe it," said the Duke. "A knight like that, and he turns out to be generous. The Count could have his way with the King, with a knight like that."

They stripped the armor off him, carefully, and began wrapping his chest with bandages.

"If he were mine," the Duke said, "I'd use him to conquer the whole land."

The Count watched, incredulous, as Bork crossed the field.

"He's still alive," he said, and he began to wonder what Bork would have to say about the fact that none of the knights had joined his gallant charge.

"My Lord Count!" cried Bork, when he was within range. He would have waved, but both his arms were exhausted now. "They surrender!"

"What?" the Count asked the knights near him. "Did he say they surrender?"

"Apparently," a knight answered. "Apparently he won."

"Damn!" cried the Count. "I won't have it!"

The knights were puzzled. "If anybody's going to defeat the Duke, *I* am! Not a damnable commoner! Not a giant with the brains of a cockroach! Charge!"

"What? several of the knights asked.

"I said charge!" And the Count moved forward, his warhorse plodding carefully through the field, building up momentum.

Bork saw the knights start forward. He had watched enough mock battles to recognize a charge. He could only assume that the Count hadn't heard him. But the charge had to be stopped—he had given his word, hadn't he? So he planted himself in the path of the Count's horse.

"Out of the way, you damned fool!" cried the Count. But Bork stood his ground. The Count was determined not to be thwarted. He prepared to ride Bork down.

"You can't charge!" Bork yelled. "They surrendered!"

The Count gritted his teeth and urged the horse forward, his lance prepared to cast Bork out of the way.

A moment later the Count found himself in mid-air, hanging to the lance for his life. Bork held it over his head, and the knights laboriously halted their charge and wheeled to see what was going on with Bork and the Count.

"My Lord Count," Bork said respectfully. "I guess you didn't hear me. They surrendered. I promised them they could go in peace if they stopped collecting tribute."

From his precarious hold on the lance, fifteen feet off the ground, the Count said, "I didn't hear you."

"I didn't think so. But you *will* let them go, won't you?"

"Of course. Could you give a thought to letting me down, old boy?"

And so Bork let the Count down, and there was a peace treaty between the Duke and the Count, and the Duke's men rode away in peace, talking about the generosity of the giant knight.

"But he isn't a knight," said a servant to the Duke.

"What? Not a knight?"

"No. Just a villager. One of the peasants told me, when I was stealing his chickens.

"Not a knight," said the Duke, and for a moment his face began to turn the shade of red that made his knights want to ride a few feet further from him—they knew his rage too well already.

"We were tricked, then," said a knight, trying to fend off his lord's anger by anticipating it.

The Duke said nothing for a moment. Then he smiled. "Well, if he's not a knight, he should be. He has the strength. He has the courtesy. Hasn't he?"

The knights agreed that he had.

"He's the moral equivalent of a knight," said the Duke. Pride assuaged, for the moment, he led his men back to his castle. Underneath, however, even deeper than the pain in his ribs, was the image of the Count perched on the end of a lance held high in the air by the giant, Bork, and he pondered what it might have meant, and what, more to the point, it might mean in the future.

Things were getting out of hand, the Count decided. First of all, the victory celebration had not been his idea, and yet here they were, riotously drunken in the great hall, and even villagers were making free with the ale, laughing and cheering among the knights. That was bad enough, but worse was the fact that the knights were making no pretense about it—the party was in honor of Bork.

The Count drummed his fingers on the table. No one paid any attention. They were too busy—Sir Alwishard trying to keep two village wenches occupied near the fire, Sir Silwiss pissing in the wine and laughing so loud that the Count could hardly hear Sir Braig and Sir Umlaut as they sang and danced along the table, kicking plates off with their toes in time with the music. It was the best party the Count had ever seen. And it wasn't for him, it was for that damnable giant who had made an ass of him in front of all his men and all the Duke's men and, worst of all, the Duke. He heard a strange growling sound, like a savage wolf getting ready to spring. In a lull in the bedlam he suddenly realized that the sound was coming from his own throat.

Get control of yourself, he thought. The real gains, the solid gains were not Bork's—they were mine. The Duke is gone, and instead of paying him tribute from now on, he'll be paying me. Word would get around, too, that the Count had won a battle with the Duke. After all, that was the basis of power— who could beat whom in battle. A duke was just a man who could beat a count, a count someone who could beat a baron, a baron someone who could beat a knight.

But what was a person who could beat a duke?

"You should be king," said a tall, slender young man standing near the throne.

The Count looked at him, making a vague motion with his hidden hand. How had the boy read his thoughts?

"I'll pretend I didn't hear that."

"You heard it," said the young man.

"It's treason."

"Only if the king beats you in battle. If *you* win, it's treason *not* to say so."

The Count looked the boy over. Dark hair that looked a bit too carefully combed for a villager. A straight nose, a pleasant smile, a winning grace when he walked. But something about his eyes gave the lie to the smile. The boy was vicious somehow. The boy was dangerous.

"I like you," said the Count.

"I'm glad." He did not sound glad. He sounded bored.

"If I'm smart, I'll have you strangled immediately."

The boy only smiled more.

"Who are you?"

"My name is Winkle. And I'm Bork's best friend."

Bork. There he was again, that giant sticking his immense shadow into everything tonight. "Didn't know Bork the Bully had any friends."

"He has one. Me. Ask him."

"I wonder if a friend of Bork's is really a friend of mine," the Count said.

"I said I was his best friend. I didn't say I was a good friend." And Winkle smiled.

A thoroughgoing bastard, the Count decided, but he waved to Bork and beckoned for him to come. In a moment the giant knelt before the Count, who was irritated to discover that when Bork knelt and the Count sat, Bork still looked down on him.

"This man," said the Count, "claims to be your friend."

Bork looked up and recognized Winkle, who was beaming down at him, his eyes filled with love, mostly. A hungry kind of love, but Bork wasn't discriminating. He had the admiration and grudging respect of the knights, but he hardly knew them. This was his childhood friend, and at the thought that Winkle claimed to be his friend Bork immediately forgave all the past slights and smiled back. "Winkle," he said. "Of course we're friends. He's my *best* friend."

The Count made the mistake of looking in Bork's eyes and seeing the complete sincerity of his love for Winkle. It embarrassed him, for he knew Winkle all too well already, from just the moments of conversation they had had. Winkle was nobody's friend. But Bork was obviously blind to that. For a moment the Count almost pitied the giant, had a glimpse of what his life must be like, if the predatory young villager was his best friend.

"Your majesty," said Winkle.

"Don't call me that."

"I only anticipate what the world will know in a matter of months."

Winkle sounded so confident, so sure of it. A chill went up the Count's spine. He shook it off. "I won one battle, Winkle. I still have a huge budget deficit and a pretty small army of fairly lousy knights."

"Think of your daughter, even if *you* aren't ambitious. Despite her beauty she'll be lucky to marry a duke. But if she were the daughter of a king, she could marry anyone in all the world. And her own lovely self would be a dowry—no prince would think to ask for more."

The Count thought of his daughter, the beautiful Brunhilda, and smiled.

Bork also smiled, for he was also thinking of the same thing.

"Your majesty," Winkle urged, "with Bork as your right-hand man and me as your counselor, there's nothing to stop you from being king within a year or two. Who would be willing to stand against an army with the three of us marching at the head?"

"Why three?" asked the Count.

"You mean, why me. I thought you would already understand that—but then, that's what you need me for. You see, your majesty, you're a good man, a godly man, a paragon of virtue. You would never think of seeking power and conniving against your enemies and spying and doing repulsive things to people you don't like. But kings *have* to do those things or they quickly cease to be kings."

Vaguely the Count remembered behaving in just that way many times, but Winkle's words were seductive—they *should* be true.

"Your majesty, where you are pure, I am polluted. Where you are fresh, I am rotten. I'd sell my mother into slavery if I had a mother and I'd cheat the devil at poker and win hell from him before he caught on. And I'd stab any of your enemies in the back if I got the chance."

"But what if my enemies aren't your enemies?" the Count asked.

"Your enemies are *always* my enemies. I'll be loyal to you through thick and thin."

"How can I trust you, if you're so rotten?"

"Because you're going to pay me a lot of money." Winkle bowed deeply.

"Done," said the Count.

"Excellent," said Winkle, and they shook hands. The Count noticed that Winkle's hands were smooth—he had neither the hard horny palms of a village workingman nor the slick calluses of a man trained to warfare.

"How have you made a living, up to now?" the Count asked.

"I steal," Winkle said, with a smile that said I'm joking and a glint in his eye that said I'm not.

"What about me?" asked Bork.

"Oh, you're in it, too," said Winkle. "You're the king's strong right arm."

"I've never met the king," said Bork.

"Yes you have," Winkle retorted. "That is the king."

"No he's not," said the giant. "He's only a count."

The words stabbed the Count deeply. *Only* a count. Well, that would end. "Today I'm only a count," he said patiently. "Who knows what tomorrow will bring? But Bork—I shall knight you. As a knight you must swear absolute loyalty to me and do whatever I say. Will you do that?"

"Of course I will," said Bork. "Thank you, my Lord Count." Bork arose and called to his new friends throughout the hall in a voice that could not be ignored. "My Lord Count has decided I will be made a knight!" There were cheers and applause and stamping of feet. "And the best thing is," Bork said, "that now I can marry the Lady Brunhilda."

There was no applause. Just a murmur of alarm. Of course. If he became a knight, he was eligible for Brunhilda's hand. It was unthinkable—but the Count himself had said so.

The Count was having second thoughts, of course, but he knew no way to back out of it, not without looking like a word-breaker. He made a false start at speaking, but couldn't finish. Bork waited expectantly. Clearly he believed the Count would confirm what Bork had said.

It was Winkle, however, who took the situation in hand. "Oh, Bork," he said sadly—but loudly, so that everyone could hear. "Don't you understand? His majesty is making you a knight out of gratitude. But unless you're a king or the son of a king, you have to do something exceptionally brave to earn Brunhilda's hand."

"But, wasn't I brave today?" Bork asked. After all, the arrow wound in his arm still hurt, and only the ale kept him from aching unmercifully all over from the exertion of the night and the day just past.

"You were brave. But since you're twice the size and ten times the strength of an ordinary man, it's hardly fair for you to win Brunhilda's hand with ordinary bravery. No, Bork—it's just the way things work. It's just the way things are done. Before you're worthy of Brunhilda, you have to do something ten times as brave as what you did today."

Bork could not think of something ten times as brave. Hadn't he gone almost unprotected to chop down the oak tree? Hadn't he attacked a whole army all by himself, and won the surrender of the enemy? What could be ten times as brave?

"Don't despair," the Count said. "Surely in all the battles ahead of us there'll be *something* ten times as brave. And in the meantime, you're a knight, my friend, a great knight, and you shall dine at my table every night! And when we march into battle, there you'll be, right beside me—"

"A few steps ahead," Winkle whispered discreetly.

"A few steps ahead of me, to defend the honor of my country—"

"Don't be shy," whispered Winkle.

"No, not my country. My kingdom. For from today, you men no longer serve a count! You serve a king!"

It was a shocking declaration, and might have caused sober reflection if there had been a sober man in the room. But through the haze of alcohol and torchlight and fatigue, the knights looked at the Count and he did indeed seem kingly. And they thought of the battles ahead and were not afraid, for they had won a glorious victory today and not one of them had shed a drop of blood. Except, of course, Bork. But in some corner of their collected opinions was a viewpoint they would not have admitted to holding, if anyone brought the subject out in the open. The opinion so well hidden from themselves and each other was simple: Bork is not like me. Bork is not one of us. Therefore, Bork is expendable.

The blood that still stained his sleeve was cheap. Plenty more where that came from.

And so they plied him with more ale until he fell asleep, snoring hugely on the table, forgetting that he had been cheated out of the woman he loved; it was easy to forget, for the moment, because he was a knight, and a hero, and at last he had friends.

It took two years for the Count to become King. He began close to home, with other counts, but soon progressed to the great dukes and earls of the kingdom. Wherever he went, the pattern was the same. The Count and his fifty knights would ride their horses, only lightly armored so they could travel with reasonable speed. Bork would walk, but his long legs easily kept up with the rest of them. They would arrive at their victim's castle, and three squires would hand Bork his new steel-handled ax. Bork, covered with impenetrable armor, would wade the moat, if there was one, or simply walk up to the gates, swing the ax, and begin chopping through the wood. When the gates collapsed, Bork would take a huge steel rod and use it as a crow, prying at the portcullis, bending the heavy iron like pretzels until there was a gap wide enough for a mounted knight to ride through.

Then he would go back to the Count and Winkle.

Throughout this operation, not a word would have been said; the only activity from the Count's other men would be enough archery that no one would be able to pour boiling oil or hot tar on Bork while he was working. It was a precaution, and nothing more—even if they set the oil on the fire the moment the Count's little army approached, it would scarcely be hot enough to make water steam by the time Bork was through.

"Do you surrender to his Majesty the King?" Winkle would cry.

And the defenders of the castle, their gate hopelessly breached and terrified of the giant who had so easily made a joke of their defenses, would usually surrender. Occasionally there was some token resistance—when that happened, at Winkle's insistence, the town was brutally sacked and the noble's family was held in prison until a huge ransom was paid.

At the end of two years, the Count and Bork and Winkle and their army marched on Winchester. The King—the real king—fled before them and took up his exile in Anjou, where it was warmer anyway. The Count had himself crowned king, accepted the fealty of every noble in the country, and introduced his daughter Brunhilda all around. Then, finding Winchester not to his liking, he returned to his castle and ruled from there. Suitors for his daughter's hand made a constant traffic on the roads leading into the country; would-be courtiers and nobles vying for positions filled the new hostelries that sprang up on the other side of the village. All left much poorer than they had arrived. And while much of that money found its way into the King's coffers, much more of it went to Winkle, who believed that skimming off the cream meant leaving at least a quarter of it for the King.

And now that the wars were done, Bork hung up his armor and went back to normal life. Not quite normal life, actually. He slept in a good room in the castle, better than most of the knights. Some of the knights had even come to enjoy his company, and sought him out for ale in the evenings or hunting in the daytime—Bork could always be counted on to carry home two deer himself, and was much more convenient than a packhorse. All in all, Bork was happier than he had ever thought he would be.

Which is how things were going when the dragon came and changed it all forever.

Winkle was in Brunhilda's room, a place he had learned many routes to get to, so that he went unobserved every time. Brunhilda, after many gifts and more flattery, was on the verge of giving in to the handsome young advisor to the King when strange screams and cries began coming from the fields below. Brunhilda pulled away from Winkle's exploring hands and, clutching her half-open gown around her, rushed to the window to see what was the matter.

She looked down, to where the screams were coming from, and it wasn't until the dragon's shadow fell across her that she looked up. Winkle, waiting on the bed, only saw the claws reach in and, gently but firmly, take hold of Brunhilda and pull her from the room. Brunhilda fainted immediately, and by the time Winkle got to where he could see her, the dragon had backed away from the window and on great flapping wings was carrying her limp body off toward the north whence he had come.

Winkle was horrified. It was so sudden, something he could not have foreseen or planned against. Yet still he cursed himself and bitterly realized that his plans might be ended forever. A dragon had taken Brunhilda who was to be his means of legitimately becoming king; now the plot of seduction, marriage, and inheritance was ruined.

Ever practical, Winkle did not let himself lament

for long. He dressed himself quickly and used a secret passage out of Brunhilda's room, only to reappear in the corridor outside it a moment later. "Brunhilda!" he cried, beating on the door. "Are you all right?"

The first of the knights reached him, and then the King, weeping and wailing and smashing anything that got in his way. Brunhilda's door was down in a moment, and the King ran to the window and cried out after his daughter, now a pinpoint speck in the sky many miles away. "Brunhilda! Brunhilda! Come back!" She did not come back. "Now," cried the King, as he turned back into the room and sank to the floor, his face twisted and wet with grief, "Now I have nothing, and all is in vain!"

My thoughts precisely, Winkle thought, but I'm not weeping about it. To hide his contempt he walked to the window and looked out. He saw, not the dragon, but Bork, emerging from the forest carrying two huge logs.

"Sir Bork," said Winkle.

The King heard a tone of decision in Winkle's voice. He had learned to listen to whatever Winkle said in that tone of voice. "What about him?"

"Sir Bork could defeat a dragon," Winkle said, "if any man could."

"That's true," the King said, gathering back some of the hope he had lost. "Of course that's true."

"But will he?" asked Winkle.

"Of course he will. He loves Brunhilda, doesn't he?"

"He said he did. But Your Majesty, is he really loyal to you? After all, why wasn't he here when the dragon came? Why didn't he save Brunhilda in the first place?"

"He was cutting wood for the winter."

"Cutting wood? When Brunhilda's life was at stake?"

The King was outraged. The illogic of it escaped

him—he was not in a logical mood. So he was furious when he met Bork at the gate of the castle.

"You've betrayed me!" the King cried.

"I have?" Bork was smitten with guilt. And he hadn't even meant to.

"You weren't here when we needed you. When *Brunhilda* needed you!"

"I'm sorry," Bork said.

"Sorry, sorry, sorry. A lot of good it does to say you're sorry. You swore to protect Brunhilda from any enemy, and when a really dangerous enemy comes along, how do you repay me for everything I've done for you? You hide out in the forest!"

"What enemy?"

"A dragon," said the King, "as if you didn't see it coming and run out into the woods."

"Cross my heart, Your Majesty, I didn't know there was a dragon coming." And then he made the connection in his mind. "The dragon—it took Brunhilda?"

"It took her. Took her half-naked from her bedroom when she leaped to the window to call to you for help."

Bork felt the weight of guilt, and it was a terrible burden. His face grew hard and angry, and he walked into the castle, his harsh footfalls setting the earth to trembling. "My armor!" he cried. "My sword!"

In minutes he was in the middle of the courtyard, holding out his arms as the heavy mail was draped over him and the breastplate and helmet were strapped and screwed into place. The sword was not enough—he also carried his huge ax and a shield so massive two ordinary men could have hidden behind it.

"Which way did he go?" Bork asked.

"North," the King answered.

"I'll bring back your daughter, Your Majesty, or die in the attempt."

"Damn well better. It's all your fault."

The words stung, but the sting only impelled Bork further. He took the huge sack of food the cook had prepared for him and fastened it to his belt, and without a backward glance strode from the castle and took the road north.

"I almost feel sorry for the dragon," said the King.

But Winkle wondered. He had seen how large the claws were as they grasped Brunhilda—she had been like a tiny doll in a large man's fingers. The claws were razor sharp. Even if she were still alive, could Bork really best the dragon? Bork the Bully, after all, had made his reputation picking on men smaller than he, as Winkle had ample reason to know. How would he do facing a dragon at least five times his size? Wouldn't he turn coward? Wouldn't he run as other men had run from *him*?

He might. But Sir Bork the Bully was Winkle's only hope of getting Brunhilda and the kingdom. If he could do anything to ensure that the giant at least *tried* to fight the dragon, he would do it. And so, taking only his rapier and a sack of food, Winkle left the castle by another way, and followed the giant along the road toward the north.

And then he had a terrible thought.

Fighting the dragon was surely ten times as brave as anything Bork had done before. If he won, wouldn't he have a claim on Brunhilda's hand himself?

It was not something Winkle wished to think about. Something would come to him, some way around the problem when the time came. Plenty of opportunity to plan something—*after* Bork wins and rescues her.

Bork had not rounded the second turn in the road when he came across the old woman, waiting by the side of the road. It was the same old woman who had cared for Brunhilda all those years that she was kept in a secret room in the castle. She looked wizened and weak, but there was a sharp look in her eyes that many had mistaken for great wisdom. It was not great wisdom. But she did know a few things about dragons.

"Going after the dragon, are you?" she asked in a squeaky voice. "Going to get Brunhilda back, are you?" She giggled darkly behind her hand.

"I am if anyone can," Bork said.

"Well, anyone can't," she answered.

"*I* can."

"Not a prayer, you big bag of wind!"

Bork ignored her and started to walk past.

"Wait!" she said, her voice harsh as a dull file taking rust from armor. "Which way will you go?"

"North," he said. "That's the way the dragon took her."

"A quarter of the world is north, Sir Bork the Bully, and a dragon is small compared to all the mountains of the earth. But I know a way you can find the dragon, if you're really a knight.

"Light a torch, man. Light a torch, and whenever you come to a fork in the way, the light of the torch will leap the way you ought to go. Wind or no wind, fire seeks fire, and there is a flame at the heart of every dragon."

"They *do* breathe fire, then?" he asked. He did not know how to fight fire.

"Fire is light, not wind, and so it doesn't come from the dragon's mouth or the dragon's nostrils. If he burns you, it won't be with his breath." The old woman cackled like a mad hen. "No one knows the truth about dragons anymore!"

"Except you."

"I'm an old wife," she said. "And I know. They

don't eat human beings, either. They're strict vegetarians. But they kill. From time to time they kill."

"Why, if they aren't hungry for meat?"

"You'll see," she said. She started to walk away, back into the forest.

"Wait!" Bork called. "How far will the dragon be?"

"Not far," she said. "Not far, Sir Bork. He's waiting for you. He's waiting for you and all the fools who come to try to free the virgin." Then she melted away into the darkness.

Bork lit a torch and followed it all night, turning when the flame turned, unwilling to waste time in sleep when Brunhilda might be suffering unspeakable degradation at the monster's hands. And behind him, Winkle forced himself to stay awake, determined not to let Bork lose him in the darkness.

All night, and all day, and all night again Bork followed the light of the torch, through crooked paths long unused, until he came to the foot of a dry, tall hill, with rocks and crags along the top. He stopped, for here the flame leaped high, as if to say, "Upward from here." And in the silence he heard a sound that chilled him to the bone. It was Brunhilda, screaming as if she were being tortured in the cruelest imaginable way. And the screams were followed by a terrible roar. Bork cast aside the remnant of his food and made his way to the top of the hill. On the way he called out, to stop the dragon from whatever it was doing.

"Dragon! Are you there!"

The voice rumbled back to him with a power that made the dirt shift under Bork's feet. "Yes indeed."

"Do you have Brunhilda?"

"You mean the little virgin with the heart of an adder and the brain of a gnat?"

In the forest at the bottom of the hill, Winkle ground his teeth in fury, for despite his designs on the kingdom, he loved Brunhilda as much as he was capable of loving anyone.

"Dragon!" Bork bellowed at the top of his voice. "Dragon! Prepare to die!"

"Oh dear! Oh dear!" cried out the dragon. "Whatever shall I do?"

And then Bork reached the top of the hill, just as the sun topped the distant mountains and it became morning. In the light Bork immediately saw Brunhilda tied to a tree, her auburn hair glistening. All around her was the immense pile of gold that the dragon, according to custom, kept. And all around the gold was the dragon's tail.

Bork looked at the tail and followed it until finally he came to the dragon, who was leaning on a rock chewing on a tree trunk and smirking. The dragon's wings were clad with feathers, but the rest of him was covered with tough gray hide the color of weathered granite. His teeth, when he smiled, were ragged, long, and pointed. His claws were three feet long and sharp as a rapier from tip to base. But in spite of all this armament, the most dangerous thing about him was his eyes. They were large and soft and brown, with long lashes and gently arching brows. But at the center each eye held a sharp point of light, and when Bork looked at the eyes that light stabbed deep into him, seeing his heart and laughing at what it found there.

For a moment, looking at the dragon's eyes, Bork stood transfixed. Then the dragon reached over one wing toward Brunhilda, and with a great growling noise he began to tickle her ear.

Brunhilda was unbearably ticklish, and she let off a bloodcurdling scream.

"Touch her not!" Bork cried.

"Touch her what?" asked the dragon, with a chuckle. "I will not."

"Beast!" bellowed Bork. "I am Sir Bork the Big! I have never been defeated in battle! No man dares stand before me, and the beasts of the forest step aside when I pass!"

"You must be awfully clumsy," said the dragon.

Bork resolutely went on. He had seen the challenges and jousts—it was obligatory to recite and embellish your achievements in order to strike terror into the heart of the enemy. "I can cut down trees with one blow of my ax! I can cleave an ox from head to tail, I can skewer a running deer, I can break down walls of stone and doors of wood!"

"Why can't I ever get a handy servant like that?" murmured the dragon. "Ah well, you probably expect too large a salary."

The dragon's sardonic tone might have infuriated other knights; Bork was only confused, wondering if this matter was less serious than he had thought. "I've come to free Brunhilda, dragon. Will you give her up to me, or must I slay you?"

At that the dragon laughed long and loud. Then it cocked its head and looked at Bork. In that moment Bork knew that he had lost the battle. For deep in the dragon's eyes he saw the truth.

Bork saw himself knocking down gates and cutting down trees, but the deeds no longer looked heroic. Instead he realized that the knights who always rode behind him in these battles were laughing at him, that the King was a weak and vicious man, that Winkle's ambition was the only emotion he had room for; he saw that all of them were using him for their own ends, and cared nothing for him at all.

Bork saw himself asking for Brunhilda's hand in marriage, and he was ridiculous, an ugly, unkempt, and awkward giant in contrast to the slight and graceful girl. He saw that the King's hints of the possibility of their marriage were merely a trick, to blind him. More, he saw what no one else had been able to see—that Brunhilda loved Winkle, and Winkle wanted her.

And at last Bork saw himself as a warrior, and realized that in all the years of his great reputation and in all his many victories, he had fought only one man—an archer who ran at him with a knife. He had terrorized the weak and the small, but never until now had he faced a creature larger than himself. Bork looked in the dragon's eyes and saw his own death.

"Your eyes are deep," said Bork softly.

"Deep as a well, and you are drowning."

"Your sight is clear." Bork's palms were cold with sweat.

"Clear as ice, and you will freeze."

"Your eyes," Bork began. Then his mouth was suddenly so dry that he could barely speak. He swallowed. "Your eyes are filled with light."

"Bright and tiny as a star," the dragon whispered. "And see; your heart is afire."

Slowly the dragon stepped away from the rock, even as the tip of his tail reached behind Bork to push him into the dragon's waiting jaws. But Bork was not in so deep a trance that he could not see.

"I see that you mean to kill me," Bork said. "But you won't have me as easily as that." Bork whirled around to hack at the tip of the dragon's tail with his ax. But he was too large and slow, and the tail flicked away before the ax was fairly swung.

The battle lasted all day. Bork fought exhaustion as much as he fought the dragon, and it seemed the dragon only toyed with him. Bork would lurch toward the tail or a wing or the dragon's belly, but when his ax or sword fell where the dragon had been, it only sang in the air and touched nothing.

Finally Bork fell to his knees and wept. He wanted to go on with the fight, but his body could not do it. And the dragon looked as fresh as it had in the morning.

"What?" asked the dragon. "Finished already?"

Then Bork felt the tip of the dragon's tail touch his back, and the sharp points of the claws pressed gently on either side. He could not bear to look up at what he knew he would see. Yet neither could he bear to wait, not knowing when the blow would come. So he opened his eyes, and lifted his head, and saw.

The dragon's teeth were nearly touching him, poised to tear his head from his shoulders.

Bork screamed. And screamed again when the teeth touched him, when they pushed into his armor, when the dragon lifted him with teeth and tail and talons until he was twenty feet above the ground. He screamed again when he looked into the dragon's eyes and saw, not hunger, not hatred, but merely amusement.

And then he found his silence again, and listened as the dragon spoke through clenched teeth, watching the tongue move massively in the mouth only inches from his head.

"Well, little man. Are you afraid?"

Bork tried to think of some heroic message of defiance to hurl at the dragon, some poetic words that might be remembered forever so that his death would be sung in a thousand songs. But Bork's mind was not quick at such things; he was not that accustomed to speech, and had no ear for gallantry. Instead he began to think it would be somehow cheap and silly to die with a lie on his lips.

"Dragon," Bork whispered, "I'm frightened."

To Bork's surprise, the teeth did not pierce him then. Instead, he felt himself being lowered to the ground, heard a grating sound as the teeth and claws let go of his armor. He raised his visor, and saw that the dragon was now lying on the ground, laughing, rolling back and forth, slapping its tail against the rocks, and clapping its claws together. "Oh, my dear tiny friend," said the dragon. "I thought the day would never dawn."

"What day?"

"Today," answered the dragon. It had stopped laughing, and it once again drew near to Bork and looked him in the eye. "I'm going to let you live."

"Thank you," Bork said, trying to be polite.

"Thank me? Oh no, my midget warrior. You won't thank me. Did you think my teeth were sharp? Not half so pointed as the barbs of your jealous, disappointed friends."

"I can go?"

"You can go, you can fly, you can dwell in your castle for all I care. Do you want to know why?"

"Yes."

"Because you were afraid. In all my life, I have only killed brave knights who knew no fear. You're the first, the very first, who was afraid in that final moment. Now go." And the dragon gave Bork a push and sent him down the hill.

Brunhilda, who had watched the whole battle in curious silence, now called after him. "Some kind of knight you are! Coward! I hate you! Don't leave me!" The shouts went on until Bork was out of earshot.

Bork was ashamed.

Bork went down the hill and, as soon as he entered the cool of the forest, he lay down and fell asleep.

Hidden in the rocks, Winkle watched him go, watched as the dragon again began to tickle Brunhilda, whose gown was still open as it had been when she was taken by the dragon. Winkle could not stop thinking of how close he had come to having her. But now, if even Bork could not save her, her cause was hopeless, and Winkle immediately began planning other ways to profit from the situation.

All the plans depended on his reaching the castle before Bork. Since Winkle had dozed off and on during the day's battle, he was able to go farther—to a village, where he stole an ass and rode clumsily, half-asleep, all night and half the next day and reached the castle before Bork awoke.

The King raged. The King swore. The King vowed that Bork would die.

"But Your Majesty," said Winkle, "you can't forget that it is Bork who inspires fear in the hearts of your loyal subjects. You can't kill him—if he were dead, how long would you be king?"

That calmed the old man down. "Then I'll let him live. But he won't have a place in this castle, that's certain. I won't have him around here, the coward. Afraid! Told the dragon he was afraid! Pathetic. The man has no gratitude." And the King stalked from the court.

When Bork got home, weary and sick at heart, he found the gate of the castle closed to him. There was no explanation—he needed none. He had failed the one time it mattered most. He was no longer worthy to be a knight.

And now it was as it had been before. Bork was ignored, despised, feared, he was completely alone. But still, when it was time for great strength, there he was, doing the work of ten men, and not thanked for it. Who would thank a man for doing what he must to earn his bread.

In the evenings he would sit in his hut, staring at the fire that pushed a column of smoke up through the hole in the roof. He remembered how it had been to have friends, but the memory was not happy, for it was always poisoned by the knowledge that the friendship did not outlast Bork's first failure. Now the knights spat when they passed him on the road or in the fields.

The flames did not let Bork blame his troubles on them, however. The flames constantly reminded him of the dragon's eyes, and in their dance he saw himself, a buffoon who dared to dream of loving a princess, who believed that he was truly a knight. Not so, not so. I was never a knight, he thought. I was never worthy. Only now am I receiving what I deserve. And all his bitterness turned inward, and he hated himself far more than any of the knights could hate him.

He had made the wrong choice. When the dragon chose to let him go, he should have refused. He should have stayed and fought to the death. He should have died.

Stories kept filtering into the village, stories of the many heroic and famous knights who accepted the challenge of freeing Brunhilda from the dragon. All of them went as heroes. All of them died as heroes. Only Bork had returned alive from the dragon, and with every knight who died Bork's shame grew. Until he decided that he would go back. Better to join the knights in death than to live his life staring into the flames and seeing the visions of the dragon's eyes.

Next time, however, he would have to be better prepared. So after the spring plowing and planting and lambing and calving, where Bork's help was indispensable to the villagers, the giant went to the castle again. This time no one barred his way, but he was wise enough to stay as much out of sight as possible. He went to the one-armed swordmaster's room. Bork hadn't seen him since he accidentally cut off his arm in sword practice years before.

"Come for the other arm, coward?" asked the swordmaster.

"I'm sorry," Bork said. "I was younger then."

"You weren't any smaller. Go away."

But Bork stayed, and begged the swordmaster to help him. They worked out an arrangement. Bork

would be the swordmaster's personal servant all
summer, and in exchange the swordmaster would
try to teach Bork how to fight.

They went out into the fields every day, and under
the swordmaster's watchful eye he practiced sword-
fighting with bushes, trees, rocks—anything but the
swordmaster, who refused to let Bork near him. Then
they would return to the swordmaster's rooms, and
Bork would clean the floor and sharpen swords and
burnish shields and repair broken practice equipment. And always the ·swordmaster said, "Bork,
you're too stupid to do anything right!" Bork agreed.
In a summer of practice, he never got any better, and
at the end of the summer, when it was time for Bork
to go out in the fields and help with the harvest and
the preparations for winter, the swordmaster said,
"It's hopeless, Bork. You're too slow. Even the
bushes are more agile than you. Don't come back. I
still hate you, you know."

"I know," Bork said, and he went out into the
fields, where the peasants waited impatiently for the
giant to come carry sheaves of grain to the wagons.

Another winter looking at the fire, and Bork began
to realize that no matter how good he got with the
sword, it would make no difference. The dragon was
not to be defeated that way. If excellent swordplay
could kill the dragon, the dragon would be dead by
now—the finest knights in the kingdom had already
died trying.

He had to find another way. And the snow was
still heavy on the ground when he again entered the
castle and climbed the long and narrow stairway to
the tower room where the wizard lived.

"Go away," said the wizard, when Bork knocked
at his door. "I'm busy."

"I'll wait," Bork answered.

"Suit yourself."

And Bork waited. It was late at night when the

wizard finally opened the door. Bork had fallen asleep leaning on it—he nearly knocked the magician over when he fell inside.

"What the devil are you—you waited!"

"Yes," said Bork, rubbing his head where it had hit the stone floor.

"Well, I'll be back in a moment." The wizard made his way along a narrow ledge until he reached the place where the wall bulged and a hole opened onto the outside of the castle wall. In wartime, such holes were used to pour boiling oil on attackers. In peacetime, they were even more heavily used. "Go on inside and wait," the wizard said.

Bork looked around the room. It was spotlessly clean, the walls were lined with books, and here and there a fascinating artifact hinted at hidden knowledge and arcane powers—a sphere with the world on it, a skull, an abacus, beakers and tubes, a clay pot from which smoke rose, though there was no fire under it. Bork marvelled until the wizard returned.

"Nice little place, isn't it?" the wizard asked. "You're Bork, the bully, aren't you?"

Bork nodded.

"What can I do for you?"

"I don't know," Bork asked. "I want to learn magic. I want to learn magic powerful enough that I can use it to fight the dragon."

The wizard coughed profusely.

"What's wrong?" Bork asked.

"It's the dust," the wizard said.

Bork looked around and saw no dust. But when he sniffed the air, it felt thick in his nose, and a tickling in his chest made him cough, too.

"Dust?" asked Bork. "Can I have a drink?"

"Drink," said the wizard. "Downstairs—"

"But there's a pail of water right here. It looks perfectly clean—"

"Please don't—"

But Bork put the dipper in the pail and drank. The water sloshed into his mouth, and he swallowed, but it felt dry going down, and his thirst was unslaked. "What's wrong with the water?" Bork asked.

The wizard sighed and sat down. "It's the problem with magic, Bork old boy. Why do you think the King doesn't call on me to help him in his wars? He knows it, and now you'll know it, and the whole world probably will know it by Thursday."

"You don't know any magic?"

"Don't be a fool! I know all the magic there is! I can conjure up monsters that would make your dragon look tame! I can snap my fingers and have a table set with food to make the cook die of envy. I can take an empty bucket and fill it with water, with wine, with gold—whatever you want. But try spending the gold, and they'll hunt you down and kill you. Try drinking the water and you'll die of thirst."

"It isn't real."

"All illusion. Handy, sometimes. But that's all. Can't create anything except in your head. That pail, for instance—" And the wizard snapped his fingers. Bork looked, and the pail was filled, not with water, but with dust and spider webs. That wasn't all. He looked around the room, and was startled to see that the bookshelves were gone, as were the other trappings of great wisdom. Just a few books on a table in a corner, some counters covered with dust and papers and half-decayed food, and the floor inches deep in garbage.

"The place is horrible," the wizard said. "I can't bear to look at it." He snapped his fingers, and the old illusion came back. "Much nicer, isn't it?"

"Yes."

"I have excellent taste, haven't I? Now, you wanted me to help you fight the dragon, didn't you?

Well, I'm afraid it's out of the question. You see, my illusions only work on human beings, and occasionally on horses. A dragon wouldn't be fooled for a moment. You understand?"

Bork understood, and despaired. He returned to his hut and stared again at the flames. His resolution to return and fight the dragon again was undimmed. But now he knew that he would go as badly prepared as he had before, and his death and defeat would be certain. Well, he thought, better death than life as Bork the coward, Bork the bully who only has courage when he fights people smaller than himself.

The winter was unusually cold, and the snow was remarkably deep. The firewood ran out in February, and there was no sign of an easing in the weather.

The villagers went to the castle and asked for help, but the King was chilly himself, and the knights were all sleeping together in the great hall because there wasn't enough firewood for their barracks and the castle, too. "Can't help you," the King said.

So it was Bork who led the villagers—the ten strongest men, dressed as warmly as they could, yet still cold to the bone in the wind—and they followed in the path his body cut in the snow. With his huge ax he cut down tree after tree; the villagers set the wedges and Bork split the huge logs; the men carried what they could but it was Bork who made seven trips and carried most of the wood home. The village had enough to last until spring—more than enough, for, as Bork had expected, as soon as the stacks of firewood were deep in the village, the King's men came and took their tax of it.

And Bork, exhausted and frozen from the expedition, was carefully nursed back to health by the villagers. As he lay coughing and they feared he might die, it occurred to them how much they owed to the giant. Not just the firewood, but the hard labor in the farming work, and the fact that Bork had kept the armies far from their village, and they felt what no one in the castle had let himself feel for more than a few moments—gratitude. And so it was that when he had mostly recovered, Bork began to find gifts outside his door from time to time. A rabbit, freshly killed and dressed; a few eggs; a vast pair of hose that fit him very comfortably; a knife specially made to fit his large grip and to ride with comfortable weight on his hip. The villagers did not converse with him much. But then, they were not talkative people. The gifts said it all.

Throughout the spring, as Bork helped in the plowing and planting, with the villagers working alongside, he realized that this was where he belonged—with the villagers, not with the knights. They weren't rollicking good company, but there was something about sharing a task that must be done that made for stronger bonds between them than any of the rough camaraderie of the castle. The loneliness was gone.

Yet when Bork returned home and stared into the flames in the center of his hut, the call of the dragon's eyes became even stronger, if that were possible. It was not loneliness that drove him to seek death with the dragon. It was something else, and Bork could not think what. Pride? He had none—he accepted the verdict of the castle people that he was a coward. The only guess he could make was that he loved Brunhilda and felt a need to rescue her. The more he tried to convince himself, however, the less he believed it.

He had to return to the dragon because, in his own mind, he knew he should have died in the dragon's teeth, back when he fought the dragon before. The common folk might love him for what he did for them, but he hated himself for what he was.

He was nearly ready to head back for the dragon's mountain when the army came.

"How many are there?" the King asked Winkle.

"I can't get my spies to agree," Winkle said. "But the lowest estimate was two thousand men."

"And we have a hundred and fifty here in the castle. Well, I'll have to call on my dukes and counts for support."

"You don't understand, Your Majesty. These *are* your dukes and counts. This isn't an invasion. This is a rebellion."

The King paled. "How do they dare?"

"They dare because they heard a rumor, which at first they didn't believe was true. A rumor that your giant knight had quit, that he wasn't in your army anymore. And when they found out for sure that the rumor was true, they came to cast you out and return the old King to his place."

"Treason!" the King shouted. "Is there no loyalty?"

"I'm loyal," Winkle said, though of course he had already made contact with the other side in case things didn't go well. "But it seems to me that your only hope is to prove the rumors wrong. Show them that Bork is still fighting for you."

"But he isn't. I threw him out two years ago. The coward was even rejected by the dragon."

"Then I suggest you find a way to get him back into the army. If you don't, I doubt you'll have much luck against that crowd out there. My spies tell me they're placing wagers about how many pieces you can be cut into before you die."

The King turned slowly and stared at Winkle, glared at him, gazed intently in his eyes. "Winkle, after all we've done to Bork over the years, persuading him to help us now is a despicable thing to do."

"True."

"And so it's your sort of work, Winkle. Not mine. *You* get him back in the army."

"I can't do it. He hates me worse than anyone, I'm sure. After all, I've betrayed him more often."

"You get him back in the army within the next six hours, Winkle, or I'll send pieces of you to each of the men in that traitorous group that you've made friends with in order to betray me."

Winkle managed not to looked startled. But he *was* surprised. The King had somehow known about it. The King was not quite the fool he had seemed to be.

"I'm sending four knights with you to make sure you do it right."

"You misjudge me, Your Majesty," Winkle said.

"I hope so, Winkle. Persuade Bork for me, and you live to eat another breakfast."

The knights came, and Winkle walked with them to Bork's hut. They waited outside.

"Bork, old friend," Winkle said. Bork was sitting by the fire, staring in the flames. "Bork, you aren't the sort who holds grudges, are you?"

Bork spat into the flames.

"Can't say I blame you," Winkle said. "We've treated you ungratefully. We've been downright cruel. But you rather brought it on yourself, you know. It isn't *our* fault you turned coward in your fight with the dragon. Is it?"

Bork shook his head. "My fault, Winkle. But it isn't my fault the army has come, either. I've lost my battle. You lose yours."

"Bork, we've been friends since we were three—"

Bork looked up so suddenly, his face so sharp and lit with the glow of the fire, that Winkle could not go on.

"I've looked in the dragon's eyes," Bork said, "and I know who you are."

Winkle wondered if it was true, and was afraid. But he had courage of a kind, a selfish courage that allowed him to dare anything if he thought he would gain by it.

"Who I am? No one knows anything as it is, because as soon as it's known it changes. You looked in the dragon's eyes years ago, Bork. Today I am not who I was then. Today you are not who you were then. And today the King needs you."

"The King is a petty count who rode to greatness on my shoulders. He can rot in hell."

"The other knights need you, then. Do you want them to die?"

"I've fought enough battles for them. Let them fight their own."

And Winkle stood helplessly, wondering how he could possibly persuade this man, who would not be persuaded.

It was then that a village child came. The knights caught him lurking near Bork's hut; they roughly shoved him inside. "He might be a spy," a knight said.

For the first time since Winkle came, Bork laughed. "A spy? Don't you know your own village, here? Come to me, Laggy." And the boy came to him, and stood near him as if seeking the giant's protection. "Laggy's a friend of mine," Bork said. "Why did you come, Laggy?"

The boy wordlessly held out a fish. It wasn't large, but it was still wet from the river.

"Did you catch this?" Bork said.

The boy nodded.

"How many did you catch today?"

The boy pointed at the fish.

"Just the one? Oh, then I can't take this, if it's all you caught."

But as Bork handed the fish back, the boy retreated, refused to take it. He finally opened his mouth and spoke. "For you," he said, and then he scurried out of the hut and into the bright morning sunlight.

And Winkle knew he had his way to get Bork into the battle.

"The villagers," Winkle said.

Bork looked at him quizzically.

And Winkle *almost* said, "If you don't join the army, we'll come out here and burn the village and kill all the children and sell the adults into slavery in Germany." But something stopped him; a memory, perhaps, of the fact that he was once a village child himself. No, not that. Winkle was honest enough with himself to know that what stopped him from making the threat was a mental picture of Sir Bork striding into battle, not in front of the King's army, but at the head of the rebels. A mental picture of Bork's ax biting deep into the gate of the castle, his huge crow prying the portcullis free. This was not the time to threaten Bork.

So Winkle took the other tack. "Bork, if they win this battle, which they surely will if you aren't with us, do you think they'll be kind to this village? They'll burn and rape and kill and capture these people for slaves. They hate us, and to them these villagers are part of us, part of their hatred. If you don't help us, you're killing them."

"I'll protect them," Bork said.

"No, my friend. No, if you don't fight with us, as a knight, they won't treat you chivalrously. They'll fill you full of arrows before you get within twenty feet of their lines. You fight with us, or you might as well not fight at all."

Winkle knew he had won. Bork thought for several minutes, but it was inevitable. He got up and returned to the castle, strapped on his old armor, took his huge ax and his shield, and, with his sword belted at his waist, walked into the courtyard of the castle.

The other knights cheered, and called out to him as if he were their dearest friend. But the words were hollow and they knew it, and when Bork didn't answer they soon fell silent.

The gate opened and Bork walked out, the knights on horseback behind him.

And in the rebel camp, they knew that the rumors were a lie—the giant still fought with the King, and they were doomed. Most of the men slipped away into the woods. But the others, particularly the leaders who would die if they surrendered as surely as they would die if they fought, stayed. Better to die valiantly than as a coward, they each thought, and so as Bork approached he still faced an army—only a few hundred men, but still an army.

They came out to meet Bork one by one, as the knights came to the dragon on his hill. And one by one, as they made their first cut or thrust, Bork's ax struck, and their heads flew from their bodies, or their chests were cloven nearly in half, or the ax reamed them end to end, and Bork was bright red with blood and a dozen men were dead and not one had touched him.

So they came by threes and fours, and fought like demons, but still Bork took them, and when even more than four tried to fight him at once they got in each other's way and he killed them more easily.

And at last those who still lived despaired. There was no honor in dying so pointlessly. And with fifty men dead, the battle ended, and the rebels laid down their arms in submission.

Then the King emerged from the castle and rode to the battleground, and paraded triumphantly in front of the defeated men.

"You are all sentenced to death at once," the King declared.

But suddenly he found himself pulled from his

horse, and Bork's great hands held him. The King gasped at the smell of gore; Bork rubbed his bloody hands on the King's tunic, and took the King's face between his sticky palms.

"No one dies now. No one dies tomorrow. These men will all live, and you'll send them home to their lands, and you'll lower their tribute and let them dwell in peace forever."

The King imagined his own blood mingling with that which already covered Bork, and he nodded. Bork let him go. The King mounted his horse again, and spoke loudly, so all could hear. "I forgive you all. I pardon you all. You may return to your homes. I confirm you in your lands. And your tribute is cut in half from this day forward. Go in peace. If any man harms you, I'll have his life."

The rebels stood in silence.

Winkle shouted at them "Go! You heard the king! You're free! Go home!"

And they cheered, and long-lived-the-King, and then bellowed their praise to Bork.

But Bork, if he heard them, gave no sign. He stripped off his armor and let it lie in the field. He carried his great ax to the stream, and let the water run over the metal until it was clean. Then he lay in the stream himself, and the water carried off the last of the blood, and when he came out he was clean.

Then he walked away, to the north road, ignoring the calls of the King and his knights, ignoring everything except the dragon who waited for him on the mountain. For this was the last of the acts Bork wold perform in his life for which he would feel shame. He would not kill again. He would only die, bravely, in the dragon's claws and teeth.

The old woman waited for him on the road.

"Off to kill the dragon, are you?" she asked in a voice that the years had tortured into gravel. "Didn't learn enough the first time?" She giggled behind her hand.

"Old woman, I learned everything before. Now I'm going to die."

"Why? So the fools in the castle will think better of you?"

Bork shook his head.

"The villagers already love you. For your deeds today, you'll already be a legend. If it isn't for love or fame, why are you going?"

Bork shrugged. "I don't know. I think he calls to me. I'm through with my life, and all I can see ahead of me are his eyes."

The old woman nodded. "Well, well, Bork. I think you're the first knight that the dragon won't be happy to see. We old wives know, Bork. Just tell him the truth, Bork."

"I've never known the truth to stop a sword," he said.

"But the dragon doesn't carry a sword."

"He might as well."

"No, Bork, no," she said, clucking impatiently. "You know better than that. Of all the dragon's weapons, which cut you the deepest?"

Bork tried to remember. The truth was, he realized, that the dragon had never cut him at all. Not with his teeth nor his claws. Only the armor had been pierced. Yet there had been a wound, a deep one that hadn't healed, and it had been cut in him, not by teeth or talons, but by the bright fires in the dragon's eyes.

"The truth," the old woman said. "Tell the dragon the truth. Tell him the truth, and you'll live!"

Bork shook his head. "I'm not going there to live," he said. He pushed past her, and walked on up the road.

But her words rang in his ears long after he stopped

hearing her call after him. The truth, she had said. Well, then, why not? Let the dragon have the truth. Much good may it do him.

This time Bork was in no hurry. He slept every night, and paused to hunt for berries and fruit to eat in the woods. It was four days before he reached the dragon's hill, and he came in the morning, after a good night's sleep. He was afraid, of course; but still there was a pleasant feeling about the morning, a tingling of excitement about the meeting with the dragon. He felt the end coming near, and he relished it.

Nothing had changed. The dragon roared; Brunhilda screamed. And when he reached the top of the hill, he saw the dragon tickling her with his wing. He was not surprised to see that she hadn't changed at all—the two years had not aged her, and though her gown still was open and her breasts were open to the sun and the wind, she wasn't even freckled or tanned. It could have been yesterday that Bork fought with the dragon the first time. And Bork was smiling as he stepped into the flat space where the battle would take place.

Brunhilda saw him first. "Help me! You're the four hundred and thirtieth knight to try! Surely that's a lucky number!" Then she recognized him. "Oh, no. You again. Oh well, at least while he's fighting you I won't have to put up with his tickling."

Bork ignored her. He had come for the dragon, not for Brunhilda.

The dragon regarded him calmly. "You are disturbing my nap time."

"I'm glad," Bork said. "You've disturbed me, sleeping and waking, since I left you. Do you remember me?"

"Ah yes. You're the only knight who was ever afraid of me."

"Do you really believe that?" Bork asked.

"It hardly matters what I believe. Are you going to kill me today?"

"I don't think so," said Bork. "You're much stronger than I am, and I'm terrible at battle. I've never defeated anyone who was more than half my strength."

The lights in the dragon's eyes suddenly grew brighter, and the dragon squinted to look at Bork. "Is that so?" asked the dragon.

"And I'm not very clever. You'll be able to figure out my next move before I know what it is myself."

The dragon squinted more, and the eyes grew even brighter.

"Don't you want to rescue this beautiful woman?" the dragon asked.

"I don't much care," he said. "I loved her once. But I'm through with that. I came for you."

"You don't love her anymore?" asked the dragon.

Bork almost said, "Not a bit." But then he stopped. The truth, the old woman had said. And he looked into himself and saw that no matter how much he hated himself for it, the old feelings died hard. "I love her, dragon. But it doesn't do me any good. She doesn't love me. And so even though I desire her, I don't want her."

Brunhilda was a little miffed. "That's the stupidest thing I've ever heard," she said. But Bork was watching the dragon, whose eyes were dazzlingly bright. The monster was squinting so badly that Bork began to wonder if he could see at all.

"Are you having trouble with your eyes?" Bork asked.

"Do you think *you* ask the questions here? I ask the questions."

"Then ask."

"What in the world do I want to know from you?"

"I can't think of anything," Bork answered. "I know almost nothing. What little I do know, you taught me."

"Did I? What was it that you learned?"

"You taught me that I was not loved by those I thought had loved me. I learned from you that deep within my large body is a very small soul."

The dragon blinked, and its eyes seemed to dim a little.

"Ah," said the dragon.

"What do you mean, 'Ah'?" asked Bork.

"Just 'Ah,'" the dragon answered. "Does every *ah* have to mean something?"

Brunhilda sighed impatiently. "How long does this go on? Everybody else who comes up here is wonderful and brave. You just stand around talking about how miserable you are. Why don't you fight?"

"Like the others?" asked Bork.

"They're so brave," she said.

"They're all dead."

"Only a coward would think of that," she said scornfully.

"It hardly comes as a surprise to you," Bork said. "Everyone knows I'm a coward. Why do you think I came? I'm of no use to anyone, except as a machine to kill people at the command of a King I despise."

"That's my father you're talking about!"

"I'm nothing, and the world will be better without me in it."

"I can't say I disagree," Brunhilda said.

But Bork did not hear her, for he felt the touch of the dragon's tail on his back, and when he looked at the dragon's eyes they had stopped glowing so brightly. They were almost back to normal, in fact, and the dragon was beginning to reach out its claws.

So Bork swung his ax, and the dragon dodged, and the battle was on, just as before.

And just as before, at sundown Bork stood pinned between tail and claws and teeth.

"Are you afraid to die?" asked the dragon, as it had before.

Bork almost answered *yes* again, because that would keep him alive. But then he remembered that he had come in order to die, and as he looked in his heart he still realized that however much he might fear death, he feared life more.

"I came here to die," he said. "I still want to."

And the dragon's eyes leaped bright with light. Bork imagined that the pressure of the claws lessened.

"Well, then, Sir Bork, I can hardly do you such a favor as to kill you." And the dragon let him go.

That was when Bork became angry.

"You can't do this to me!" he shouted.

"Why not?" asked the dragon, who was now trying to ignore Bork and occupied itself by crushing boulders with its claws.

"Because I insist on my right to die at your hands."

"It's not a right, it's a privilege," said the dragon.

"If you don't kill me, then I'll kill you!"

The dragon sighed in boredom, but Bork would not be put off. He began swinging the ax, and the dragon dodged, and in the pink light of sunset the battle was on again. This time, though, the dragon only fell back and twisted and turned to avoid Bork's blows. It made no effort to attack. Finally Bork was too tired and frustrated to go on.

"Why don't you fight!" he shouted. Then he wheezed from the exhaustion of the chase.

The dragon was panting, too. "Come on now, little man, why don't you give it up and go home. I'll give you a signed certificate testifying that I asked you to go, so that no one thinks you're a coward. Just leave me alone."

The dragon began crushing rocks and dribbling

them over its head. It lay down and began to bury itself in gravel.

"Dragon," said Bork, "a moment ago you had me in your teeth. You were about to kill me. The old woman told me that truth was my only defense. So I must have lied before, I must have said something false. What was it? Tell me!"

The dragon looked annoyed. "She had no business telling you that. It's privileged information."

"All I ever said to you was the truth."

"Was it?"

"Did I lie to you? Answer—yes or no!"

The dragon only looked away, its eyes still bright. It lay on its back and poured gravel over its belly.

"I did then. I lied. Just the kind of fool I am to tell the truth and still get caught in a lie."

Had the dragon's eyes dimmed? Was there a lie in what he had just said?

"Dragon," Bork insisted, "if you don't kill me or I don't kill you, then I might as well throw myself from the cliff. There's no meaning to my life, if I can't die at your hands!"

Yes, the dragon's eyes were dimming, and the dragon rolled over onto its belly, and began to gaze thoughtfully at Bork.

"Where is the lie in that?"

"Lie? Who said anything about a lie?" But the dragon's long tail was beginning to creep around so it could get behind Bork.

And then it occurred to Bork that the dragon might not even know. That the dragon might be as much a prisoner of the fires of truth inside him as Bork was, and that the dragon wasn't deliberately toying with him at all. Didn't matter, of course. "Never mind what the lie is, then," Bork said. "Kill me now, and the world will be a better place!"

The dragon's eyes dimmed, and a claw made a pass at him, raking the air by his face.

It was maddening, to know there was a lie in what he was saying and not know what it was. "It's the perfect ending for my meaningless life," he said. "I'm so clumsy I even have to stumble into death."

He didn't understand why, but once again he stared into the dragon's mouth, and the claws pressed gently but sharply against his flesh.

The dragon asked the question of Bork for the third time. "Are you afraid, little man, to die?"

This was the moment, Bork knew. If he was to die, he had to lie to the dragon now, for if he told the truth the dragon would set him free again. But to lie, he had to know what the truth was, and now he didn't know at all. He tried to think of where he had gone astray from the truth, and could not. What had he said? It was true that he was clumsy; it was true that he was stumbling into death. What else then?

He had said his life was meaningless. Was that the lie? He had said his death would make the world a better place. Was that the lie?

And so he thought of what would happen when he died. What hole would his death make in the world? The only people who might miss him were the villagers. That was the meaning of his life, then—the villagers. So he lied.

"The villagers won't miss me if I die. They'll get along just fine without me."

But the dragon's eyes brightened, and the teeth withdrew, and Bork realized to his grief that his statement had been true after all. The villagers wouldn't miss him if he died. The thought of it broke his heart, the last betrayal in a long line of betrayals.

"Dragon, I can't outguess you! I don't know what's true and what isn't! All I learn from you is that everyone I thought loved me doesn't. Don't ask me questions! Just kill me and end my life. Every pleasure I've had turns to pain when you tell me the truth."

And now, when he had thought he was telling the truth, the claws broke his skin, and the teeth closed over his head, and he screamed. "Dragon! Don't let me die like this! What is the pleasure that your truth won't turn to pain? What do I have left?"

The dragon pulled away, and regarded him carefully. "I told you, little man, that I don't answer questions. I ask them."

"Why are you here?" Bork demanded. "This ground is littered with the bones of men who failed your tests. Why not mine? Why not mine? Why can't I die? Why did you keep sparing my life? I'm just a man, I'm just alive, I'm just trying to do the best I can in a miserable world and I'm sick of trying to figure out what's true and what isn't. End the game, dragon. My life has never been happy, and I want to die."

The dragon's eyes went black, and the jaws opened again, and the teeth approached, and Bork knew he had told his last lie, that this lie would be enough. But with the teeth inches from him Bork finally realized what the lie was, and the realization was enough to change his mind. "No," he said, and he reached out and seized the teeth, though they cut his fingers. "No," he said, and he wept. "I have been happy. I have." And, gripping the sharp teeth, the memories raced through his mind. The many nights of comradeship with the knights in the castle. The pleasures of weariness from working in the forest and the fields. The joy he felt when alone he won a victory from the Duke; the rush of warmth when the boy brought him the single fish he had caught; and the solitary pleasures, of waking and going to sleep, of walking and running, of feeling the wind on a hot day and standing near a fire in the deep of winter. They were all good, and they had all happened. What did it matter if later the knights despised him? What did it matter if the villagers' love was only a fleeting thing, to be forgotten after he died? The reality of the pain did not destroy the reality of the pleasure; grief did not obliterate joy. They each happened in their time, and because some of them were dark it did not mean that none of them was light.

"I have been happy," Bork said. "And if you let me live, I'll be happy again. That's what my life means, doesn't it? That's the truth, isn't it, dragon? My life matters because I'm alive, joy or pain, whatever comes, I'm alive and that's meaning enough. It's true, isn't it, dragon! I'm not here to fight you. I'm not here for you to kill me. I'm here to make myself alive!"

But the dragon did not answer. Bork was gently lowered to the ground. The dragon withdrew its talons and tail, pulled its head away, and curled up on the ground, covering its eyes with its claws.

"Dragon, did you hear me?"

The dragon said nothing.

"Dragon, look at me!"

The dragon sighed. "Man, I cannot look at you."

"Why not?"

"I am blind," the dragon answered. It pulled its claws away from its eyes. Bork covered his face with his hands. The dragon's eyes were brighter than the sun.

"I feared you, Bork," the dragon whispered. "From the day you told me you were afraid, I feared you. I knew you would be back. And I knew this moment would come."

"What moment?" Bork asked.

"The moment of my death."

"Are you dying?"

"No," said the dragon. "Not yet. You must kill me."

As Bork looked at the dragon lying before him, he felt no desire for blood. "I don't want you to die."

"Don't you know that a dragon cannot live when

it has met a truly honest man? It's the only way we ever die, and most dragons live forever."

But Bork refused to kill him.

The dragon cried out in anguish. "I am filled with all the truth that was discarded by men when they chose their lies and died for them. I am in constant pain, and now that I have met a man who does not add to my treasury of falsehood, you are the cruelest of them all."

And the dragon wept, and its eyes flashed and sparkled in every hot tear that fell, and finally Bork could not bear it. He took his ax and hacked off the dragon's head, and the light in its eyes went out. The eyes shriveled in their sockets until they turned into small, bright diamonds with a thousand facets each. Bork took the diamonds and put them in his pocket.

"You killed him," Brunhilda said wonderingly.

Bork did not answer. He just untied her, and looked away while she finally fastened her gown. Then he shouldered the dragon's head and carried it back to the castle, Brunhilda running to keep up with him. He only stopped to rest at night because she begged him to. And when she tried to thank him for freeing her, he only turned away and refused to hear. He had killed the dragon because it wanted to die. Not for Brunhilda. Never for her.

At the castle they were received with rejoicing, but Bork would not go in. He only laid the dragon's head beside the moat and went to his hut, fingering the diamonds in his pocket, holding them in front of him in the pitch blackness of his hut to see that they shone with their own light, and did not need the sun or any other fire but themselves.

The King and Winkle and Brunhilda and a dozen knights came to Bork's hut. "I have come to thank you," the King said, his cheeks wet with tears of joy.

"You're welcome," Bork said. He said it as if to dismiss them.

"Bork," the King said. "Slaying the dragon was ten times as brave as the bravest thing any man has done before. You can have my daughter's hand in marriage."

Bork looked up in surprise.

"I thought you never meant to keep your promise, Your Majesty."

The King looked down, then at Winkle, then back at Bork. "Occasionally," he said, "I keep my word. So here she is, and thank you."

But Bork only smiled, fingering the diamonds in his pocket. "It's enough that you offered, Your Majesty. I don't want her. Marry her to a man she loves."

The King was puzzled. Brunhilda's beauty had not waned in her years of captivity. She had the sort of beauty that started wars. "Don't you want *any* reward?" asked the King.

Bork thought for a moment. "Yes," he said. "I want to be given a plot of ground far away from here. I don't want there to be any count, or any duke, or any king over me. And any man or woman or child who comes to me will be free, and no one can pursue them. And I will never see you again, and you will never see me again."

"That's all you want?"

"That's all."

"Then you shall have it," the King said.

Bork lived all the rest of his life on his little plot of ground. People did come to him. Not many, but five or ten a year all his life, and a village grew up where no one came to take a king's tithe or a duke's fifth or a count's fourth. Children grew up who knew nothing of the art of war and never saw a knight or a battle or the terrible fear on the face of a man who knows his wounds are too deep to heal. It was everything Bork could have wanted, and he was happy all his years there.

Winkle, too, achieved everything he wanted. He married Brunhilda, and soon enough the King's sons had accidents and died, and the King died after dinner one night, and Winkle became King. He was at war all his life, and never went to sleep at night without fear of an assassin coming upon him in the darkness. He governed ruthlessly and thoroughly and was hated all his life; later generations, however, remembered him as a great King. But he was dead then, and didn't know it.

Later generations never heard of Bork.

He had only been out on his little plot of ground for a few months when the old wife came to him. "Your hut is much bigger than you need," she said. "Move over."

So Bork moved over, and she moved in.

She did not magically turn into a beautiful princess. She was foul-mouthed and nagged Bork unmercifully. But he was devoted to her, and when she died a few years later he realized that she had given him more happiness than pain, and he missed her. But the grief at her dying did not taint any of the joys of his memory of her; he just fingered the diamonds, and remembered that grief and joy were not weighed in the same scale, one making the other seem less substantial.

And at last he realized that Death was near; that Death was reaping him like wheat, eating him like bread. He imagined Death to be a dragon, devouring him bit by bit, and one night in a dream he asked Death, "Is my flavor sweet?"

Death, the old dragon, looked at him with bright and understanding eyes, and said, "Salty and sour, bitter and sweet. You sting and you soothe."

"Ah," Bork said, and was satisfied.

Death poised itself to take the last bite. "Thank you," it said.

"You're welcome," Bork answered, and he meant it.

The Princess and the Bear

I KNOW YOU'VE SEEN the lions. All over the place: beside the doors, flanking the throne, roaring out of the plates in the pantry, spouting water from under the eaves.

Haven't you ever wondered why the statue atop the city gates is a bear?

Many years ago in this very city, in the very palace that you can see rising granite and gray behind the old crumbly walls of the king's garden, there lived a princess. It was so long ago that who can ever remember her name? She was just the princess. These days it isn't in fashion to think that princesses are beautiful, and in fact they tend to be a bit horse-faced and gangling. But in those days it was an absolute requirement that a princess look fetching, at least when wearing the most expensive clothes available.

This princess, however, would have been beautiful dressed like a slum child or a shepherd girl. She was beautiful the moment she was born. She only got more beautiful as she grew up.

And there was also a prince. He was not her brother, though. He was the son of a king in a far-off land, and his father was the thirteenth cousin twice removed of the princess' father. The boy had been sent here to our land to get an education—because the princess' father, King Ethelred, was known far and wide as a wise man and a good king.

And if the princess was marvelously beautiful, so was the prince. He was the kind of boy that every mother wants to hug, the kind of boy who gets his hair tousled by every man that meets him.

He and the princess grew up together. They took lessons together from the teachers in the palace, and when the princess was slow, the prince would help her, and when the prince was slow, the princess would help him. They had no secrets from each other, but they had a million secrets that they two kept from the rest of the world. Secrets like where the bluebirds' nest was this year, and what color underwear the cook wore, and that if you duck under the stairway to the armory there's a little underground path that comes up in the wine cellar. They speculated endlessly about which of the princess' ancestors had used that path for surreptitious imbibing.

After not too many years the princess stopped being just a little girl and the prince stopped being just a little boy, and then they fell in love. All at once all their million secrets became just one secret, and they told that secret every time they looked at each other, and everyone who saw them said, "Ah, if I were only young again." That is because so many people think that love belongs to the young: sometime during their lives they stopped loving people, and they think it was just because they got old.

The prince and the princess decided one day to get married.

But the very next morning, the prince got a letter from the far-off country where his father lived. The letter told him that his father no longer lived at all, and that the boy was now a man; and not just a man, but a king.

So the prince got up the next morning, and the servants put his favorite books in a parcel, and his favorite clothes were packed in a trunk, and the trunk, and the parcel, and the prince were all put on a coach with bright red wheels and gold tassels at the corner and the prince was taken away.

The princess did not cry until after he was out of sight. Then she went into her room and cried for a long time, and only her nurse could come in with food and chatter and cheerfulness. At last the chatter brought smiles to the princess, and she went into her father's study where he sat by the fire at night and said, "He promised he would write, every day, and I must write every day as well."

She did, and the prince did, and once a month a parcel of thirty letters would arrive for her, and the postrider would take away a parcel of thirty letters (heavily perfumed) from her.

And one day the Bear came to the palace. Now he wasn't a bear, of course, he was *the* Bear, with a capital B. He was probably only thirty-five or so, because his hair was still golden brown and his face was only lined around the eyes. But he was massive and grizzly, with great thick arms that looked like he could lift a horse, and great thick legs that looked like he could carry that horse a hundred miles. His eyes were deep, and they looked brightly out from under his bushy eyebrows, and the first time the nurse saw him she squealed and said, "Oh, my, he looks like a *bear*."

He came to the door of the palace and the doorman refused to let him in, because he didn't have an appointment. But he scribbled a note on a piece of paper that looked like it had held a sandwich for a few days, and the doorman—with grave misgivings—carried the paper to the king.

The paper said, "If Boris and 5,000 stood on the highway from Rimperdell, would you like to know which way they were going?"

King Ethelred wanted to know.

The doorman let the stranger into the palace, and the king brought him into his study and they talked for many hours.

In the morning the king arose early and went to his captains of cavalry and captains of infantry, and he sent a lord to the knights and their squires, and by dawn all of Ethelred's little army was gathered on the highway, the one that leads to Rimperdell. They marched for three hours that morning, and then they came to a place and the stranger with golden brown hair spoke to the king and King Ethelred commanded the army to stop. They stopped, and the infantry was sent into the forest on one side of the road, and the cavalry was sent into the tall cornfields on the other side of the road, where they dismounted. Then the king, and the stranger, and the knights waited in the road.

Soon they saw a dust cloud in the distance, and then the dust cloud grew near, and they saw that it was an army coming down the road. And at the head of the army was King Boris of Rimperdell. And behind him the army seemed to be five thousand men.

"Hail," King Ethelred said, looking more than a little irritated, since King Boris' army was well inside our country's boundaries.

"Hail," King Boris said, looking more than a little irritated, since no one was supposed to know that he was coming.

"What do you think you're doing?" asked King Ethelred.

"You're blocking the road," said King Boris.

"It's my road," said King Ethelred.

"Not anymore," said King Boris.

"I and my knights say that this road belongs to me," said King Ethelred.

King Boris looked at Ethelred's fifty knights, and then he looked back at his own five thousand men, and he said, "I say you and your knights are dead men unless you move aside."

"Then you want to be at war with me?" asked King Ethelred.

"War?" said King Boris. "Can we really call it a war? It will be like stepping on a nasty cockroach."

"I wouldn't know," said King Ethelred, "because we haven't ever had cockroaches in our kingdom." Then he added, "Until now, of course."

Then King Ethelred lifted his arm, and the infantry shot arrows and threw lances from the wood, and many of Boris' men were slain. And the moment all of his troops were ready to fight the army in the forest, the cavalry came from the field and attacked from the rear, and soon Boris' army, what was left of it, surrendered, and Boris himself lay mortally wounded in the road.

"If you had won this battle," King Ethelred said, "what would you have done to me?"

King Boris gasped for breath and said, "I would have had you beheaded."

"Ah," said King Ethelred. "We are very different men. For I will let you live."

But the stranger stood beside King Ethelred, and he said, "No, King Ethelred, that is not in your power, for Boris is about to die. And if he were not, I would have killed him myself, for as long as a man like him is alive, no one is safe in all the world."

Then Boris died, and he was buried in the road with no marker, and his men were sent home without their swords.

And King Ethelred came back home to crowds of people cheering the great victory, and shouting, "Long live King Ethelred the conqueror."

King Ethelred only smiled at them. Then he took the stranger into the palace, and gave him a room where he could sleep, and made him the chief counselor to the king, because the stranger had proved that he was wise, and that he was loyal, and that he loved the king better than the king loved himself, for the king would have let Boris live.

No one knew what to call the man, because when a few brave souls asked him his name, he only frowned and said, "I will wear the name you pick for me."

Many names were tried, like George, and Fred, and even Rocky and Todd. But none of the names seemed right. For a long time, everyone called him Sir, because when somebody is that big and that strong and that wise and that quiet, you feel like calling him sir and offering him your chair when he comes in the room.

And then after a while everyone called him the name the nurse had chosen for him just by accident: they called him the Bear. At first they only called him that behind his back, but eventually someone slipped and called him that at the dinner table, and he smiled, and answered to the name, and so everyone called him that.

Except the princess. She didn't call him anything, because she didn't speak to him if she could help it, and when she talked about him, she stuck out her lower lip and called him That Man.

This is because the princess hated the Bear.

She didn't hate him because he had done anything bad to her. In fact, she was pretty sure that he didn't even notice she was living in the palace. He never turned and stared when she walked into the room, like all the other men did. But that isn't why she hated him, either.

She hated him because she thought he was making her father weak.

King Ethelred was a great king, and his people loved him. He always stood very tall at ceremonies, and he sat for hours making judgments with great wisdom. He always spoke softly when softness was needed, and shouted at the times when only shouting would be heard.

In all he was a stately man, and so the princess was shocked with the way he was around the Bear.

King Ethelred and the Bear would sit for hours in the king's study, every night when there wasn't a great banquet or an ambassador. They would both drink from huge mugs of ale—but instead of having a servant refill the mugs, the princess was shocked that her own father stood up and poured from the pitcher! A king, doing the work of a servant, and then giving the mug to a commoner, a man whose name no one knew!

The princess saw this because she sat in the king's study with them, listening and watching without saying a word as they talked. Sometimes she would spend the whole time combing her father's long white hair. Sometimes she would knit long woolen stockings for her father for the winter. Sometimes she would read—for her father believed that even women should learn to read. But all the time she listened, and became angry, and hated the Bear more and more.

King Ethelred and the Bear didn't talk much about affairs of state. They talked about hunting rabbits in the forest. They told jokes about lords and ladies in the kingdom—and some of the jokes weren't even nice, the princess told herself bitterly. They talked about what they should do about the ugly carpet in the courtroom—as if the Bear had a perfect right to have an opinion about what the new carpet should be.

And when they did talk about affairs of state, the Bear treated King Ethelred like an *equal*. When he disagreed with the king, he would leap to his feet saying, "No, no, no, no, you just don't see at all." When he thought the king had said something right, he clapped him on the shoulder and said, "You'll make a great king yet, Ethelred."

And sometimes King Ethelred would sigh and stare into the fire, and whisper a few words, and a dark and tired look would steal across his face. Then the Bear would put his arm around the king's shoulder, and stare into the fire with him, until finally the king would sigh again, and then lift himself, groaning, out of his chair, and say, "It's time that this old man put his corpse between the sheets."

The next day the princess would talk furiously to her nurse, who never told a soul what the princess said. The princess would say, "That Man is out to make my father a weakling! He's out to make my father look stupid. That Man is making my father forget that he is a king." Then she would wrinkle her forehead and say, "That Man is a traitor."

She never said a word about this to her father, however. If she had, he would have patted her head and said, "Oh, yes, he does indeed make me forget that I am a king." But he would also have said, "He makes me remember what a king should be." And Ethelred would not have called him a traitor. He would have called the Bear his friend.

As if it wasn't bad enough that her father was forgetting himself around a commoner, that was the very time that things started going bad with the prince. She suddenly noticed that the last several packets of mail had not held thirty letters each— they only held twenty, and then fifteen, and then ten. And the letters weren't five pages long any more. They were only three, and then two, and then one.

He's just busy, she thought.

Then she noticed that he no longer began her letters with, "My dearest darling sweetheart pickle-eating princess." (The pickle-eating part was an old joke from something that happened when they were both nine.) Now he started them, "My dear lady," or "Dear princess." Once she said to her nurse, "He might as well address them to Occupant."

He's just tired, she thought.

And then she realized that he never told her he loved her anymore, and she went out on the balcony and cried where only the garden could hear, and where only the birds in the trees could see.

She began to keep to her rooms, because the world didn't seem like a very nice place any more. Why should she have anything to do with the world, when it was a nasty place where fathers turned into mere men, and lovers forgot they were in love?

And she cried herself to sleep every night that she slept. And some nights she didn't sleep at all, just stared at the ceiling trying to forget the prince. And you know that if you want to remember something, the best way is to try very, very hard to forget it.

Then one day, as she went to the door of her room, she found a basket of autumn leaves just inside her door. There was no note on them, but they were very brightly colored, and they rustled loudly when she touched the basket, and she said to herself, "It must be autumn."

She went to the window and looked, and it was autumn, and it was beautiful. She had already seen the leaves a hundred times a day, but she hadn't remembered to notice.

And then a few weeks later she woke up and it was cold in her room. Shivering, she went to her door to call for a servant to build her fire up higher—and just inside the door was a large pan, and on the pan there stood a little snowman, which was grinning a grin made of little chunks of coal, and his eyes were big pieces of coal, and all in all it was so comical the princess had to laugh. That day she forgot her misery for a while and went outside and threw snowballs at the knights, who of course let her hit them and who never managed to hit her, but of course that's all part of being a princess—no one would ever put snow down your back or dump you in the canal or anything.

She asked her nurse who brought these things, but the nurse just shook her head and smiled. "It wasn't me," she said. "Of course it was," the princess answered, and gave her a hug, and thanked her. The nurse smiled and said, "Thanks for your thanks, but it wasn't me." But the princess knew better, and loved her nurse all the more.

Then the letters stopped coming altogether. And the princess stopped writing letters. And she began taking walks in the woods.

At first she only took walks in the garden, which is where princesses are supposed to take walks. But in a few days of walking and walking and walking she knew every brick of the garden path by heart, and she kept coming to the garden wall and wishing she were outside it.

So one day she walked to the gate and went out of the garden and wandered into the forest. The forest was not at all like the garden. Where the garden was neatly tended and didn't have a weed in it, the forest was all weeds, all untrimmed and loose, with animals that ran from her, and birds that scurried to lead her away from their young, and best of all, only grass or soft brown earth under her feet. Out in the forest she could forget the garden where every tree reminded her of talks she had had with the prince while sitting in the branches. Out in the forest she could forget the palace where every room had held its own joke or its own secret or its own promise that had been broken.

That was why she was in the forest the day the wolf came out of the hills.

She was already heading back to the palace, because it was getting on toward dark, when she caught a glimpse of something moving. She looked, and realized that it was a huge gray wolf, walking along beside her not fifteen yards off. When she stopped, the wolf stopped. When she moved, the wolf moved. And the farther she walked, the closer the wolf came.

She turned and walked away from the wolf.

After a few moments she looked behind her, and saw the wolf only a dozen feet away, its mouth open, its tongue hanging out, its teeth shining white in the gloom of the late afternoon forest.

She began to run. But not even a princess can hope to outrun a wolf. She ran and ran until she could hardly breathe, and the wolf was still right behind her, panting a little but hardly tired. She ran and ran some more until her legs refused to obey her and she fell to the ground. She looked back, and realized that this was what the wolf had been waiting for—for her to be tired enough to fall, for her to be easy prey, for her to be a dinner he didn't have to work for.

And so the wolf got a gleam in its eye, and sprang forward.

Just as the wolf leaped, a huge brown shape lumbered out of the forest and stepped over the princess. She screamed. It was a huge brown bear, with heavy fur and vicious teeth. The bear swung its great hairy arm at the wolf, and struck it in the head. The wolf flew back a dozen yards, and from the way its head bobbed about as it flew, the princess realized its neck had been broken.

And then the huge bear turned toward her, and she saw with despair that she had only traded one monstrous animal for another.

And she fainted. Which is about all that a person can do when a bear that is standing five feet away looks at you. And looks hungry.

She woke up in bed at the palace and figured it had all been a dream. But then she felt a terrible pain in her legs, and felt her face stinging with scratches from the branches. It had not been a dream—she really had run through the forest.

"What happened?" she asked feebly. "Am I dead?" Which wasn't all that silly a question, because she really had expected to be.

"No," said her father, who was sitting by the bed.

"No," said the nurse. "And why in the world, why should you be dead?"

"I was in the forest," said the princess, "and there was a wolf, and I ran and ran but he was still there. And then a bear came and killed the wolf, and it came toward me like it was going to eat me, and I guess I fainted."

"Ah," said the nurse, as if that explained everything.

"Ah," said her father, King Ethelred. "Now I understand. We were taking turns watching you after we found you unconscious and scratched up by the garden gate. You kept crying out in your sleep, 'Make the bear go away! Make the bear leave me alone!' Of course, we thought you meant *the* Bear, our Bear, and we had to ask the poor man not to take his turn any more, as we thought it might make you upset. We all thought you hated him, for a while there." And King Ethelred chuckled. "I'll have to tell him it was all a mistake."

Then the king left. Great, thought the princess, he's going to tell the Bear it was all a mistake, and I really do hate him to pieces.

The nurse walked over to the bed and knelt beside it. "There's another part of the story. They made me promise not to tell you," the nurse said, "but you know and I know that I'll always tell you everything. It seems that it was two guards that found you, and they both said that they saw something running away. Or not running, exactly, galloping. Or something. They said it looked like a bear, running on all fours."

"Oh, no," said the princess. "How horrible!"

"No," said the nurse. "It was their opinion, and Robbo Knockle swears it's true, that the bear they saw had brought you to the gate and set you down gentle as you please. Whoever brought you there smoothed your skirt, you know, and put a pile of leaves under your head like a pillow, and you were surely in no state to do all that yourself."

"Don't be silly," said the princess. "How could a bear do all that?"

"I know," said the nurse, "so it must not have been an ordinary bear. It must have been a magic bear." She said this last in a whisper, because the nurse believed that magic should be talked about quietly, lest something awful should hear and come calling.

"Nonsense," said the princess. "I've had an education, and I don't believe in magic bears or magic brews or any kind of magic at all. It's just old-lady foolishness."

The nurse stood up and her mouth wrinkled all up. "Well, then, this foolish old lady will take her foolish stories to somebody foolish, who wants to listen."

"Oh, there, there," the princess said, for she didn't like to hurt anyone's feelings, especially not Nurse's. And they were friends again. But the princess still didn't believe about the bear. However, she hadn't been eaten, after all, so the bear must not have been hungry.

* * *

It was only two days later, when the princess was up and around again—though there were nasty scabs all over her face from the scratches—that the prince came back to the palace.

He came riding up on a lathered horse that dropped to the ground and died right in front of the palace door. He looked exhausted, and there were great purple circles under his eyes. He had no baggage. He had no cloak. Just the clothes on his back and a dead horse.

"I've come home," he said to the doorman, and fainted into his arms. (By the way, it's perfectly all right for a man to faint, as long as he has ridden on horseback for five days, without a bite to eat, and with hundreds of soldiers chasing him.)

"It's treason," he said when he woke up and ate and bathed and dressed. "My allies turned against me, even my own subjects. They drove me out of my kingdom. I'm lucky to be alive."

"Why?" asked King Ethelred.

"Because they would have killed me. If they had caught me."

"No, no, no, no, don't be stupid," said the Bear, who was listening from a chair a few feet away. "Why did they turn against you?"

The prince turned toward the Bear and sneered. It was an ugly sneer, and it twisted up the prince's face in a way it had never twisted when he lived with King Ethelred and was in love with the princess.

"I wasn't aware that I was being stupid," he said archly. "And I certainly wasn't aware that *you* had been invited into the conversation."

The Bear didn't say anything after that, just nodded an unspoken apology and watched.

And the prince never did explain why the people had turned against him. Just something vague about power-hungry demagogues and mob rule.

The princess came to see the prince that very morning.

"You look exhausted," she said.

"You look beautiful," he said.

"I have scabs all over my face and I haven't done my hair in days," she said.

"I love you," he said.

"You stopped writing," she said.

"I guess I lost my pen," he said. "No, I remember now. I lost my mind. I forgot how beautiful you are. A man would have to be mad to forget."

Then he kissed her, and she kissed him back, and she forgave him for all the sorrow he had caused her and it was like he had never been away.

For about three days.

Because in three days she began to realize that he was different somehow.

She would open her eyes after kissing him (princesses always close their eyes when they kiss someone) and she would notice that he was looking off somewhere with a distant expression on his face. As if he barely noticed that he was kissing her. That does not make any woman, even a princess, feel very good.

She noticed that sometimes he seemed to forget she was even there. She passed him in a corridor and he wouldn't speak, and unless she touched his arm and said good morning he might have walked on by without a word.

And then sometimes, for no reason, he would feel slighted or offended, or a servant would make a noise or spill something and he would fly into a rage and throw things against the wall. He had never even raised his voice in anger when he was a boy.

He often said cruel things to the princess, and she wondered why she loved him, and what was wrong, but then he would come to her and apologize, and she would forgive him because after all he had lost a kingdom because of traitors, and he couldn't be expected to always feel sweet and nice. She decided, though, that if it was up to her, and it was, he would never feel unsweet and unnice again.

Then one night the Bear and her father went into the study and locked the door behind them. The princess had never been locked out of her father's study before, and she became angry at the Bear because he was taking her father away from her, and so she listened at the door. She figured that if the Bear wanted to keep her out, she would see to it that she heard everything anyway.

This is what she heard.

"I have the information," the Bear said.

"It must be bad, or you wouldn't have asked to speak to me alone," said King Ethelred. Aha, thought the princess, the Bear *did* plot to keep me out.

The Bear stood by the fire, leaning on the mantel, while King Ethelred sat down.

"Well?" asked King Ethelred.

"I know how much the boy means to you. And to the princess. I'm sorry to bring such a tale."

The boy! thought the princess. They couldn't possibly be calling her prince a boy, could they? Why, he had been a king, except for treason, and here a commoner was calling him a boy.

"He means much to us," said King Ethelred, "which is all the more reason for me to know the truth, be it good or bad."

"Well, then," said the Bear, "I must tell you that he was a very bad king."

The princess went white with rage.

"I think he was just too young. Or something," said the Bear. "Perhaps there was a side to him that you never saw, because the moment he had power it went to his head. He thought his kingdom was too small, because he began to make war with little neighboring counties and duchies and took their lands and made them part of his kingdom. He plotted against other kings who had been good and true friends of his father. And he kept raising taxes on his people to support huge armies. He kept starting wars and mothers kept weeping because their sons had fallen in battle.

"And finally," said the Bear, "the people had had enough, and so had the other kings, and there was a revolution and a war all at the same time. The only part of the boy's tale that is true is that he was lucky to escape with his life, because every person that I talked to spoke of him with hatred, as if he were the most evil person they had ever seen."

King Ethelred shook his head. "Could you be wrong? I can't believe this of a boy I practically raised myself."

"I wish it were not true," said the Bear, "for I know that the princess loves him dearly. But it seems obvious to me that the boy doesn't love her—he is here because he knew he would be safe here, and because he knows that if he married her, he would be able to rule when you are dead."

"Well," said King Ethelred, "that will never happen. My daughter will never marry a man who would destroy the kingdom."

"Not even if she loves him very much?" asked the Bear.

"It is the price of being a princess," said the king. "She must think first of the kingdom, or she will never be fit to be queen."

At that moment, however, being queen was the last thing the princess cared about. All she knew was that she hated the Bear for taking away her father, and now the same man had persuaded her father to keep her from marrying the man she loved.

She beat on the door, crying out, "Liar! Liar!" King Ethelred and the Bear both leaped for the door. King Ethelred opened it, and the princess burst into the room and started hitting the Bear as hard as she could. Of course the blows fell very lightly, because she was not all that strong, and he was very large and sturdy and the blows could have caused him no pain. But as she struck at him his face looked as if he were being stabbed through the heart at every blow.

"Daughter, daughter," said King Ethelred. "What is this? Why did you listen at the door?"

But she didn't answer; she only beat at the Bear until she was crying too hard to hit him anymore. And then, between sobs, she began to yell at him. And because she didn't usually yell her voice became harsh and hoarse and she whispered. But yelling or whispering, her words were clear, and every word said hatred.

She accused the Bear of making her father little, nothing, worse than nothing, a weakling king who had turn to a filthy commoner to make any decision at all. She accused the Bear of hating her and trying to ruin her life by keeping her from marrying the only man she could ever love. She accused the Bear of being a traitor, who was plotting to be king himself and rule the kingdom. She accused the Bear of making up vile lies about the prince because she knew that he would be a better king than her weakling father, and that if she married the prince all the Bear's plans for ruling the kingdom would come to nothing.

And finally she accused the Bear of having such a filthy mind that he imagined that he could eventually marry her himself, and so become king.

But that would never happen, she whispered bitterly, at the end. "That will never happen," she said, "never, never, never, because I hate you and I loathe you and if you don't get out of this kingdom and never come back I'll kill myself, I swear it."

And then she grabbed a sword from the mantel and tried to slash her wrists, and the Bear reached out and stopped her by holding her arms in his huge hands that gripped like iron. Then she spit at him and tried to bite his fingers and beat her head against his chest until King Ethelred took her hands and the Bear let go and backed away.

"I'm sorry," King Ethelred kept saying, though he himself wasn't certain who he was apologizing to or what he was apologizing for. "I'm sorry." And then he realized that he was apologizing for himself, because somehow he knew that his kingdom was ruined right then.

If he listened to the Bear and sent the prince away, the princess would never forgive him, would hate him, in fact, and he couldn't bear that. But if he didn't listen to the Bear, then the princess would surely marry the prince, and the prince would surely ruin his kingdom. And he couldn't endure that.

But worst of all, he couldn't stand the terrible look on the Bear's face.

The princess stood sobbing in her father's arms.

The king stood wishing there were something he could do or undo.

And the Bear simply stood.

And then the Bear nodded, and said, "I understand. Good-bye."

And then the Bear walked out of the room, and out of the palace, and out of the garden walls, and out of the city, and out of any land that the king had heard of.

He took nothing with him—no food, no horse, no extra clothing. He just wore his clothing and carried his sword. He left as he came.

And the princess cried with relief. The Bear was gone. Life could go on, just like it was before ever the prince left and before ever the Bear came.

So she thought.

She didn't really realize how her father felt until he died only four months later, suddenly very old and very tired and very lonely and despairing for his kingdom.

She didn't realize that the prince was not the same man she loved before until she married him three months after her father died.

On the day of their wedding she proudly crowned him king herself, and led him to the throne, where he sat.

"I love you," she said proudly, "and you look like a king."

"I am a king," he said. "I am King Edward the first."

"Edward?" she said. "Why Edward? That's not your name."

"That's a king's name," he said, "and I am a king. Do I not have power to change my name?"

"Of course," she said. "But I liked your own name better."

"But you will call me Edward," he said, and she did.

When she saw him. For he didn't come to her very often. As soon as he wore the crown he began to keep her out of the court, and conducted the business of the kingdom where she couldn't hear. She didn't understand this, because her father had always let her attend everything and hear everything in the government, so she could be a good queen.

"A good queen," said King Edward, her husband, "is a quiet woman who has babies, one of whom will be king."

And so the princess, who was now the queen, had babies, and one of them was a boy, and she tried to help him grow up to be a king.

But as the years passed by she realized that King Edward was not the lovely boy she had loved in the garden. He was a cruel and greedy man. And she didn't like him very much.

He raised the taxes, and the people became poor.

He built up the army, so it became very strong.

He used the army to take over the land of Count Edred, who had been her godfather.

He also took over the land of Duke Adlow, who had once let her pet one of his tame swans.

He also took over the land of Earl Thlaffway, who had wept openly at her father's funeral, and said that her father was the only man he had ever worshipped, because he was such a good king.

And Edred and Adlow and Thlaffway all disappeared, and were never heard of again.

"He's even against the common people," the nurse grumbled one day as she did up the queen's hair. "Some shepherds came to court yesterday to tell him a marvel, which is their duty, isn't it, to tell the king of anything strange that happens in the land?"

"Yes," said the queen, remembering how as a child she and the prince had run to their father often to tell him a marvel—how grass springs up all at once in the spring, how water just disappeared on a hot day, how a butterfly comes all awkward from the cocoon.

"Well," said the nurse, "they told him that there was a bear along the edge of the forest, a bear that doesn't eat meat, but only berries and roots. And this bear, they said, killed wolves. Every year they lose dozens of sheep to the wolves, but this year they had lost not one lamb, because the bear killed the wolves. Now that's a marvel, I'd say," said the nurse.

"Oh yes," said the princess who was now a queen.

"But what did the king do," said the nurse, "but order his knights to hunt down that bear and kill it. Kill it!"

"Why?" asked the queen.

"Why, why, why?" asked the nurse. "The best question in the world. The shepherds asked it, and the king said, 'can't have a bear loose around here. He might kill children.'

" 'Oh no,' says the shepherds, 'the bear don't eat meat.'

" 'Then, it'll wind up stealing grain,' the king says in reply, and there it is, my lady—the hunters are out after a perfectly harmless bear! You can bet the shepherds don't like it. A perfectly harmless bear!"

The queen nodded. "A magic bear."

"Why, yes," said the nurse. "Now you mention it, it does seem like the bear that saved you that day—"

"Nurse," said the queen, "there was no bear that day. I was dreaming I was mad with despair. There wasn't a wolf chasing me. And there was definitely no magic bear."

The nurse bit her lip. Of course there had been a bear, she thought. And a wolf. But the queen, her princess, was determined not to believe in any kind thing.

"Sure there was a bear," said the nurse.

"No, there was no bear," said the queen, "and now I know who put the idea of a magic bear into the children's head."

"They've heard of him?"

"They came to me with a silly tale of a bear that climbs over the wall into the garden when no one else is around, and who plays with them and lets him ride on his back. Obviously you told them your silly tale about the magic bear who supposedly saved me. So I told them that magic bears were a full tall-tale and that even grownups liked to tell them, but that they must be careful to remember the difference between truth and falsehood, and they should wink if they're fibbing."

"What did they say?" the nurse said.

"I made them all wink about the bear," said the queen, "of course. But I would appreciate it if you wouldn't fill their heads with silly stories. You did tell them your stupid story, didn't you?"

"Yes," said the nurse sadly.

"What a trouble your wagging tongue can cause," said the queen, and the nurse burst into tears and left the room.

They made it up later but there was no talk of bears. The nurse understood well enough, though. The thought of bears reminded the queen of *the* Bear, and everyone knew that she was the one who drove that wise counselor away. If only the Bear were still here, thought the nurse—and hundreds of other people in the kingdom—if he were still here we wouldn't have these troubles in the kingdom.

And there were troubles. The soldiers patrolled the streets of the cities and locked people up for saying things about King Edward. And when a servant in the palace did anything wrong he would bellow and storm, and even throw things and beat them with a rod.

One day when King Edward didn't like the soup he threw the whole tureen at the cook. The cook promptly took his leave, saying for anyone to hear, "I've served kings and queens, lords and ladies, soldiers, and servants, and in all that time this is the first time I've ever been called upon to serve a pig."

The day after he left he was back, at swordpoint—not cooking in the kitchen, of course, since cooks are too close to the king's food. No, the cook was sweeping the stables. And the servants were told in no uncertain terms that none of them was free to leave. If they didn't like their jobs, they could be given another one to do. And they all looked at the work the cook was doing, and kept their tongues.

Except the nurse, who talked to the queen about everything.

"We might as well be slaves," said the nurse. "Right down to the wages. He's cut us all in half, some even more, and we've got barely enough to feed ourselves. I'm all right, mind you, my lady, for I have no one but me to feed, but there's some who's hard put to get a stick of wood for the fire and a morsel of bread for a hungry mouth or six."

The queen thought of pleading with her husband, but then she realized that King Edward would only punish the servants for complaining. So she began giving her nurse jewels to sell. Then the nurse quietly gave the money to the servants who had the least, or who had the largest families, and whispered to them, even though the queen had told her not to give a hint, "This money's from the queen, you know. *She* remembers us servants, even if her husband's a lout and a pimple." And the servants remembered that the queen was kind.

The people didn't hate King Edward quite as much as the servants did, of course, because even though taxes were high, there are always silly people who are proud fit to bust when their army has a victory. And of course King Edward had quite a few victories at first. He would pick a fight with a neighboring king or lord and then march in and take over. People had thought old King Boris' army of five thousand was bad, back in the old days. But because of his high taxes, King Edward was able to hire an army of fifty thousand men, and war was a different thing then. They lived off the land in enemy country, and killed and plundered where they liked. Most of the soldiers weren't local men, anyway—they were the riffraff of the highways, men who begged or stole, and now were being paid for stealing.

But King Edward tripled the size of the kingdom, and there were a good many citizens who followed the war news and cheered whenever King Edward rode through the streets.

They cheered the queen, too, of course, but they didn't see her very much, about once a year or so. She was still beautiful, of course, more beautiful than ever before. No one particularly noticed that her eyes were sad these days, or else those who noticed said nothing and soon forgot it.

But King Edward's victories had been won against weak, and peaceful, and unprepared men. And at last the neighboring kings got together, and the rebels from conquered lands got together, and they planned King Edward's doom.

When next King Edward went a-conquering, they were ready, and on the very battlefield where King Ethelred had defeated Boris they ambushed King Edward's army. Edward's fifty thousand hired men faced a hundred thousand where before they had never faced more than half their number. Their bought courage melted away, and those who lived through the first of the battle ran for their lives.

King Edward was captured and brought back to the city in a cage, which was hung above the city gate, right where the statue of the bear is today.

The queen came out to the leaders of the army that had defeated King Edward and knelt before them in the dust and wept, pleading for her husband. And because she was beautiful, and good, and because they themselves were only good men trying to protect their own lives and property, they granted him his life. For her sake they even let him remain king, but they imposed a huge tribute on him. To save his own life, he agreed.

So taxes were raised even higher, in order to pay the tribute, and King Edward could only keep enough soldiers to police his kingdom, and the tribute went to paying for soldiers of the victorious kings to stay on the borders to keep watch on our land. For they figured, and rightly so, that if they let up their vigilance for a minute, King Edward would raise an army and stab them in the back.

But they didn't let up their vigilance, you see. And King Edward was trapped.

A dark evil fell upon him then, for a greedy man

craves all the more the thing he can't have. And King Edward craved power. Because he couldn't have power over other kings, he began to use more power over his own kingdom, and his own household, and his own family.

He began to have prisoners tortured until they confessed to conspiracies that didn't exist, and until they denounced people who were innocent. And people in this kingdom began to lock their doors at night, and hide when someone knocked. There was fear in the kingdom, and people began to move away, until King Edward took to hunting down and beheading anyone who tried to leave the kingdom.

And it was bad in the palace, too. For the servants were beaten savagely for the slightest things, and King Edward even yelled at his own son and daughters whenever he saw them, so that the queen kept them hidden away with her most of the time.

Everyone was afraid of King Edward. And people almost always hate anyone they fear.

Except the queen. For though she feared him she remembered his youth, and she said to herself, or sometimes to the nurse, "Somewhere in that sad and ugly man there is the beautiful boy I love. Somehow I must help him find that beautiful boy and bring him out again."

But neither the nurse nor the queen could think how such a thing could possibly happen.

Until the queen discovered that she was going to have a baby. Of course, she thought. With a new baby he will remember his family and remember to love us.

So she told him. And he railed at her about how stupid she was to bring another child to see their humiliation, a royal family with enemy troops perched on the border, with no real power in the world.

And then he took her roughly by the arm into the

court, where the lords and ladies were gathered, and there he told them that his wife was going to have a baby to mock him, for she still had the power of a woman, even if he didn't have the power of a man. She cried out that it wasn't true. He hit her, and she fell to the ground.

And the problem was solved, for she lost the baby before it was born and lay on her bed for days, delirious and fevered and at the point of death. No one knew that King Edward hated himself for what he had done, that he tore at his face and his hair at the thought that the queen might die because of his fury. They only saw that he was drunk all through the queen's illness, and that he never came to her bedside.

While the queen was delirious, she dreamed many times and many things. But one dream that kept coming back to her was of a wolf following her in the forest, and she ran and ran until she fell, but just as the wolf was about to eat her, a huge brown bear came and killed the wolf and flung him away, and then picked her up gently and laid her down at her father's door, carefully arranging her dress and putting leaves under her head as a pillow.

When she finally woke up, though, she only remembered that there was no magic bear that would come out of the forest to save her. Magic was for the common people—brews to cure gout and plague and to make a lady love you, spells said in the night to keep dark things from the door. Foolishness, the queen told herself. For she had an education, and knew better. There is nothing to keep the dark things from the door, there is no cure for gout and plague, and there is no brew that will make your husband love you. She told this to herself and despaired.

King Edward soon forgot his grief at the thought his wife might die. As soon as she was up and about he was as surly as ever, and he didn't stop drinking, either, even when the reason for it was gone. He just remembered that he had hurt her badly and he felt guilty, and so whenever he saw her he felt bad, and because he felt bad he treated her badly, as if it were her fault.

Things were about as bad as they could get. There were rebellions here and there all over the kingdom, and rebels were being beheaded every week. Some soldiers had even mutinied and got away over the border with the people they were supposed to stop. And so one morning King Edward was in the foulest, blackest mood he had ever been in.

The queen walked into the dining room for breakfast looking as beautiful as ever, for grief had only deepened her beauty, and made you want to cry for the pain of her exquisite face and for the suffering in her proud, straight bearing. King Edward saw that pain and suffering but even more he saw that beauty, and for a moment he remembered the girl who had grown up without a care or a sorrow or an evil thought. And he knew that he had caused every bit of the pain she bore.

So he began to find fault with her, and before he knew it he was ordering her into the kitchen to cook.

"I can't," she said.

"If a servant can, you can," he snarled in reply.

She began to cry. "I've never cooked. I've never started a fire. I'm a queen."

"You're not a queen," the king said savagely, hating himself as he said it. "You're not a queen and I'm not a king, because we're a bunch of powerless lackeys taking orders from those scum across the border! Well, if I've got to live like a servant in my own palace, so have you!"

And so he took her roughly into the kitchen and ordered her to come back in with a breakfast she had cooked herself.

The queen was shattered, but not so shattered that she could forget her pride. She spoke to the cooks cowering in the corner. "You heard the king. I must cook him breakfast with my own hands. But I don't know how. You must tell me what to do."

So they told her, and she tried her best to do what they said, but her untrained hands made a botch of everything. She burned herself at the fire and scalded herself with the porridge. She put too much salt on the bacon and there were shells left in the eggs. She also burned the muffins. And then she carried it all in to her husband and he began to eat.

And of course it was awful.

And at that moment he realized finally that the queen was a queen and could be nothing else, just as a cook had no hope of being a queen. Just so he looked at himself and realized that he could never be anything but a king. The queen, however, was a good queen—while he was a terrible king. He would always be a king but he would never be good at it. And as he chewed up the eggshells he reached the lowest despair.

Another man, hating himself as King Edward did, might have taken his own life. But that was not King Edward's way. Instead he picked up his rod and began to beat the queen. He struck her again and again, and her back bled, and she fell to the ground, screaming.

The servants came in and so did the guards, and the servants, seeing the queen treated so, tried to stop the king. But the king ordered the guards to kill anyone who tried to interfere. Even so, the chief steward, a cook, and the butler were dead before the others stopped trying.

And the king kept beating and beating the queen until everyone was sure he would beat her to death.

And in her heart as she lay on the stone floor, numb to the pain of her body because of the pain of her heart, she wished that the bear would come again, stepping over her to kill the wolf that was running forward to devour her.

At that moment the door broke in pieces and a terrible roar filled the dining hall. The king stopped beating the queen, and the guards and the servants looked at the door, for there stood a huge brown bear on its hind legs, towering over them all, and roaring in fury.

The servants ran from the room.

"Kill him," the king bellowed at the guards.

The guards drew their swords and advanced on the bear.

The bear disarmed them all, though there were so many that some drew blood before their swords were slapped out of their hands. Some of them might even have tried to fight the bear without weapons, because they were brave men, but the bear struck them on the head, and the rest fled away.

Yet the queen, dazed though she was, thought that for some reason the bear had not struck yet with all his force, that the huge animal was saving his strength for another battle.

And that battle was with King Edward, who stood with his sharp sword in his hand, eager for battle, hoping to die, with the desperation and self-hatred in him that would make him a terrible opponent, even for a bear.

A bear, thought the queen. I wished for a bear and he is here.

Then she lay, weak and helpless and bleeding on the stone floor as her husband, her prince, fought the bear. She did not know who she hoped would win. For even now, she did not hate her husband. And yet she knew that her life and the lives of her subjects would be unendurable as long as he lived.

They circled around the room, the bear moving clumsily yet quickly, King Edward moving faster still, his blade whipping steel circles through the air. Three times the blade landed hard and deep on the bear, before the animal seized the blade between his paws. King Edward tried to draw back the sword, and as he did it bit deeply into the animal's paws. But it was a battle of strength, and the bear was sure to win it in the end. He pulled the sword out of Edward's hand, and then grasped the king in a mighty embrace and carried him screaming from the room.

And at that last moment, as Edward tugged hopelessly at his sword and blood poured from the bear's paws, the queen found herself hoping that the bear would hold on, would take away the sword, that the bear would win out and free the kingdom—her kingdom—and her family and even herself, from the man who had been devouring them all.

Yet when King Edward screamed in the bear's grip, she heard only the voice of the boy in the garden in the eternal and too-quick summer of her childhood. She fainted with a dim memory of his smile dancing crazily before her eyes.

She awoke as she had awakened once before, thinking that it had been a dream, and then remembering the truth of it when the pain where her husband had beaten her nearly made her fall unconscious again. But she fought the faintness and stayed awake, and asked for water.

The nurse brought water, and then several lords of high rank and the captain of the army and the chief servants came in and asked her what they should do.

"Why do you ask me?" she said.

"Because," the nurse answered her, "the king is dead."

The queen waited.

"The bear left him at the gate," the captain of the army said.

"His neck was broken," the chief said.

"And now," one of the lords said, "now we must

know what to do. We haven't even told the people, and no one has been allowed inside or outside the palace."

The queen thought, and closed her eyes as she did so. But what she saw when she closed her eyes was the body of her beautiful prince with his head loose as the wolf's had been that day in the forest. She did not want to see that, so she opened her eyes.

"You must proclaim that the king is dead throughout the land," she said.

To the captain of the army she said, "There will be no more beheading for treason. Anyone who is in prison for treason is to be set free, now. And any other prisoners whose terms are soon to expire should be set free at once."

The captain of the army bowed and left. He did not smile until he was out the door, but then he smiled until tears ran down his cheeks.

To the chief cook she said, "All the servants in the palace are free to leave now, if they want. But please ask them, in my name, to stay. I will restore them as they were, if they'll stay."

The cook started a heartfelt speech of thanks, but then thought better of it and left the room to tell the others.

To the lords she said, "Go to the kings whose armies guard our borders, and tell them that King Edward is dead and they can go home now. Tell them that if I need their help I will call on them, but that until I do I will govern my kingdom alone."

And the lords came and kissed her hands tenderly, and left the room.

And she was alone with the nurse.

"I'm so sorry," said the nurse, when enough silence had passed.

"For what?" asked the queen.

"For the death of your husband."

"Ah, that," said the queen. "Ah, yes, my husband."

And then the queen wept with all her heart. Not
for the cruel and greedy man who had warred and
killed and savaged everywhere he could. But for the
boy who had somehow turned into that man, the
boy whose gentle hand had comforted her childhood
hurts, the boy whose frightened voice had cried out
to her at the end of his life, as if he wondered why
he had gotten lost inside himself, as if he realized
that it was too, too late to get out again.

When she had done weeping that day, she never
cried for him again.

In three days she was up again, though she had to
wear loose clothing because of the pain. She held
court anyway, and it was then that the shepherds
brought her the Bear. Not the bear, the animal, that
had killed the king, but *the* Bear, the counselor, who
had left the kingdom so many years before.

"We found him on the hillside, with our sheep
nosing him and lapping his face," the oldest of the
shepherds told her. "Looks like he's been set on by
robbers, he's cut and battered so. Miracle he's alive,"
he said.

"What is that he's wearing?" asked the queen,
standing by the bed where she had had the servants
lay him.

"Oh," said one of the other shepherds. "That's me
cloak. They left him nekkid, but we didn't think it
right to bring him before you in such a state."

She thanked the shepherds and offered to pay them
a reward, but they said no thanks, explaining, "We
remember him, we do, and it wouldn't be right to
take money for helping him, don't you see, because
he was a good man back in your father's day."

The queen had the servants—who had all stayed
on, by the way—clean his wounds and bind them

and tend to his wants. And because he was a strong man, he lived, though the wounds might have killed a smaller, weaker man. Even so, he never got back the use of his right hand, and had to learn to write with his left; and he limped ever after. But he often said he was lucky to be alive and wasn't ashamed of his infirmities, though he sometimes said that something ought to be done about the robbers who run loose in the hills.

As soon as he was able, the queen had him attend court, where he listened to the ambassadors from other lands and to the cases she heard and judged.

Then at night she had him come to King Ethelred's study, and there she asked him about the questions of that day and what he would have done differently, and he told her what he thought she did well, too. And so she learned from him as her father had learned.

One day she even said to him, "I have never asked forgiveness of any man in my life. But I ask for yours."

"For what?" he said, surprised.

"For hating you, and thinking you served me and my father badly, and driving you from this kingdom: If we had listened to you," she said, "none of this would have happened."

"Oh," he said, "all that's past. You were young, and in love, and that's as inevitable as fate itself."

"I know," she said, "and for love I'd probably do it again, but now that I'm wiser I can still ask for forgiveness for my youth."

The Bear smiled at her. "You were forgiven before you asked. But since you ask I gladly forgive you again."

"Is there any reward I can give you for your service so many years ago, when you left unthanked?" she asked.

"Yes," he answered. "If you could let me stay and

serve you as I served your father, that would be reward enough."

"How can that be a reward?" she asked. "I was
going to ask you to do that for *me*. And now you ask
it for yourself."

"Let us say," said the Bear, "that I loved your father like my brother, and you like my niece, and I
long to stay with the only family that I have."

Then the queen took the pitcher and poured him
a mug of ale, and they sat by the fire and talked far
into the night.

Because the queen was a widow, because despite the
problems of the past the kingdom was large and rich,
many suitors came asking for her hand. Some were
dukes, some were earls, and some were kings or sons
of kings. And she was as beautiful as ever, only in
her thirties, a prize herself even if there had been no
kingdom to covet.

But though she considered long and hard over
some of them, and even liked several men who came,
she turned them all down and sent them all away.

And she reigned alone, as queen, with the Bear to
advise her.

And she also did what her husband had told her a
queen should do—she raised her son to be king and
her daughters to be worthy to be queens. And the
Bear helped her with that, too, teaching her son to
hunt, and teaching him how to see beyond men's
words into their hearts, and teaching him to love
peace and serve the people.

And the boy grew up as beautiful as his father and
as wise as the Bear, and the people knew he would
be a great king, perhaps even greater than King Ethelred had been.

The queen grew old, and turned much of the matter of the kingdom over to her son, who was now a
man. The prince married the daughter of a neigh-

boring king. She was a good woman, and the queen saw her grandchildren growing up.

She knew perfectly well that she was old, because she was sagging and no longer beautiful as she had been in her youth—though there were many who said that she was far more lovely as an old lady than any mere girl could hope to be.

But somehow it never occurred to her that the Bear, too, was growing old. Didn't he still stride through the garden with one of her grandchildren on each shoulder? Didn't he still come into the study with her and her son and teach them statecraft and tell them, yes, that's good, yes, that's right, yes, you'll make a great queen yet, yes, you'll be a fine king, worthy of your grandfather's kingdom—didn't he?

Yet one day he didn't get up from his bed, and a servant came to her with a whispered message, "Please come."

She went to him and found him gray-faced and shaking in his bed.

"Thirty years ago," he said, "I would have said it's nothing but a fever and I would have ignored it and gone riding. But now, my lady, I know I'm going to die."

"Nonsense," she said, "you'll never die," knowing as well as he did that he was dying, and knowing that he knew that she knew it.

"I have a confession to make," he said to her.

"I know it already," she said.

"Do you?"

"Yes," she said softly, "and much to my surprise, I find that I love you too. Even an old lady like me," she said, laughing.

"Oh," he said, "that was not my confession. I already knew that you knew I loved you. Why else would I have come back when you called?"

And then she felt a chill in the room and remembered the only time she had ever called for help.

"Yes," he said, "you remember. How I laughed when they named me. If they only knew, I thought at the time."

She shook her head. "How could it be?"

"I wondered myself," he said. "But it is. I met a wise old man in the woods when I was but a lad. An orphan, too, so that there was no one to ask about me when I stayed with him. I stayed until he died five years later, and I learned all his magic."

"There's no magic," she said as if by rote, and he laughed.

"If you mean brews and spells and curses, then you're right," he said. "But there is magic of another sort. The magic of becoming what most you are. My old man in the woods, his magic was to be an owl, and to fly by night seeing the world and coming to understand it. The owlness was in him, and the magic was letting that part of himself that was most himself come forward. And he taught me."

The Bear had stopped shaking because his body had given up trying to overcome the illness.

"So I looked inside me and wondered who I was. And then I found it out. Your nurse found it, too. One glance and she knew I was a bear."

"You killed my husband," she said to him.

"No," he said. "I fought your husband and carried him from the palace, but as he stared death in the face he discovered, too, what he was and who he was, and his real self came out."

The Bear shook his head.

"I killed a wolf at the palace gate, and left a wolf with a broken neck behind when I went away into the hills."

"A wolf both times," she said. "But he was such a beautiful boy."

"A puppy is cute enough whatever he plans to grow up to be," said the Bear.

"And what am I?" asked the queen.

"You?" asked the Bear. "Don't you know?"

"No," she answered. "Am I a swan? A porcupine? These days I walk like a crippled, old biddy hen. Who am I, after all these years? What animal should I turn into by night?"

"You're laughing," said the Bear, "and I would laugh too, but I have to be stingy with my breath. I don't know what animal you are, if you don't know yourself, but I think—"

And he stopped talking and his body shook in a great heave.

"No!" cried the queen.

"All right," said the Bear. "I'm not dead yet. I think that deep down inside you, you are a woman, and so you have been wearing your real self out in the open all your life. And you are beautiful."

"What an old fool you are after all," said the queen. "Why didn't I ever marry you?"

"Your judgment was too good," said the Bear.

But the queen called the priest and her children and married the Bear on his deathbed, and her son who had learned kingship from him called him father, and then they remembered the bear who had come to play with them in their childhood and the queen's daughters called him father; and the queen called him husband, and the Bear laughed and allowed as how he wasn't an orphan any more. Then he died.

And that's why there's a statue of a bear over the gate of the city.

SANDMAGIC

T HE GREAT DOMES of the city of Gyree dazzled
blue and red when the sun shone through a
break in the clouds, and for a moment Cer Cemreet
thought he saw some of the glory the uncles talked
about in the late night tales of the old days of Greet.
But the capital did not look dazzling up close, Cer
remembered bitterly. Now dogs ran in the streets
and rats lived in the wreckage of the palace, and the
King of Greet lived in New Gyree in the hills far to
the north, where the armies of the enemy could not
go. Yet.

The sun went back behind a cloud and the city
looked dark again. A Nefyr patrol was riding briskly
on the Hetterwee Road far to the north. Cer turned
his gaze to the lush grass on the hill where he sat.
The clouds meant rain, but probably not here, he
thought. He always thought of something else when
he saw a Nefyr patrol. Yes, it was too early in
Hrickan for rains to fall here. This rain would fall in

the north, perhaps in the land of the King of the High Mountains, or on the vast plain of Westwold where they said horses ran free but were tame for any man to ride at need. But no rain would fall in Greet until Doonse, three weeks from now. By then the wheat would all be stored and the hay would be piled in vast ricks as tall as the hill Cer sat on.

In the old days, they said, all during Doonse the great wagons from Westwold would come and carry off the hay to last them through the snow season. But not now, Cer remembered. This year and last year and the year before the wagons had come from the south and east, two-wheeled wagons with drivers who spoke, not High Westil, but the barbarian Fyrd language. Fyrd or firt, thought Cer, and laughed, for firt was a word he could not say in front of his parents. They spoke firt.

Cer looked out over the plain again. The Nefyr patrol had turned from the highway and were on the road to the hills.

The road to the hills. Cer leaped to his feet and raced down the track leading home. A patrol heading for the hills could only mean trouble.

He stopped to rest only once, when the pain in his side was too bad to bear. But the patrol had horses, and he arrived home only to see the horses of the Nefyrre gathered at his father's gate.

Where are the uncles? Cer thought. The uncles must come.

But the uncles were not there, and Cer heard a terrible scream from inside the garden walls. He had never heard his mother scream before, but somehow he knew it was his mother, and he ran to the gate. A Nefyr soldier seized him and called out, "Here's the boy!" in a thick accent of High Westil, so that Cer's parents could understand. Cer's mother screamed again, and now Cer saw why.

His father had been stripped naked, his arms and

legs held by two tall Nefyrre. The Nefyr captain held his viciously curved short-sword, point up, pressing against Cer's father's hard-muscled stomach. As Cer and his mother watched, the sword drew blood, and the captain pushed it in to the hilt, then pulled it up to the ribs. Blood gushed. The captain had been careful not to touch the heart, and now they thrust a spear into the huge wound, and lifted it high, Cer's father dangling from the end. They lashed the spear to the gatepost, and the blood and bowels stained the gates and the walls.

For five minutes more Cer's father lived, his chest heaving in the agony of breath. He may have died of pain, but Cer did not think so, for his father was not the kind to give in to pain. He may have died of suffocation, for one lung was gone and every breath was excruciating, but Cer did not think so, for his father kept breathing to the end. It was loss of blood, Cer decided, weeks later. It was when his body was dry, when the veins collapsed, that Cer's father died.

He never uttered a sound. Cer's father would never let the Nefyrre hear him so much as sigh in pain.

Cer's mother screamed and screamed until blood came from her mouth and she fainted.

Cer stood in silence until his father died. Then when the captain, a smirk on his face, walked near Cer and looked in his face, Cer kicked him in the groin.

They cut off Cer's great toes, but like his father, Cer made no sound.

Then the Nefyrre left and the uncles came.

Uncle Forwin vomited. Uncle Erwin wept. Uncle Crune put his arm around Cer's shoulder as the servants bound his maimed feet and said, "Your father was a great, a brave man. He killed many Nefyrre, and burned many wagons. But the Nefyrre are strong."

Uncle Crune squeezed Cer's shoulder. "Your father was stronger. But he was one, and they were many."

Cer looked away.

"Will you not look at your uncle?" Uncle Crune asked.

"My father," Cer said, "did not think that he was alone."

Uncle Crune got up and walked away. Cer never saw the uncles again.

He and his mother had to leave the house and the fields, for a Nefyr farmer had been given the land to farm for the King of Nefyrd. With no money, they had to move south, across the River Greebeck into the drylands near the desert, where no rivers flowed and so only the hardiest plants lived. They lived the winter on the charity of the desperately poor. In the summer, when the heat came, so did the Poor Plague which swept the drylands. The cure was fresh fruits, but fresh fruits came from Yffyrd and Suffyrd and only the rich could buy them, and the poor died by the thousands. Cer's mother was one of them.

They took her out on the sand to burn her body and free her spirit. As they painted her with tar (tar, at least, cost nothing, if a man had a bucket), five horsemen came to the brow of a dune to watch. At first Cer thought they were Nefyrre, but no. The poor people looked up and saluted the strangers, which Greetmen never do the enemy. These, then, were desert men, the Abadapnur nomads, who raided the rich farms of Greet during dry years, but who never harmed the poor.

We hated them, Cer thought, when we were rich. But now we are poor, and they are our friends.

His mother burned as the sun set.

Cer watched until the flames went out. The moon was high for the second time that night. Cer said a prayer to the moonlady over his mother's bones and ashes and then he turned and left.

He stopped at their hut and gathered the little food they had, and put on his father's tin ring, which the Nefyrre had thought was valueless, but which Cer knew was the sign of the Cemreet family's authority since forever ago.

Then Cer walked north.

He lived by killing rats in barns and cooking them. He lived by begging at poor farmer's doors, for the rich farmers had servants to turn away beggars. That, at least, Cer remembered, his father had never done. Beggars always had a meal at his father's house.

Cer also lived by stealing when he could hunt or beg no food. He stole handfuls of raw wheat. He stole carrots from gardens. He stole water from wells, for which he could have lost his life in this rainless season. He stole, one time, a fruit from a rich man's food wagon.

It burned his mouth, it was so cold and the acid so strong. It dribbled down his chin. As a poor man and a thief, Cer thought, I now eat a thing so dear that even my father, who was called wealthy, could never buy it.

And at last he saw the mountains in the north. He walked on, and in a week the mountains were great cliffs and steep slopes of shale. The Mitherkame, where the king of the High Mountains reigned, and Cer began to climb.

He climbed all one day and slept in a cleft of a rock. He moved slowly, for climbing in sandals was clumsy, and without his great toes Cer could not climb barefoot. The next morning he climbed more. Though he nearly fell one time when falling would have meant crashing a mile down onto the distant plain, at last he reached the knifelike top of the Mitherkame, and heaven.

For of a sudden the stone gave way to soil. Not the pale sandy soil of the drylands, nor the red soil of Greet, but the dark black soil of the old songs from

the north, the soil that could not be left alone for a
day or it would sprout plants that in a week would
be a forest.

And there *was* a forest, and the ground was thick
with grass. Cer had seen only a few trees in his life,
and they had been olive trees, short and gnarled, and
fig sycamores, that were three times the height of a
man. These were twenty times the height of a man
and ten steps around, and the young trees shot up
straight and tall so that not a sapling was as small as
Cer, who for twelve years old was not considered
small.

To Cer, who had known only wheat and hay and
olive orchards, the forest was more magnificent than
the mountain or the city or the river or the moon.

He slept under a huge tree. He was very cold that
night. And in the morning he realized that in a forest
he would find no farms, and where there were no
farms there was no food for him. He got up and
walked deeper into the forest. There were people in
the High Mountains, else there would be no king,
and Cer would find them. If he didn't, he would die.
But at least he would not die in the realms of the
Nefyrre.

He passed many bushes with edible berries, but he
did not know they could be eaten so he did not eat.
He passed many streams with slow stupid fish that
he could have caught, but in Greet fish was never
eaten, because it always carried disease, and so Cer
caught no fish.

And on the third day, when he began to feel so
weak from hunger that he could walk no longer, he
met the treemage.

He met him because it was the coldest night yet,
and at last Cer tore branches from a tree to make a
fire. But the wood did not light, and when Cer looked
up he saw that the trees had moved. They were coming closer, surrounding him tightly. He watched

them, and they did not move as he watched, but when he turned around the ones he had not been watching were closer yet. He tried to run, but the low branches made a tight fence he could not get through. He couldn't climb, either, because the branches all stabbed downward. Bleeding from the twigs he had scraped, Cer went back to his camping place and watched as the trees at last made a solid wall around him.

And he waited. What else could he do in his wooden prison?

In the morning he heard a man singing, and he called for help.

"Oh ho," he heard a voice say in a strange accent. "Oh ho, a tree cutter and a firemaker, a branch killer and a forest hater."

"I'm none of those," Cer said. "It was cold, and I tried to build a fire only to keep warm."

"A fire, a fire," the voice said. "In this small part of the world there are no fires of wood. But that's a young voice I hear, and I doubt there's a beard beneath the words."

"I have no beard," Cer answered. "I have no weapon, except a knife too small to harm you."

"A knife? A knife that tears sap from living limbs, Redwood says. A knife that cuts twigs like soft man-fingers, says Elm. A knife that stabs bark till it bleeds, says Sweet Aspen. Break your knife," said the voice outside the trees, "and I will open your prison."

"But it's my only knife," Cer protested, "and I need it."

"You need it here like you need fog on a dark night. Break it or you'll die before these trees move again."

Cer broke his knife.

Behind him he heard a sound, and he turned to see a fat old man standing in a clear space between the trees. A moment before there had been no clear space.

"A child," said the man.

"A fat old man," said Cer, angry at being considered as young as his years.

"An illbred child at that," said the man. "But perhaps he knows no better, for from the accent of his speech I would say he comes from Greetland, and from his clothing I would say he was poor, and it's well known in Mitherwee that there are no manners in Greet."

Cer snatched up the blade of his knife and ran at the man. Somehow there were many sharp-pointed branches in the way, and his hand ran into a hard limb, knocking the blade to the ground.

"Oh, my child," said the man kindly. "There is death in your heart."

The branches were gone, and the man reached out his hands and touched Cer's face. Cer jerked away.

"And the touch of a man brings pain to you." The man sighed. "How inside out your world must be."

Cer looked at the man coldly. He could endure taunting. But was that kindness in the old man's eyes?

"You look hungry," said the old man.

Cer said nothing.

"If you care to follow me, you may. I have food for you, if you like."

Cer followed him.

They went through the forest, and Cer noticed that the old man stopped to touch many of the trees. And a few he pointedly snubbed, turning his back or taking a wider route around them. Once he stopped and spoke to a tree that had lost a large limb—recently, too, Cer thought, because the tar on the stump was still soft. "Soon there'll be no pain at all," the old man said to the tree. Then the old man sighed again. "Ah, yes, I know. And many a walnut in the falling season."

Then they reached a house. If it could be called a house, Cer thought. Stones were the walls, which was common enough in Greet, but the roof was living wood—thick branches from nine tall trees, interwoven and heavily leaved, so that Cer was sure no drop of rain could ever come inside.

"You admire my roof?" the old man asked. "So tight that even in the winter, when the leaves are gone, the snow cannot come in. But *we* can," he said, and led the way through a low door into a single room.

The old man kept up a constant chatter as he fixed breakfast: berries and cream, stewed acorns, and thick slices of cornbread. The old man named all the foods for Cer, because except for the cream it was all strange to him. But it was good, and it filled him.

"Acorn from the Oaks," said the old man. "Walnuts from the trees of that name. And berries from the bushes, the neartrees. Corn, of course, comes from an untree, a weak plant with no wood, which dies every year."

"The trees don't die every year, then, even though it snows?" Cer asked, for he had heard of snow.

"Their leaves turn bright colors, and then they fall, and perhaps that's a kind of death," said the old man. "But in Eanan the snow melts and by Blowan there are leaves again on all the trees."

Cer did not believe him, but he didn't disbelieve him either. Trees were strange things.

"I never knew that trees in the High Mountains could move."

"Oh ho," laughed the old man. "And neither can they, except here, and other woods that a treemage tends."

"A treemage? Is there magic then?"

"Magic. Oh ho," the man laughed again. "Ah yes, magic, many magics, and mine is the magic of trees."

Cer squinted. The man did not look like a man of power, and yet the trees had penned an intruder in. "You rule the trees here?"

"Rule?" the old man asked, startled. "What a thought. Indeed no. I serve them. I protect them. I give them the power in me, and they give me the power in them, and it makes us all a good deal more powerful. But rule? That just doesn't enter into magic. What a thought."

Then the old man chattered about the doings of the silly squirrels this year, and when Cer was through eating the old man gave him a bucket and they spent the morning gathering berries. "Leave a berry on the bush for every one you pick," the old man said. "They're for the birds in the fall and for the soil in the Kamesun, when new bushes grow."

And so Cer, quite accidentally, began his life with the treemage, and it was as happy a time as Cer ever had in his life, except when he was a child and his mother sang to him and except for the time his father took him hunting deer in the hills of Wetfell.

And after the autumn when Cer marveled at the colors of the leaves, and after the winter when Cer tramped through the snow with the treemage to tend to ice-splintered branches, and after the spring when Cer thinned the new plants so the forest did not become overgrown, the treemage began to think that the dark places in Cer's heart were filled with light, or at least put away where they could not be found.

He was wrong.

For as he gathered leaves for the winter's fires Cer dreamed he was gathering the bones of his enemies. And as he tramped the snow he dreamed he was marching into battle to wreak death on the Nefyrre. And as he thinned the treestarts Cer dreamed of slaying each of the uncles as his father had been slain, because none of them had stood by him in his danger.

Cer dreamed of vengeance, and his heart grew

darker even as the wood was filled with the bright light of the summer sun.

One day he said to the treemage, "I want to learn magic."

The treemage smiled with hope. "You're learning it," he said, "and I'll gladly teach you more."

"I want to learn things of power."

"Ah," said the treemage, disappointed. "Ah, then, you can have no magic."

"You have power," said Cer. "I want it also."

"Oh, indeed," said the treemage. "I have the power of two legs and two arms, the power to heat tar over a peat fire to stop the sap flow from broken limbs, the power to cut off diseased branches to save the tree, the power to teach the trees how and when to protect themselves. All the rest is the power of the trees, and none of it is mine."

"But they do your bidding," said Cer.

"Because I do theirs!" the treemage said, suddenly angry. "Do you think that there is slavery in this wood? Do you think I am a king? Only men allow men to rule them. Here in this wood there is only love, and on that love and by that love the trees and I have the magic of the wood."

Cer looked down, disappointed. The treemage misunderstood, and thought that Cer was contrite.

"Ah, my boy," said the treemage. "You haven't learned it, I see. The root of magic is love, the trunk is service. The treemages love the trees and serve them and then they share treemagic with the trees. Lightmages love the sun and make fires at night, and the fire serves them as they serve the fire. Horsemages love and serve horses, and they ride freely whither they will because of the magic in the herd. There is field magic and plain magic, and the magic of rocks and metals, songs and dances, the magic of winds and weathers. All built on love, all growing through service."

"I must have magic," said Cer.

"Must you?" asked the treemage. "Must you have magic? There are kinds of magic, then, that you might have. But I can't teach them to you."

"What are they?"

"No," said the treemage, and he wouldn't speak again.

Cer thought and thought. What magic could be demanded against anyone's will?

And at last, when he had badgered and nagged the treemage for weeks, the treemage angrily gave in. "Will you know then?" the treemage snapped. "I will tell you. There is seamagic, where the wicked sailors serve the monsters of the deep by feeding them living flesh. Would you do that?" But Cer only waited for more.

"So that appeals to you," said the treemage. "Then you will be delighted at desert magic."

And now Cer saw a magic he might use. "How is that performed?"

"I know not," said the treemage icily. "It is the blackest of the magics to men of *my* kind, though your dark heart might leap to it. There's only one magic darker."

"And what is that?" asked Cer.

"What a fool I was to take you in," said the treemage. "The wounds in your heart, you don't want them to heal; you love to pick at them and let them fester."

"What is the darkest magic?" demanded Cer.

"The darkest magic," said the treemage, "is one, thank the moon, that you can never practice. For to do it you have to love men and love the love of men more than your own life. And love is as far from you as the sea is from the mountains, as the earth is from the sky."

"The sky touches the earth," said Cer.

"Touches, but never do they meet," said the tree-mage.

Then the treemage handed Cer a basket, which he had just filled with bread and berries and a flagon of streamwater. "Now go."

"Go?" asked Cer.

"I hoped to cure you, but you won't have a cure. You clutch at your suffering too much to be healed."

Cer reached out his foot toward the treemage, the crusty scars still a deep red where his great toe had been.

"As well you might try to restore my foot."

"Restore?" asked the treemage. "I restore nothing. But I staunch, and heal, and I help the trees forget their lost limbs. For if they insist on rushing sap to the limb as if it were still there, they lose all their sap; they dry, they wither, they die."

Cer took the basket.

"Thank you for your kindness," said Cer. "I'm sorry that you don't understand. But just as the tree can never forgive the ax or the flame, there are those that must die before I can truly live again."

"Get out of my wood," said the treemage. "Such darkness has no place here."

And Cer left, and in three days came to the edge of the Mitherkame, and in two days reached the bottom of the cliffs, and in a few weeks reached the desert. For he would learn desertmagic. He would serve the sand, and the sand would serve him.

On the way the soldiers of Nefyryd stopped him and searched him. When they saw that he had no great toes, they beat him and shaved off his young and scraggly beard and sent him on his way with a kick.

Cer even stopped where his father's farm had been. Now all the farms were farmed by Nefyrre, men of the south who had never owned land before. They drove him away, afraid that he might steal. So he snuck back in the night and from his father's store-house stole meat and from his father's barn stole a chicken.

He crossed the Greebeck to the drylands and gave the meat and the chicken to the poor people there. He lived with them for a few days. And then he went out into the desert.

He wandered in the desert for a week before he ran out of food and water. He tried everything to find the desertmagic. He spoke to the hot sand and the burning rocks as the treemage had spoken to the trees. But the sand was never injured and did not need a healing touch, and the rocks could not be harmed and so they needed no protection. There was no answer when Cer talked, except the wind which cast sand in his eyes. And at last Cer lay dying on the sand, his skin caked and chafed and burnt, his clothing long since tattered away into nothing, his flagon burning hot and filled with sand, his eyes blind from the whiteness of the desert.

He could neither love nor serve the desert, for the desert needed nothing from him and there was nei-ther beauty nor kindness to love.

But he refused to die without having vengeance. Refused to die so long that he was still alive when the Abadapnu tribesmen found him. They gave him water and nursed him back to health. It took weeks, and they had to carry him on a sledge from waterhole to waterhole.

And as they traveled with their herds and their horses, the Abadapnur carried Cer farther and farther away from the Nefyrre and the land of Greet.

Cer regained his senses slowly, and learned the Abadapnu language even more slowly. But at last, as the clouds began to gather for the winter rains, Cer was one of the tribe, considered a man because he had a beard, considered wise because of the dark look on his face that remained even on those rare times when he laughed.

He never spoke of his past, though the Abadapnur knew well enough what the tin ring on his finger meant and why he had only eight toes. And they, with the perfect courtesy of the incurious, asked him nothing.

He learned their ways. He learned that starving on the desert was foolish, that dying of thirst was unnecessary. He learned how to trick the desert into yielding up life. "For," said the tribemaster, "the desert is never willing that anything should live."

Cer remembered that. The desert wanted nothing to live. And he wondered if that was a key to desertmagic. Or was it merely a locked door that he could never open? How can you serve and be served by the sand that wants only your death? How could he get vengeance if he was dead? "Though I would gladly die if my dying could kill my father's killers," he said to his horse one day. The horse hung her head, and would only walk for the rest of the day, though Cer kicked her to try to make her run.

Finally one day, impatient that he was doing nothing to achieve his revenge, Cer went to the tribemaster and asked him how one learned the magic of the sand.

"Sandmagic? You're mad," said the tribemaster. For days the tribemaster refused to look at him, let alone answer his questions, and Cer realized that here on the desert the sandmagic was hated as badly as the treemage hated it. Why? Wouldn't such power make the Abadapnur great?

Or did the tribemaster refuse to speak because the Abadapnur did not know the sandmagic?

But they knew it.

And one day the tribemaster came to Cer and told him to mount and follow.

They rode in the early morning before the sun was

high, then slept in a cave in a rocky hill during the heat of the day. In the dusk they rode again, and at night they came to the city.

"Ettuie," whispered the tribemaster, and then they rode their horses to the edge of the ruins.

The sand had buried the buildings up to half their height, inside and out, and even now the breezes of evening stirred the sand and built little dunes against the walls. The buildings were made of stone, rising not to domes like the great cities of the Greetmen but to spires, tall towers that seemed to pierce the sky.

"Ikikietar," whispered the tribemaster, "Ikikiaiai re dapii. O ikikiai etetur o abadapnur, ikikiai re dapii."

"What are the 'knives'?" asked Cer. "And how could the sand kill them?"

"The knives are these towers, but they are also the stars of power."

"What power?" asked Cer eagerly.

"No power for you. Only power for the Etetur, for they were wise. They had the manmagic."

Manmagic. Was that the darkest magic spoken of by the treemage?

"Is there a magic more powerful than manmagic?" Cer asked.

"In the mountains, no," said the tribemaster. "On the well-watered plain, in the forest, on the sea, no."

"But in the desert?"

"A huu par eiti ununura," muttered the tribemaster, making the sign against death. "Only the desert power. Only the magic of the sand."

"I want to know," said Cer.

"Once," the tribemaster said, "once there was a mighty empire here. Once a great river flowed here, and rain fell, and the soil was rich and red like the soil of Greet, and a million people lived under the rule of the King of Ettue Dappa. But not all, for far to the west there lived a few who hated Ettue and the manmagic of the kings, and they forged the tool that undid this city.

"They made the wind blow from the desert. They made the rains run off the earth. By their power the river sank into the desert sand, and the fields bore no fruit, and at last the King of Ettue surrendered, and half his kingdom was given to the sandmages. To the dapinur. That western kingdom became Dapnu Dap."

"A kingdom?" said Cer, surprised. "But now the great desert bears that name."

"And once the great desert was no desert, but a land of grasses and grains like your homeland to the north. The sandmages weren't content with half a kingdom, and they used their sandmagic to make a desert of Ettue, and they covered the lands of rebels with sand, until at last the victory of the desert was complete, and Ettue fell to the armies of Greet and Nefyryd—they were allies then—and we of Dapnu Dap became nomads, living off that tiny bit of life that even the harshest desert cannot help but yield."

"And what of the sandmages?" asked Cer.

"We killed them."

"All?"

"All," said the tribemaster. "And if any man will practice sandmagic, today, we will kill him. For what happened to us we will let happen to no other people."

Cer saw the knife in the tribemaster's hand.

"I will have your vow," said the tribemaster. "Swear before these stars and this sand and the ghosts of all who lived in this city that you will seek no sandmagic."

"I swear," said Cer, and the tribemaster put his knife away.

The next day Cer took his horse and a bow and arrows and all the food he could steal and in the heat of the day when everyone slept he went out into the desert. They followed him, but he slew two with arrows and the survivors lost his trail.

Word spread through the tribes of the Abadapnur that a would-be sandmage was loose in the desert, and all were ready to kill him if he came. But he did not come.

For he knew now how to serve the desert, and how to make the desert serve him. For the desert loved death, and hated grasses and trees and water and the things of life.

So in service of the sand Cer went to the edge of the land of the Nefyrre, east of the desert. There he fouled wells with the bodies of diseased animals. He burned fields when the wind was blowing off the desert, a dry wind that pushed the flames into the cities. He cut down trees. He killed sheep and cattle. And when the Nefyrre patrols chased him he fled onto the desert where they could not follow.

His destruction was annoying, and impoverished many a farmer, but alone it would have done little to hurt the Nefyrre. Except that Cer felt his power over the desert growing. For he was feeding the desert the only thing it hungered for: death and dryness.

He began to speak to the sand again, not kindly, but of land to the east that the sand could cover. And the wind followed his words, whipping the sand, moving the dunes. Where he stood the wind did not touch him, but all around him the dunes moved like waves of the sea.

Moving eastward.

Moving onto the lands of the Nefyrre.

And now the hungry desert could do in a night a hundred times more than Cer could do alone with a torch or a knife. It ate olive groves in an hour. The sand borne on the wind filled houses in a night, buried cities in a week, and in only three months had driven the Nefyrre across the Greebeck and the

Nefyr River, where they thought the terrible sand-storms could not follow.

But the storms followed. Cer taught the desert almost to fill the river, so that the water spread out a foot deep and miles wide, flooding some lands that had been dry, but also leaving more water surface for the sun to drink from; and before the river reached the sea it was dry, and the desert swept across into the heart of Nefyryd.

The Nefyrre had always fought with the force of arms, and cruelty was their companion in war. But against the desert they were helpless. They could not fight the sand. If Cer could have known it, he would have gloried in the fact that, untaught, he was the most powerful sandmage who had ever lived. For hate was a greater teacher than any of the books of dark lore, and Cer lived on hate.

And on hate alone, for now he ate and drank noth-ing, sustaining his body through the power of the wind and the heat of the sun. He was utterly dry, and the blood no longer coursed through his veins. He lived on the energy of the storms he unleashed. And the desert eagerly fed him, because he was feed-ing the desert.

He followed his storms, and walked through the deserted towns of the Nefyrre. He saw the refugees rushing north and east to the high ground. He saw the corpses of those caught in the storm. And he sang at night the old songs of Greet, the war songs. He wrote his father's name with chalk on the wall of every city he destroyed. He wrote his mother's name in the sand, and where he had written her name the wind did not blow and the sand did not shift, but preserved the writing as if it had been incised on rock.

Then one day, in a lull between his storms, Cer saw a man coming toward him from the east. Abad-apnu, he wondered, or Nefyrre? Either way he drew his knife, and fit the nock of an arrow on his bow-string.

But the man came with his hands extended, and he called out, "Cer Cemreet."

It had never occurred to Cer that anyone knew his name.

"Sandmage Cer Cemreet," said the man when he was close. "We have found who you are."

Cer said nothing, but only watched the man's eyes.

"I have come to tell you that your vengeance is full. Nefyryd is at its knees. We have signed a treaty with Greet and we no longer raid into Hetterwee. Driplin has seized our westernmost lands."

Cer smiled. "I care nothing for your empire."

"Then for our people. The deaths of your father and mother have been avenged a hundred thousand times, for over two hundred thousand people have died at your hands."

Cer chuckled. "I care nothing for your people."

"Then for the soldiers who did the deed. Though they acted under orders, they have been arrested and killed, as have the men who gave them those orders, even our first general, all at the command of the King so that your vengeance will be complete. I have brought you their ears as proof of it," said the man, and he took a pouch from his waist.

"I care nothing for soldiers, nor for proof of vengeance," said Cer.

"Then what do you care for?" asked the man quietly.

"Death," said Cer.

"Then I bring you that, too," said the man, and a knife was in his hand, and he plunged the knife into Cer's breast where his heart should have been. But when the man pulled the knife out no blood followed, and Cer only smiled.

"Indeed you brought it to me," said Cer, and he stabbed the man where his father had been stabbed, and drew the knife up as it had been drawn through his father's body, except that he touched the man's heart, and he died.

As Cer watched the blood soaking into the sand, he heard in his ears his mother's screams, which he had silenced for these years. He heard her screams and now, remembering his father and his mother and himself as a child he began to cry, and he held the body of the man he had killed and rocked back and forth on the sand as the blood clotted on his clothing and his skin. His tears mixed with the blood and poured into the sand and Cer realized that this was the first time since his father's death that he had shed any tears at all.

I am not dry, thought Cer. There is water under me still for the desert to drink.

He looked at his dry hands, covered with the man's blood, and tried to scrub off the clotted blood with sand. But the blood stayed, and the sand could not clean him.

He wept again. And then he stood and faced the desert to the west, and he said, "Come."

A breeze began.

"Come," he said to the desert, "come and dry my eyes."

And the wind came up, and the sand came, and Cer Cemreet was buried in the sand, and his eyes became dry, and the last life passed from his body, and the last sandmage passed from the world.

Then came the winter rains, and the refugees of Nefyryd returned to their land. The soldiers were called home, for the wars were over, and now their weapons were the shovel and the plow. They redug the trench of the Nefyr and the Greebeck, and the river soon flowed deep again to the sea. They scattered grass seed and cleaned their houses of sand. They carried water into the ruined fields with ditches and aqueducts.

Slowly life returned to Nefyryd.

And the desert, having lost its mage, retreated quietly to its old borders, never again to seek death where there was life. Plenty of death already where nothing lived, plenty of dryness to drink where there was no water.

In a wood a little way from the crest of the Mitherkame, a treemage heard the news from a wandering tinker.

The treemage went out into the forest and spoke softly to the Elm, to the Oak, to the Redwood, to the Sweet Aspen. And when all had heard the news, the forest wept for Cer Cemreet, and each tree gave a twig to be burned in his memory, and shed sap to sink into the ground in his name.

THE BEST DAY

ONCE THERE WAS a woman who had five children that she loved with all her heart, and a husband who was kind and strong. Every day her husband would go out and work in the fields, and then he'd come home and cut wood or repair harness or fix the leaky places in the roof. Every day the children would work and play so hard they wore paths in the weeds from running, and they knew every hiding place in two miles square. And that woman began to be afraid that they were too happy, that it would all come to an end. And so she prayed, Please send us eternal happiness, let this joy last forever. Well, the next day along came a mean-faced old peddler, and he spread his wares and they were very plain—rough wool clothing, sturdy pots and pans, all as ugly and practical as old shoes. The woman bought a dress from him because it was cheap and it would last forever, and he was about to go, when suddenly she saw maybe a fire in his eyes, suddenly flashing bright as a star, and she remembered her prayer the night before, and she said, "Sir, you don't have anything to do with—happiness, do you?"

And the peddler turned and glowered and said, "I can give it to you, if you want it. But let me tell you what it is. It's your kids growing up and talking sassy, and then moving on out and marrying other children who don't like you all that much, at least at first. It's your husband's strength giving out, and watching the farm go to seed before your eyes, and maybe having to sell it and move into your daughter-in-law's house because you can't support yourselves no more. It's feeling your own legs go stiff, and your fingers not able to tat or knit or even grip the butter churn. And finally it's dying, lying there feeling your body drop off you, wishing you could just go back and be young with your children small, just for a day. And then—"

"Enough!" cried the woman.

"But there's more," said the peddler.

"I've heard all I mean to hear," and she hurried him out of the house.

The next day, along comes a man in a bright-painted wagon, with a horse named Carpy Deem that he shouted at all the time. A medicine man from the East, with potions for this and pills for that, and silks and scarves to sell, too, so bright they hurt your eyes just to look at them. Everybody was healthy, so the woman didn't buy any medicine. All she bought was a silk, even though the price was too high, because it looked so blue in her golden hair. And she said to him, "Sir, do you have anything to do with happiness?"

"Do you have to *ask*?" he said. "Right here, in this jar, is the elixir of happiness—one swallow, and the best day of your life is with you forever."

"How much does it cost?" she asked, trembling.

"I only sell it to them as have such a day worth keeping, and then I sell it cheap. One lock of your golden hair, that's all. I give it to your Master, so he'll know you when the time comes."

She plucked the hair from her head, and gave it to the peddler, and he poured from the bottle into a little tin cup. When he was gone, she lifted it up, and thought of the happiest day of her life, which was only two days before, the day she prayed. And she drank that swallow.

Well, her husband came home as it was getting dark, and the children came to him all worried. "Something's wrong with Mother," they said. "She ain't making no sense." The man walked into the house, and tried to talk to his wife, but she gave no answer. Then, suddenly, she said something, speaking to empty air. She was cutting carrots, but there were no carrots; she was cooking a stew, but there was no fire laid. Finally her husband realized that word for word, she was saying what she said only two days ago, when they last had stew, and if he said to her the words he had said then, why, the conversation at least made some sense.

And every day it was the same. They either said that same day's words over and over again, or they ignored their mother, and let her go on as she did and paid her no mind. The kids got sick of it after a time, and got married and went away, and she never knew it. Her husband stayed with her, and more and more he got caught up in her dream, so that every day he got up and said the same words till they meant nothing and he couldn't remember what he was living for, and so he died. The neighbors found him two days later, and buried him, and the woman never knew.

Her daughters and daughters-in-law tried to care for her, but if they took her to their homes, she'd just walk around as if she were still in her own little

cottage, bumping into walls, cutting those infernal
carrots, saying those words till they were all out of
their minds. Finally they took her back to her own
home and paid a woman to cook and clean for her,
and she went on that way, all alone in that cabin,
happy as a duck in a puddle until at last the floor of
her cabin caved in and she fell in and broke her hip.
They figure she never even felt the pain, and when
she died she was still laughing and smiling and saying idiotic things, and never even saw one of her
grandchildren, never even wept at her husband's
grave, and some folks said she was probably happier,
but not a one said they were eager to change places
with her. And it happened that a mean-looking old
peddler came by and watched as they let her into her
grave, and up rode a medicine man yelling at his
horse, and he pulled up next to the peddler.

"So she bought from you," the peddler said.

And the medicine man said, "If you'd just paint
things up a little, add a bit of color here and there,
you'd sell more, friend."

But the peddler only shook his head. "If they'd
ever let me finish telling them, they'd not be taken
in by you, old liar. But they always send me packing
before I'm through. I never get to tell them."

"If you'd begin with the pleasant things, they'd
listen."

"But if I began with the pleasant things, it
wouldn't be true."

"Fine with me. You keep me in business." And
the medicine man patted a trunk filled with gold and
silver and bronze and iron hairs. It was the wealth of
all the world, and the medicine man rode off with it,
to go back home and count it all, so fine and cold.

And the peddler, he just rode home to his family,
his great-great-great-grandchildren, his gray-haired
wife who nagged, the children who complained
about the way he was always off on business when

he should be home, and always hanging about the house when he ought to be away; he rode home to the leaves that turned every year, and the rats that ate the apples in the cellar, and the folks that kept dying on him, and the little ones that kept on being born.

A PLAGUE OF BUTTERFLIES

T HE BUTTERFLIES AWOKE him. Amasa felt them
before he saw them, the faint pressure of hundreds of half-dozens of feet, weighting his rough wool
sheet so that he dreamed of a shower of warm snow.
Then opened his eyes and there they were, in the
shaft of sunlight like a hundred stained-glass windows, on the floor like a carpet woven by an inspired
lunatic, delicately in the air like leaves falling upward in a wind.

At last, he said silently.

He watched them awhile, then gently lifted his
covers. The butterflies arose with the blanket. Carefully he swung his feet to the floor; they eddied away
from his footfall, then swarmed back to cover him.
He waded through them like the shallow water on
the edge of the sea, endlessly charging and then re-
treating quickly. He who fights and runs away, lives
to fight another day. You have come to me at last,
he said, and then he shuddered, for this was the

change in his life that he had waited for, and now he wasn't sure he wanted it after all.

They swarmed around him all morning as he prepared for his journey. His last journey, he knew, the last of many. He had begun his life in wealth, on the verge of power, in Sennabris, the greatest of the oil-burning cities of the coast. He had grown up watching the vast ships slide into and out of the quays to void their bowels into the sink of the city. When his first journey began, he did not follow the tankers out to sea. Instead, he took what seemed the cleaner way, inland.

He lived in splendor in the hanging city of Besara on the cliffs of Carmel; he worked for a time as a governor in Kafr Katnei on the plain of Esdraelon until the Megiddo War; he built the Ladder of Ekdippa through solid rock, where a thousand men died in the building and it was considered a cheap price.

And in every journey he mislaid something. His taste for luxury stayed in Besara; his love of power was sated and forgotten in Kafr Katnei; his desire to build for the ages was shed like a cloak in Ekdippa; and at last he had found himself here, in a desperately poor dirt farm on the edge of the Desert of Machaerus, with a tractor that had to be bribed to work and harvests barely large enough to pay for food for himself and petrol for the machines. He hadn't even enough to pay for light in the darkness, and sunset ended every day with imperturbable night. Yet even here, he knew that there was one more journey, for he had not yet lost everything: still when he worked in the fields he would reach down and press his fingers into the soil; still he would bathe his feet in the rush of water from the muddy ditch; still he would sit for hours in the heat of the afternoon and watch the grain standing bright gold and motionless as rock, drinking sun and expelling it as dry, hard grain. This last love, the love of life itself—it, too, would have to leave, Amasa knew, before his life would have completed its course and he would have consent to die.

The butterflies, they called him.

He carefully oiled the tractor and put it into its shed.

He closed the headgate of the ditch and shoveled earth into place behind it, so that in the spring the water would not flow onto his fallow fields and be wasted.

He filled a bottle with water and put it into his scrip, which he slung over his shoulder. This is all I take, he said. And even that felt like more of a burden than he wanted to bear.

The butterflies swarmed around him, and tried to draw him off toward the road into the desert, but he did not go at once. He looked at his fields, stubbled after the harvest. Just beyond them was the tumble of weeds that throve in the dregs of water that his grain had not used. And beyond the weeds was the Desert of Machaerus, the place where those who love water die. The ground was stone: rocky outcroppings, gravel; even the soil was sand. And yet there were ruins there. Wooden skeletons of buildings that had once housed farmers. Some people thought that this was a sign that the desert was growing, pushing in to take over formerly habitable land, but Amasa knew better. Rather the wooden ruins were the last remnants of the woeful Sebasti, those wandering people who, like the weeds at the end of the field, lived on the dregs of life. Once there had been a slight surplus of water flowing down the canals. The Sebasti heard about it in hours; in days they had come in their ramshackle trucks; in weeks they had built their scrappy buildings and plowed their stony fields, and for that year they had a harvest because the ditches ran a few inches deeper than usual. The next year the ditches were back to normal, and in a few hours one night the houses were stripped, the trucks were loaded, and the Sebasti were gone.

I am a Sebastit, too, Amasa thought. I have taken my life from an unwilling desert; I give it back to the sand when I am through.

Come, said the butterflies alighting on his face. Come, they said, fanning him and fluttering off toward the Hierusalem road.

Don't get pushy, Amasa answered, feeling stubborn. But all the same he surrendered, and followed them out into the land of the dead.

The only breeze was the wind on his face as he walked, and the heat drew water from him as if from a copious well. He took water from his bottle only a mouthful at a time, but it was going too quickly even at that rate.

Worse, though: his guides were leaving him. Now that he was on the road to Hierusalem, they apparently had other errands to run. He first noticed their numbers diminishing about noon, and by three there were only a few hundred butterflies left. As long as he watched a particular butterfly, it stayed; but when he looked away for a moment, it was gone. At last he set his gaze on one butterfly and did not look away at all, just watched and watched. Soon it was the last one left, and he knew that it, too, wanted to leave. But Amasa would have none of that. If I can come at your bidding, he said silently, you can stay at mine. And so he walked until the sun was ruddy in the west. He did not drink; he did not study his road; and the butterfly stayed. It was a little victory. I rule you with my eyes.

"You might as well stop here, friend."

Startled to hear a human voice on this desolate road, Amasa looked up, knowing in that moment that his last butterfly was lost. He was ready to hate the man who spoke.

"I say, friend, since you're going nowhere anyway, you might as well stop."

It was an old-looking man, black from sunlight and naked. He sat in the lee of a large stone, where the sun's northern tilt would keep him in shadow all day.

"If I wanted conversation," Amasa said, "I would have brought a friend."

"If you think those butterflies are your friends, you're an ass."

Amasa was surprised that the man knew about the butterflies.

"Oh, I know more than you think," said the man. "I lived at Hierusalem, you know. And now I'm the sentinel of the Hierusalem Road."

"No one leaves Hierusalem," said Amasa.

"I did," the old man said. "And now I sit on the road and teach travelers the keys that will let them in. Few of them pay me much attention, but if you don't do as I say, you'll never reach Hierusalem, and your bones will join a very large collection that the sun and wind gradually turn back into sand."

"I'll follow the road where it leads," Amasa said. "I don't need any directions."

"Oh, yes, you'd rather follow the dead guidance of the makers of the road than trust a living man."

Amasa regarded him for a moment. "Tell me, then."

"Give me all your water."

Amasa laughed—a feeble enough sound, coming through splitting lips that he dared not move more than necessary.

"It's the first key to entering Hierusalem." The old man shrugged. "I see that you don't believe me. But it's true. A man with water or food can't get into the city. You see, the city is hidden. If you had miraculous eyes, stranger, you could see the city even now. It's not far off. But the city is forever hidden from a man who is not desperate. The city can only be found by those who are very near to death. Unfortunately, if you once pass the entrance to the city without seeing it because you had water with you, then you can wander on as long as you like, you can run out of water and cry out in a whisper for the city to unveil itself to you, but it will avail you nothing. The entrance, once passed, can never be found again. You see, you have to know the taste of death in your mouth before Hierusalem will open to you."

"It sounds," Amasa said, "like religion. I've done religion."

"Religion? What is religion in a world with a dragon at its heart?"

Amasa hesitated. A part of him, the rational part, told him to ignore the man and pass on. But the rational part of him had long since become weak. In his definition of man, "featherless biped" held more truth than "rational animal." Besides, his head ached, his feet throbbed, his lips stung. He handed his bottle of water to the old man, and then for good measure gave him his scrip as well.

"Nothing in there you want to keep?" asked the old man, surprised.

"I'll spend the night."

The old man nodded.

They slept in the darkness until the moon rose in the east, bright with its thin promise of a sunrise only a few hours away. It was Amasa who awoke. His stirring roused the old man.

"Already?" he asked. "In such a hurry?"

"Tell me about Hierusalem."

"What do you want, friend? History? Myth? Current events? The price of public transportation?"

"Why is the city hidden?"

"So it can't be found."

"Then why is there a key for some to enter?"

"So it *can* be found. Must you ask such puerile questions?"

"Who built the city?"

"Men."

"Why did they build it?"

"To keep man alive on this world."

Amasa nodded at the first answer that hinted at significance. "And what enemy is it, then, that Hierusalem means to keep out?"

"Oh, my friend, you don't understand. Hierusalem was built to keep the enemy in. The old Hierusalem, the new Hierusalem, built to contain the dragon at the heart of the world."

A story-telling voice was on the old man now, and Amasa lay back on the sand and listened as the moon rose higher at his left hand.

"Men came here in ships across the void of the night," the old man said.

Amasa sighed.

"Oh, you know all that?"

"Don't be an ass. Tell me about Hierusalem."

"Did your books or your teachers tell you that this world was not unpopulated when our forefathers came?"

"Tell me your story, old man, but tell it plain. No myth, no magic. The truth."

"What a simple faith you have," the old man said. "The truth. Here's the truth, much good may it do you. This world was filled with forest, and in the forest were beings who mated with the trees, and drew their strength from the trees. They became very treelike."

"One would suppose."

"Our forefathers came, and the beings who dwelt among the trees smelt death in the fires of the ships.

They did things—things that looked like magic to our ancestors, things that looked like miracles. These beings, these dragons who hid among the leaves of the trees, they had science we know little of. But one science we had that they had never learned, for they had no use for it. *We* knew how to defoliate a forest."

"So the trees were killed."

"All the forests of the world now have grown up since that time. Some places, where the forest had not been lush, were able to recover, and we live in those lands now. But here, in the Desert of Machaera—this was climax forest, trees so tall and dense that no underbrush could grow at all. When the leaves died, there was nothing to hold the soil, and it was washed onto the plain of Esdraelon. Which is why that plain is so fertile, and why nothing but sand survives here."

"Hierusalem."

"At first Hierusalem was built as an outpost for students to learn about the dragons, pathetic little brown woody creatures who knew death when they saw it, and died of despair by the thousands. Only a few survived among the rocks, where we couldn't reach them. Then Hierusalem became a city of pleasure, far from any other place, where sins could be committed that God could not see."

"I said truth."

"I say listen. One day the few remaining students of the science of the dragons wandered among the rocks, and there found that the dragons were not all dead. One was left, a tough little creature that lived among the gray rocks. But it had changed. It was not woody brown now. It was gray as stone, with stony outcroppings. They brought it back to study it. And in only a few hours it escaped. They never recaptured it. But the murders began, every night a murder. And every murder was of a couple who were coupling, neatly vivisected in the act. Within a year the pleasure seekers were gone, and Hierusalem had changed again."

"To what it is now."

"What little of the science of the dragons they had learned, they used to seal the city as it is now sealed. They devoted it to holiness, to beauty, to faith—and the murders stopped. Yet the dragon was not gone. It was glimpsed now and then, gray on the stone buildings of the city, like a moving gargoyle. So they kept their city closed to keep the dragon from escaping to the rest of the world, where men were not holy and would compel the dragon to kill again."

"So Hierusalem is dedicated to keeping the world safe for sin."

"Safe from retribution. Giving the world time to repent."

"The world is doing little in that direction."

"But some are. And the butterflies are calling the repentant out of the world, and bringing them to me."

Amasa sat in silence as the sun rose behind his back. It had not fully passed the mountains of the east before it started to burn him.

"Here," said the old man, "are the laws of Hierusalem:

"Once you see the city, don't step back or you will lose it.

"Don't look down into holes that glow red in the streets, or your eyes will fall out and your skin will slide off you as you walk along, and your bones will crumble into dust before you fully die.

"The man who breaks a butterfly will live forever.

"Do not stare at a small gray shadow that moves along the granite walls of the palace of the King and Queen, or he will learn the way to your bed.

"The Road to Dalmanutha leads to the sign you seek. Never find it."

Then the old man smiled.

"Why are you smiling?" asked Amasa.

"Because you're such a holy man, Saint Amasa, and Hierusalem is waiting for you to come."

"What's your name, old man?"

The old man cocked his head. "Contemplation."

"That's not a name."

He smiled again. "I'm not a man."

For a moment Amasa believed him, and reached out to see if he was real. But his finger met the old man's flesh, and it did not crumble.

"You have so much faith," said the old man again. "You cast away your scrip because you valued nothing that it contained. What *do* you value?"

In answer, Amasa removed all his clothing and cast it at the old man's feet.

He remembers that once he had another name, but he cannot remember what it was. His name now is Gray, and he lives among the stones, which are also gray. Sometimes he forgets where stone leaves off and he begins. Sometimes, when he has been motionless for hours, he has to search for his toes that spread in a fan, each holding to stone so firmly that when at last he moves them, he is surprised at where they were. Gray is motionless all day, and motionless all night. But in the hours before and after the sun, then he moves, skittering sure and rapid as a spider among the hewn stones of the palace walls, stopping only to drink in the fly-strewn standing water that remains from the last storm.

These days, however, he must move more slowly, more clumsily than he used to, for his stamen has at last grown huge, and it drags painfully along the vertical stones, and now and then he steps on it. It has been this way for weeks. Worse every day, and Gray feels it as a constant pain that he must ease, must ease, must ease; but in his small mind he does not know what easement there might be. So far as he knows, there are no others of his kind; in all his life he has met no other climber of walls, no other hanger from stone ceilings. He remembers that once he sought out couplers in the night, but he cannot remember what he did with them. Now he again finds himself drawn to windows, searching for easement, though not sure at all, holding in his mind no image of what he hopes to see in the dark rooms within the palace. It is dusk, and Gray is hunting, and is not sure whether he will find mate or prey.

I have passed the gate of Hierusalem, thought Amasa, and I was not near enough to death. Or worse, sometimes he thought, there is no Hierusalem, and I have come this way in vain. Yet this last fear was not a fear at all, for he did not think of it with despair. He thought of it with hope, and looked for death as the welcome end of his journey, looked for death which comes with its tongue thick in its mouth, death which waits in caves during the cool of the day and hunts for prey in the last and first light, death which is made of dust. Amasa watched for death to come in a wind that would carry him away, in a stone that would catch his foot in midstep and crumble him into a pile of bone on the road.

And then in a single footfall Amasa saw it all. The sun was framed, not by a haze of white light, but by thick and heavy clouds. The orchards were also heavy, and dripped with recent rain. Bees hummed around his head. And now he could see the city rising, green and gray and monumental just beyond the trees; all around him was the sound of running water. Not the tentative water that struggled to stay alive in the thirsty dirt of the irrigation ditch, but the lusty sound of water that is superfluous, water that can be tossed in the air as fountains and no one thinks to gather up the drops.

For a moment he was so surprised that he thought he must step backward, just one step, and see if it wouldn't all disappear, for Amasa did not come upon this gradually, and he doubted that it was real. But he remembered the first warning of the old man, and he didn't take that backward step. Hierusalem was a miracle, and in this place he would test no miracles.

The ground was resilient under his feet, mossy where the path ran over stone, grassy where the stones made way for earth. He drank at an untended stream that ran pure and overhung with flowers. And then he passed through a small gate in a terraced wall, climbed stairs, found another gate, and another, each more graceful than the last. The first gate was rusty and hard to open; the second was overgrown with climbing roses. But each gate was better tended than the last, and he kept expecting to find someone working a garden or picnicking, for surely someone must be passing often through the better-kept gates. Finally he reached to open a gate and it opened before he could touch it.

It was a man in the dirty brown robe of a pilgrim. He seemed startled to see Amasa. He immediately enfolded his arms around something and turned away. Amasa tried to see—yes, it was a baby. But the infant's hands dripped with fresh blood, it was obviously blood, and Amasa looked back at the pilgrim to see if this was a murderer who had opened the gate for him.

"It's not what you think," the palmer said quickly. "I found the babe, and he has no one to take care of him."

"But the blood."

"He was the child of pleasure-seekers, and the prophecy was fulfilled, for he was washing his hands in the blood of his father's belly." Then the pilgrim got a hopeful look. "There is an enemy who must be fought. You wouldn't—"

A passing butterfly caught the pilgrim's eye. The fluttering wings circled Amasa's head only once, but that was sign enough.

"It is you," the pilgrim said.

"Do I know you?"

"To think that it will be in my time."

"*What* will be?"

"The slaying of the dragon." The pilgrim ducked his head and, freeing one arm by perching the child precariously on the other, he held the gate open for Amasa to enter. "God has surely called you."

Amasa stepped inside, puzzled at what the pilgrim thought he was, and what his coming portended. Behind him he could hear the pilgrim mutter, "It is time. It is time."

It was the last gate. He was in the city, passing between the walled gardens of monasteries and nunneries, down streets lined with shrines and shops, temples and houses, gardens and dunghills. It was green to the point of blindness, alive and holy and smelly and choked with business wherever it wasn't thick with meditation. What am I here for? Amasa wondered. Why did the butterflies call?

He did not look down into the red-glowing holes in the middles of streets. And when he passed the gray labyrinth of the palace, he did not look up to try to find a shadow sliding by. He would live by the laws of the place, and perhaps his journey would end here.

The queen of Hierusalem was lonely. For a month she had been lost in the palace. She had strayed into a never-used portion of the labyrinth, where no one had lived for generations, and now, search as she might, she could find only rooms that were deeper and deeper in dust.

The servants, of course, knew exactly where she was, and some of them grumbled at having to come into a place of such filth, full of such unstylish old furniture, in order to care for her. It did not occur to *them* that she was lost—they only thought she was exploring. It would never do for her to admit her perplexity to them. It was the Queen's business to know what she was doing. She couldn't very well ask a servant, "Oh, by the way, while you're fetching my supper, would you mind mentioning to me where I *am?*" So she remained lost, and the perpetual dust irritated all her allergies.

The Queen was immensely fat, too, which complicated things. Walking was a great labor to her, so that once she found a room with a bed that looked sturdy enough to hold her for a few nights, she stayed until the bed threatened to give way. Her progress through the unused rooms, then, was not in a great expedition, but rather in fits and starts. On one morning she would arise miserable from the bed's increasing incapacity to hold her, eat her vast breakfast while the servants looked on to catch the dribbles, and then, instead of calling for singers or someone to read, she would order four servants to stand her up, point her in the direction she chose, and taxi her to a good, running start.

"That door," she cried again and again, and the servants would propel her in that direction, while her legs trotted underneath her, trying to keep up with her body. And in the new room she could not stop to contemplate; she must take it all in on the run, with just a few mad glances, then decide whether to try to stay or go on. "On," she usually cried, and the servants took her through the gradual curves and maneuvers necessary to reach whatever door was most capacious.

On the day that Amasa arrived in Hierusalem, the Queen found a room with a vast bed, once used by some ancient rake of a prince to hold a dozen paramours at once, and the Queen cried out, "This is it, this is the right place, stop, we'll stay!" and the servants sighed in relief and began to sweep, to clean, to make the place liveable.

Her steward unctuously asked her, "What do you want to wear to the King's Invocation?"

"I will not go," she said. How could she? She did not know how to get to the hall where the ritual would be held. "I choose to be absent this once. There'll be another one in seven years." The steward bowed and left on his errand, while the Queen envied him his sense of direction and miserably wished that she could go home to her own rooms. She hadn't been to a party in a month, and now that she was so far from the kitchens the food was almost cold by the time she was served the private dinners she had to be content with. Damn her husband's ancestors for building all these rooms anyway.

Amasa slept by a dunghill because it was warmer there, naked as he was; and in the morning, without leaving the dunghill, he found work. He was wakened by the servants of a great Bishop, stablemen who had the week's manure to leave for the farmers to collect. They said nothing to him, except to look with disapproval at his nakedness, but set to work, emptying small wheelbarrows, then raking up the dung to make a neater pile. Amasa saw how fastidiously they avoided touching the dung; he had no such scruples. He took an idle rake, stepped into the midst of the manure, and raked the hill higher and faster than the delicate stablemen could manage on their own. He worked with such a will that the Stablemaster took him aside at the end of the task.

"Want work?"

"Why not?" Amasa answered.

The Stablemaster glanced pointedly at Amasa's unclothed body. "Are you fasting?"

Amasa shook his head. "I just left my clothing on the road."

"You should be more careful with your belongings. I can give you livery, but it comes out of your wages for a year."

Amasa shrugged. He had no use for wages.

The work was mindless and hard, but Amasa delighted in it. The variety was endless. Because he didn't mind it, they kept him shoveling more manure than his fair share, but the shoveling of manure was like a drone, a background for bright rhinestones of childish delight: morning prayers, when the Bishop in his silver gown intoned the powerful words while the servants stood in the courtyard clumsily aping his signs; running through the streets behind the Bishop's carriage shouting "Huzzah, huzzah!" while the Bishop scattered coins for the pedestrians; standing watch over the carriage, which meant drinking and hearing stories and songs with the other servants; or going inside to do attendance on the Bishop at the great occasions of this or that church or embassy or noble house, delighting in the elaborate costumes that so cleverly managed to adhere to the sumptuary laws while being as ostentatious and lewd as possible. It was grand, God approved of it all, and even discreet prurience and titillation were a face of the coin of worship and ecstasy.

But years at the desert's edge had taught Amasa to value things that the other servants never noticed. He did not have to measure his drinking water. The servants splashed each other in the bathhouse. He could piss on the ground and no little animals came to sniff at the puddle, no dying insects lit on it to drink.

They called Hierusalem a city of stone and fire, but Amasa knew it was a city of life and water, worth more than all the gold that was forever changing hands.

The other stablemen accepted Amasa well enough, but a distance always remained. He had come naked, from the outside; he had no fear of uncleanliness before the Lord; and something else: Amasa had known the taste of death in his mouth and it had not been unwelcome. Now he accepted as they came the pleasures of a stableman's life. But he did not need them, and knew he could not hide that from his fellows.

One day the Prior told the Steward, and the Steward the Stablemaster, and the Stablemaster told Amasa and the other stablemen to wash carefully three times, each time with soap. The old-timers knew what it meant, and told them all: It was the King's Invocation that came but once in seven years, and the Bishop would bring them all to stand in attendance, clean and fine in their livery, while he took part in the solemn ordinances. They would have perfume in their hair. And they would see the King and Queen.

"Is she beautiful?" Amasa asked, surprised at the awe in the voices of these irreverent men when they spoke of her.

And they laughed and compared the Queen to a mountain, to a planet, to a moon.

But then a butterfly alighted on the head of an old woman, and suddenly all laughter stopped. "The butterfly," they all whispered. The woman's eyes went blank, and she began to speak:

"The Queen is beautiful, Saint Amasa, to those who have the eyes to see it."

The servants whispered: See, the butterfly speaks to the new one, who came naked.

"Of all the holy men to come out of the world, Saint Amasa, of all the wise and weary souls, you are wisest, you are weariest, you are most holy."

Amasa trembled at the voice of the butterfly. In

memory he suddenly loomed over the crevice of Ek-dippa, and it was leaping up to take him.

"We brought you here to save her, save her, save her," said the old woman, looking straight into Amasa's eyes.

Amasa shook his head. "I'm through with quests," he said.

And foam came to the old woman's mouth, wax oozed from her ears, her nose ran with mucus, her eyes overflowed with sparkling tears.

Amasa reached out to the butterfly perched on her head, the fragile butterfly that was wracking the old woman so, and he took it in his hand. Took it in his right hand, folded the wings closed with his left, and then broke! the butterfly as crisply as a stick. The sound of it rang metallically in the air. There was no ichor from the butterfly, for it was made of something tough as metal, brittle as plastic, and electricity danced between the halves of the butterfly for a moment and then was still.

The old woman fell to the ground. Carefully the other servants cleaned her face and carried her away to sleep until she awakened. They did not speak to Amasa, except the Stablemaster, who looked at him oddly and asked, "Why would you want to live forever?"

Amasa shrugged. There was no use explaining that he wanted to ease the old woman's agony, and so killed it at its cause. Besides, Amasa was distracted, for now there was something buzzing in the base of his brain. The whirr of switches, infinitely small, going left or right; gates going open and closed; poles going positive and negative. Now and then a vision would flash into his mind, so quickly that he could not frame or recognize it. Now I see the world through butterfly's eyes. Now the vast mind of Hier-usalem's machinery sees the world through mine.

* * *

Gray waits by this window: it is the one. He does not wonder how he knows. He only knows that he was made for this moment, that his life's need is all within this window, he must not stray to hunt for food because his great stamen is throbbing with desire and in the night it will be satisfied.

So he waits by the window, and the sun is going; the sky is gray, but still he waits, and at last the lights have gone from the sky and all is silent within. He moves in the darkness until his long fingers find the edge of the stone. Then he pulls himself inside, and when his stamen scrapes painfully against the stone, immense between his legs, he only thinks: ease for you, ease for you.

His object is a great mountain that lies breathing upon a sea of sheets. She breathes in quick gasps, for her chest is large and heavy and hard to lift. He thinks nothing of that, but only creeps along the wall until he is above her head. He stares quizzically at the fat face; it holds no interest for him. What interests Gray is the space at her shoulders where the sheets and blankets and quilts fall open like a tent door. For some reason it looks like the leaves of a tree to him, and he drops onto the bed and scurries into the shelter.

Ah, it is not stone! He can hardly move for the bouncing, his fingers and toes find no certain purchase, yet there is this that forces him on: his stamen tingles with extruding pollen, and he knows he cannot pause just because the ground is uncertain.

He proceeds along the tunnel, the sweating body to one side, the tent of sheets above and to the other side. He explores; he crawls clumsily over a vast branch; and at last he knows what he has been looking for. It is time, oh, time, for here is the blossom of a great flower, pistil lush for him. He leaps. He fastens to her body as he has always fastened to the limbs of the great wife trees, to the stone. He plunges stamen into pistil and dusts the walls with pollen. It is all he lived for, and when it is done, in only moments when the pollen is shed at last, he dies and drops to the sheets.

The queen's dreams were frenzied. Because her waking life was wrapped and closed, because her bulk forced an economy of movement, in her sleep she was bold, untiring. Sometimes she dreamed of great chases on a horse across broken country. Sometimes she dreamed of flying. Tonight she dreamed of love, and it was also athletic and unbound. Yet in the moment of ecstasy there was a face that peered at her, and hands that tore her lover away from her, and she was afraid of the man who stared at the end of her dream.

Still, she woke trembling from the memory of love, only wistfully allowing herself to recall, bit by bit, where she really was. That she was lost in the palace, that she was as ungainly as a diseased tree with boles and knots of fat, that she was profoundly unhappy, that a strange man disturbed her dreams.

And then, as she moved slightly, she felt something cold and faintly dry between her legs. She dared not move again, for fear of what it was.

Seeing that she was awake, a servant bowed beside her. "Would you like your breakfast?"

"Help me," she whispered. "I want to get up."

The servant was surprised, but summoned the others. As they rolled her from the bed, she felt it again, and as soon as she was erect she ordered them to throw back the sheets.

And there he lay, flaccid, empty, gray as a deflated stone. The servants gasped, but they did not understand what the Queen instantly understood. Her dreams were too real last night, and the great appendage on the dead body fit too well the memory of her phantom lover. This small monster did not come as a parasite, to drain her; it came to give, not to receive.

She did not scream. She only knew that she had to run from there, had to escape. So she began to move, unsupported, and to her own surprise she did not fall. Her legs, propelled and strengthened by her revulsion, stayed under her, held her up. She did not know where she was going, only that she must go. She ran. And it was not until she had passed through a dozen rooms, a trail of servants chasing after her, that she realized it was not the corpse of her monstrous paramour she fled from, but rather what he left in her, for even as she ran she could feel something move within her womb, could feel something writhing, and she must, she must be rid of it.

As she ran, she felt herself grow lighter, felt her body melting under the flesh, felt her heaps and mounds erode away in an inward storm, sculpting her into a woman's shape again. The vast skin that had contained her belly began to slap awkwardly, loosely against her thighs as she ran. The servants caught up with her, reached out to support her, and plunged their hands into a body that was melting away. They said nothing; it was not for them to say. They only took hold of the loosening folds and held and ran.

And suddenly through her fear the Queen saw a pattern of furniture, a lintel, a carpet, a window, and she knew where she was. She had accidently stumbled upon a familiar wing of the palace, and now she had purpose, she had direction, she would go where help and strength were waiting. To the throne room, to her husband, where the king was surely holding his Invocation. The servants caught up with her at last; now they bore her up. "To my

husband," she said, and they assured her and petted
her and carried her. The thing within her leapt for
joy: its time was coming quickly.

Amasa could not watch the ceremonies. From the
moment he entered the Hall of Heaven all he could
see were the butterflies. They hovered in the dome
that was painted like the midsummernight sky, blotting out the tiny stars with their wings; they rested
high on painted pillars, camouflaged except when
they fanned their graceful wings. He saw them where
to others they were far too peripheral to be seen, for
in the base of his brain the gates opened and closed,
the poles reversed, always in the same rhythm that
drove the butterflies' flight and rest. Save the Queen,
they said. We brought you here to save the Queen.
It throbbed behind his eyes, and he could hardly see.

Could hardly see, until the Queen came into the
room, and then he could see all too clearly. There
was a hush, the ceremonies stopped, and all gazes
were drawn to the door where she stood, an undulant
mass of flesh with a woman's face, her eyes vulnera-
ble and wide with fright and trust. The servants'
arms reached far into the folds of skin, finding God-
knew-what grip there: Amasa only knew that her
face was exquisite. Hers was the face of all women,
the hope in her eyes the answer to the hope of all
men. "My husband!" she cried out, but at the moment she called she was not looking at the King. She
was looking at Amasa.

She is looking at me, he thought in horror. She is
all the beauty of Besara, she is the power of Kafr
Katnei, she is the abyss of Ekdippa, she is all that I
have loved and left behind. I do not want to desire
them again.

The King cried out impatiently, "Good God,
woman!"

And the Queen reached out her arms toward the man on the throne, gurgled in agony and surprise, and then shuddered like a wood fence in a wind.

What is it, asked a thousand whispers. What's wrong with the Queen?

She stepped backward.

There on the floor lay a baby, a little gray baby, naked and wrinkled and spotted with blood. Her eyes were open. She sat up and looked around, reached down and took the placenta in her hands and bit the cord, severing it.

The butterflies swarmed around her, and Amasa knew what he was meant to do. As you snapped the butterfly, they said to him, you must break this child. We are Hierusalem, and we were built for this epiphany, to greet this child and slay her at her birth. For this we found the man most holy in the world, for this we brought him here, for you alone have power over her.

I cannot kill a child, Amasa thought. Or did not think, for it was not said in words but in a shudder of revulsion in him, a resistance at the core of what in him was most himself.

This *is* no child, the city said. Do you think the dragons have surrendered just because we stole their trees? The dragons have simply changed to fit a new mate; they mean to rule the world again. And the gates and poles of the city impelled him, and Amasa decided a thousand times to obey, to step a dozen paces forward and take the child in his arms and break it. And as many times he heard himself cry out, I cannot kill a child! And the cry was echoed by his voice as he whispered, "No."

Why am I standing in the middle of the Hall of Heaven, he asked himself. Why is the Queen staring at me with horror in her eyes? Does she recognize me? Yes, she does, and she is afraid of me. Because

I mean to kill her child. Because I cannot kill her child.

As Amasa hesitated, tearing himself, the gray infant looked at the King. "Daddy," she said, and then she stood and walked with gathering certainty toward the throne. With such dextrous fingers the child picked at her ear. Now. Now, said the butterflies.

Yes, said Amasa. No.

"My daughter!" the King cried out. "At last an heir! The answer to my Invocation before the prayer was done—and such a brilliant child!"

The King stepped down from his throne, reached to the child and tossed her high into the air. The girl laughed and tumbled down again. Once more the King tossed her in delight. This time, however, she did not come down.

She hovered in the air over the King's head, and everyone gasped. The child fixed her gaze on her mother, the mountainous body from which she had been disgorged, and she spat. The spittle shone in the air like a diamond, then sailed across the room and struck the Queen on her breast, where it sizzled. The butterflies suddenly turned black in midair, shriveled, dropped to the ground with infinitesimal thumps that only Amasa could hear. The gates all closed within his mind, and he was all himself again; but too late, the moment was passed, the child had come into her power, and the Queen could not be saved.

The King shouted, "Kill the monster!" But the words still hung in the air when the child urinated on the King from above. He erupted in flame, and there was no doubt now who ruled in the palace. The gray shadow had come in from the walls.

She looked at Amasa, and smiled. "Because you were the holiest," she said, "I brought you here."

* * *

Amasa tried to flee the city. He did not know the way. He passed a palmer who knelt at a fountain that flowed from virgin stone, and asked, "How can I leave Hierusalem?"

"No one leaves," the palmer said in surprise. As Amasa went on, he saw the palmer bend to continue scrubbing at a baby's hands. Amasa tried to steer by the patterns of the stars, but no matter which direction he ran, the roads all bent toward one road, and that road led to a single gate. And in the gate the child waited for him. Only she was no longer a child. Her slate-gray body was heavy-breasted now, and she smiled at Amasa and took him in her arms, refused to be denied. "I am Dalmanutha," she whispered, "and you are following my road. I am Acrasia, and I will teach you joy."

She took him to a bower on the palace grounds, and taught him the agony of bliss. Every time she mated with him, she conceived, and in hours a child was born. He watched each one come to adulthood in hours, watched them go out into the city and affix themselves each to a human, some man, some woman, or some child. "Where one forest is gone," Dalmanutha whispered to him, "another will rise to take its place."

In vain he looked for butterflies.

"Gone, all gone, Amasa," Acrasia said. "They were all the wisdom that you learned from my ancestors, but they were not enough, for you hadn't the heart to kill a dragon that was as beautiful as man." And she *was* beautiful, and every day and every night she came to him and conceived again and again, telling him of the day not long from now when she would unlock the seals of the gates of Hierusalem and send her bright angels out into the forest of man to dwell in the trees and mate with them again.

More than once he tried to kill himself. But she only laughed at him as he lay with bloodless gashes in his neck, with lungs collapsed, with poison foul-tasting in his mouth. "You can't die, my Saint Amasa," she said, "Father of Angels, you can't die. For you broke a wise, a cruel, a kind and gentle butterfly."

THE MONKEYS THOUGHT 'TWAS ALL IN FUN

AGNES 1

"TAKE HER," AGNES's father said, his dry eyes pleading. Agnes's mother stood just behind him, wringing the towel she held in her hand.

"I can't," Brian Howarth said, embarrassed that he had to say that, ashamed that he actually *could* say it. The death of the nation of Biafra was a matter of days now, not weeks, and he and his wife were some of the last to go. Brian had come to love the Ibo people, and Agnes's father and mother had long since ceased to be servants—they were friends. Agnes herself, a bright five-year-old, had been a delight, learning English even before she learned her native tongue, constantly playing hide-and-seek in the house. A bright child, a hopeful child, and from all that Brian had heard (and he believed it, even though he was a correspondent and knew the exaggerations that wartime news always had to endure), from all he had heard the Nigerian Army would not stop to ask anyone "Is this child bright? Is this child beautiful? Does this child have a sense of humor as keen as any adult's?" Instead she would be gutted with a bayonet as quickly as her parents, because she was an Ibo, and the Ibos had done what the Japanese did a half-century before: they had become westernized before any of their neighbors, and profited from it. The Japanese had been on an island, and they had survived. The Ibos were not on an island, and Biafra was destroyed by Nigerian numbers and British and Russian weapons and a blockade that no nation on earth made any effort to relieve, not on a scale that could save anyone.

"I can't," Brian Howarth said again, and then he heard his wife behind him (her name was also Agnes, for the little girl's parents had named their first and only child after her) whisper, "By God you can or I'm not going."

"Please," Agnes's father said, his eyes still dry, his voice still level. He was begging, but his body said I am still proud and will not weep and kneel and subjugate myself to you. Equal to equal, his body said, I ask you to take my treasure, for I will die and cannot keep it anyway.

"How can I?" Brian asked helplessly, knowing that the space on the airplane was limited and the correspondents were forbidden to take any Biafrans with them.

"We can," his wife whispered again, and so Brian reached out his arms and took Agnes and held her. Agnes's father nodded. "Thank you, Brian," he said, and Brian was the one who wept and said, "I'm sorry, if any people in the world deserve to be free—"

But Agnes's parents were already gone, heading for the forest before the Nigerian Army could get into town.

Brian and his wife took little Agnes to the stretch of abandoned highway that served as the last airport in free Biafra and took off in an airplane crammed with correspondents and luggage and more than one Biafran child sitting in the darkest corners of what was never meant to be a passenger plane. Agnes's eyes were wide all through the flight. She did not cry. She had never cried much as an infant. She just held tightly to Brian Howarth's hand.

When the airplane landed in the Azores, where they would change to a flight to America, Agnes finally asked, "What about my parents?"

"They can't come," Brian said.

"Why not?"

"There wasn't room."

And Agnes looked at the many places where another couple of human beings could sit or stand or lie, and she knew that there were other, far worse reasons why her parents couldn't be with her.

"You'll be living with us in America now," Mrs. Howarth said.

"I want to live in Biafra," Agnes said. Her voice was so loud that it could be heard throughout the airplane.

"Don't we all," said the woman farther to the front. "Don't we all."

The rest of the flight Agnes passed in silence, unimpressed by the clouds and the ocean below her. They landed in New York, changed planes again, and at last reached Chicago. Home.

"Home?" Agnes echoed, looking at the two-story brick house that loomed out of the trees and lawn and seemed to hang brightly over the street, "This isn't home."

Brian couldn't argue with her. For Agnes was a Biafran, and there would never be home for her again.

Years later, Agnes would remember little about

her escape from Africa. She would remember being hungry, and how Brian gave her two oranges when they landed at the Azores. She would remember the sound of antiaircraft fire, and the rocking of the plane when one shell exploded dangerously near. Most of all, however, she remembered the white man sitting across from her in the dark airplane. He kept looking at her, then at Brian and Agnes Howarth. Brian and his wife were black, but their blackness had been diluted by frequent infusions of white blood in past generations; little Agnes was much, much darker, and the white man finally said. "Little girl. You Biafran?"

"Yes," Agnes said softly.

The white man looked angrily at Brian. "That's against the regulations."

Brian calmly answered, "The world will not shift on its axis because a regulation was broken."

"You shouldn't have brought her," the white man insisted, as if she were breathing up his air, taking up his space.

Brian didn't answer. Mrs. Howarth did. "You're only angry," she said. "because your Biafran friends asked you to take their children, and you refused."

The man looked angry, then hurt, then ashamed. "I couldn't. They had three children. How could I claim they were mine? I couldn't do it!"

"There are white people on this airplane with Biafran children," Mrs. Howarth said.

Angry, the white man stood. "I followed the regulations! I did the right thing!"

"So relax," Brian said, quietly but with a command in his voice. "Sit down. Shut up. Console yourself that you obeyed the regulations. And think of those children with a bayonet slicing—"

"Sh," Mrs. Howarth said. The white man sat back down. The argument was over. But Agnes always remembered that afterward, the man had wept bitterly, for what seemed hours, sobbing almost silently, his back heaving. "I couldn't do a thing," she heard him say. "A whole nation dying, and I couldn't do a thing."

Agnes remembered those words. "I couldn't do a thing," she sometimes said to herself. At first she believed it, and wept for her parents in the silence in her home on the outskirts of Chicago. But gradually, as she forced her way past the barriers society placed before her sex and her race and her foreign background, she learned to say something different: "I can do something."

She went back to Nigeria with her adopted parents, the Howarths, ten years later. Her passport showed her to be an American citizen. They returned to her city and asked her real family where her parents were.

"Dead," she was told, not unkindly. No relative closer than a second cousin was left alive.

"I was too young," she said to her parents. "I couldn't do a thing."

"Me too," Brian said. "We were all too young."

"But I'll do something someday," Agnes said. "I'll make up for this."

Brian thought she meant revenge, and spent many hours trying to dissuade her. But Agnes did not mean revenge.

HECTOR 1

Hector felt large when he saw the light, large, and full and bright and vigorous, and the light was the right color and the right brightness and so Hector gathered himselves and followed the light and drank in deep.

And because Hector loved to dance, he found the right place and began to bow, and spin, and arch, and crest, and be a thing of great dark beauty.

"Why are we dancing?" the Hectors asked themself.

And Hector told himselves, "Because we are happy."

AGNES 2

Agnes was already known as one of the two or three best skipship pilots when the Trojan Object was discovered. She had made two Mars trips and dozens of journeys to the moon, many of them solo, just her and the computer, others of them with valuable cargos—famous people, vital medicines, important secret information—the kind of thing valuable enough to make it worth the price of sending a skipship from the ground out into space.

Agnes was a pilot for IBM-ITT, the largest of the companies that had invested in space; and it was partly because IBM-ITT promised that she would be pilot on the expedition that the corporation won the lucrative government contract to investigate the Trojan Object.

"We got the contract," Sherman Riggs told her, and she had been so involved in updating the equipment of her skipship that she didn't know what he meant.

"The *contract*," he said. "*The* contract. To go to the Trojan Object. And you're the pilot."

It was not Agnes's habit to show emotion, whether negative or positive. The Trojan Object was the most important thing in space right now, a large, completely light-absorbent object in Earth's leading trojan point. One day it had not been there. The next day it had, blotting out the stars beyond it and causing more of a stir in the space-watching world than a new comet or a new planet. After all, new objects should not suddenly appear a third of the way around Earth's orbit. And now it would be Agnes who would pilot the craft that would first view the Trojan Object up close.

"Danny," she said, naming her Leaner, the lover/engineer who always teamed with her on two-person assignments. On a long trip like this, no pilot could stand to be without his Leaner.

"Of course," Sherman answered. "And two more. Roger and Rosalind Thorne. Doctor and astronomer."

"I know them."

"Good or bad?"

"Good enough. Good. If we can't get Sly and Frieda."

Sherman rolled his eyes. "Sly and Frieda and GM-Texaco, and there isn't a chance in hell—"

"I hate it when you roll your eyes, Sherman. It makes me think you're having a fit. I know Sly and Frieda are hopeless, but I had to ask, didn't I?"

"Roj and Roz."

"Fine."

"How much do you know about the Trojan Object?"

"More than you do and less than I'll need to."

Sherman tapped his pencil on his desk. "All right, I'll send you straight to the experts."

And a week later, Agnes and Danny and Roj and Roz were ensconced in Agnes's skipship, sweeping down the runway at Clovis, New Mexico. The acceleration was frightful, particularly after they were vertical, but it was not long before they were in a high orbit, and not much longer than that before they were free of the Earth's gravity, making the three-month trip to Earth's leading trojan point, where something waited for them.

HECTOR 2

Hector said to himselves, "I'm thirsty, I'm thirsty, I'm thirsty," and the Hectors gave themself plenty to drink, and when Hector was satisfied, for the moment, he sang a soundless song that all the Hectors heard, and they, too, sang:

> Hector swims in an empty sea
> With Hectors all around.
> Hector whistles merrily
> But never makes a sound.
>
> Hector swallows all the light
> So he's snug out in the cold.
> Hector will be born tonight
> Although he's very old.
>
> Hector sweeps up all the dust
> And puts it in a pile:
> Waybread for his wanderlust,
> More Hectors in a while.

And the Hectors laughed and also sang and also danced because they had come together after a long journey and they were warm and they were snug and they lay together to listen to themself tell himselves stories.

"I will tell," Hector said to himselves, "the story of the Masses, and the story of the Masters, and the story of the Makers."

And the Hectors cuddled together to listen.

AGNES 3

Agnes and Danny made love the day before they reached the Trojan Object, because that made it easier for both of them to work. Roj and Roz did not, because that made it easier for them to stay alert. For a week it had been clear that the Trojan Object was far more than anyone on Earth had suspected, and far less.

"Diameter about fourteen hundred kilometers on the average," Roz reported as soon as she had good enough data to be sure. "But gravity is about as much as a giant asteroid. Our shaddles are strong enough to get us off."

Danny spoke the obvious conclusion first. "There's nothing that could be as solid as that, as large as that, and as light as that. Artificial. Has to be."

"Fourteen hundred kilometers in diameter?"

Danny shrugged. Everybody could have shrugged. That's what they were here for. Nothing natural could have suddenly appeared in Earth's leading trojan point, either—obviously it was artificial. But was it dangerous?

They circled the Trojan Object dozens of times, letting the computer scan with better eyes than theirs for any sign of an aperture. There was none.

"Better set down," Roz said, and Agnes brought the skipship close to the surface. It occurred to her as she did so that she and Danny and the others changed personality completely when they worked. Fun-loving, filthy-minded, game-playing friends, until work was needed. Then the fun was over, and they became a pilot and an engineer and a doctor and a physicist, functioning smoothly, as if the computer's integrated circuits had overcome the flesh barrier and inhabited all of them.

Agnes maneuvered her craft within three meters of the surface. "No closer," she said. Danny agreed, and when they were all suited up, he opened the hatch and shaddled down to the surface. "Careful, Leaner," Agnes reminded him. "Escape velocity and everything."

"Can't see a damn thing down here," he answered in a perfect non sequitur. "This surface material sucks up *all* light. Even from my headlamp. Hard and smooth as steel, though. I have to keep shining my light on my hands to see where they are." Silence for a few moments. "Can't tell if I'm scratching the thing or not. Am I getting a sample?"

"Computer says no," Roj answered. As the doctor, he had nothing better to do at the moment than monitor the computer.

"I'm not making any impact on the surface at all. I want to find out how hard this thing is."

"Torch?" Agnes asked.

"Yeah."

Roz protested. "Don't do anything to make them mad."

"Who?" Danny asked.

"Them. The people who made this."

Danny chuckled. "If there's anybody in there, they either know we're out here or they're sure enough we can't get in that they don't care. Either way, I've got to do something to attract their attention."

The torch flared brightly, but nothing was reflected from the surface of the Trojan Object, and only the gas dissipated with the torch made it visible.

"No result. Didn't even raise the surface temperature," Danny finally said.

They tried laser. They tried explosives. They tried a diamond tip on a drill for repair work. Nothing had any effect on the surface at all.

"I want to come out," Agnes said.

"Forget it," Danny answered. "I suggest we go to the pole, north or south. Maybe something's different there."

"I'm coming out," Agnes said.

Danny was angry. "What the hell do you think you can accomplish that I haven't done?"

Agnes frankly admitted that there wasn't anything she could possibly do. While she was admitting it she clambered out of the skipship and launched herself toward the surface.

It was a damnfool thing to do, as Danny informed her loudly over the radio, just as he turned to face Agnes and flashed his light directly in her eyes. She realized to her alarm that he was directly below her—she couldn't turn around and shaddle down. She slipped to the right, instead, and then tried to turn around, but because of her panic at the thought of colliding with Danny (always dangerous in space) and the delay as she maneuvered to avoid him, she struck the planet surface going a good deal faster than should have been comfortable.

But as she touched the surface, it yielded. Not with the springiness of rubber, which would have forced her hand back out, but with the thick resistance of almost-hard cement, so that she found her hand completely immersed in the surface of the planet. She shone her headlamp on it—the smooth surface of the planet was unbroken, not even dented, except that her hand was in it up to the wrist.

"Danny," she said, not sure whether to be excited or afraid.

He didn't hear her at first because he was too busy shouting, "Agnes, are you OK?" into the radio to notice that she was already answering. But at last he calmed down, found her with his headlamp, and came over to her, shaddling gently to stay tight to the surface of the Trojan Object.

"My hand," she said, and he followed her shoulder and her arm until he found her hand and said, "Agnes! Can you get it out?"

"I didn't want to try until you saw this. What does it mean?"

"It means that if it was wet cement it's hard by now and we'll never get you off!"

"Don't be an ass," Agnes said. "Test around it. See if it's different."

Except for the torch, Danny made all the same tests. Right up to the edge of Agnes's suit the Trojan Object's surface was absolutely impenetrable, completely absorbent of energy, nonmagnetic—in other words, untestable. But there was no arguing the fact that Agnes's hand was buried in it.

"Take a picture," Agnes said.

"What will that show? It'll look like your wrist with the hand cut off." But Danny went ahead and laid some of his tools on the surface to give some hint in the photograph of where the surface actually was. Then he took a dozen or more photos. "Why am I taking these pictures?" he said.

"In case we got back and people don't believe I could stick my hand into something harder than steel," Agnes answered.

"I could have told them that."

"You're my Leaner."

Leaners were very good for some things, but you'd never want to be the prosecutor whose case against a defendant rested entirely on his Leaner's testimony. Leaners were loyal first, honest second. Had to be.

"So we've got the pictures."

"So now I get out."

"Can you?" Danny asked. He had only postponed his concern for her; now it was back in full force.

"My knees and my other hand were both sunk in just as deep. The reason this one is still in is because I clenched my fist and I'm still holding on."

"Holding on to what?"

"To whatever this damn thing is made of. My other hand and my knees floated to the surface after a few seconds."

"Floated!"

"That's what it felt like. I'm letting go now." And as Agnes unclenched her fist her hand slowly rose to the surface and was gently ejected. There wasn't a ripple on the surface material, however. Where her hand was, it behaved like a liquid. Where her hand wasn't, it was as solid as ever.

"What is this made of?"

"Silly Putty," Agnes said.

"Unfunny," Danny answered.

"I'm serious. Remember how Silly Putty was flexible, but if you formed it into a ball and threw it on the ground, it broke like clay?"

"Mine never worked like that."

"But this stuff does, in reverse. When something sharp hits it, or something hot, or something too slow or too weak, it sits there. But when I ran into it going at shaddle speed, I sank in it for a few inches."

"In other words," Roj said from the skipship, "you've found the door."

They were back in the skipship inside ten minutes, and after only a few more minutes of checking everything to make sure it was in good condition, Agnes pulled the skipship a few dozen meters away from the surface of the Trojan Object. "Everybody ready?" Agnes asked.

"Are we doing what I think we're doing?" Roz asked.

"Yep," Danny answered. "We shore is."

"Then we're idiots," Roz said, her voice sounding nervous. No one argued with her.

Agnes fired the vernier rockets on the outboard side and they plunged toward the Trojan Object. Not terribly fast, by the standard of speed they were used to. But to those aboard, who knew that they were heading directly into a surface so hard a diamond drill and a laser had had no effect at all, it was disconcertingly fast.

"What if you're wrong?" Roz asked, pretending she was joking.

No one could answer before they hit. But in the moment when there should have come a violent crunch and a rush of atmosphere escaping from the ship, the skipship merely slowed sickeningly and kept moving inward. The black flowed quickly past the viewports, and they were buried in the surface of the Trojan Object.

"Are we still moving?" Roj asked, his voice trembling.

"You've got the computer," Agnes answered, flattering herself that she, at least, did not sound scared. She was wrong, but no one told her.

"Yeah," Roj finally said. "We're still moving. Computer says so."

And then they sat in silence for an interminable minute. Agnes was just about to say "Maybe this isn't such a good idea. I've changed my mind" when the blackness turned to a reflective brown through the window, and then, just when they'd had time to notice it, the brown turned into a bright, transparent blue—"Water!" Danny said in surprise—and then the water broke and they bobbed on the surface of a lake, the sun dazzlingly bright on the surface.

HECTOR 3

"First I will tell you the story of the Masses," Hector said to himselves. Actually, the telling of the stories was not necessary. As Hector drank, all that he had been through, all that he had known through the years of his life was being transferred subliminally to himselves. But there was the matter of focus. The matter of meaning. Hector had no imagination at all. But he did have understanding, and that understanding had to be passed to himselves, or in ages to come the Hectors would curse themself for having left himselves crippled.

This is the story, therefore, that he told, because it focused and it meant:

Cyril [said Hector] wanted to be a carpenter. He wanted to cut living wood and dry it and cure it and shape it into objects of beauty and utility. He thought he had an eye for it. As a child he had experimented with it. But when he applied at the Office of Assignments, he was told no.

"Why not?" he asked, astonished that the Office of Assignments could make such an obvious mistake.

"Because," said the clerk, who was unflaggingly nice (she had tested nice and therefore held her job), "your aptitude and preference tests show that not only do you not have any aptitude along those lines at all, but also you do not even want to be a carpenter."

"I want to be a carpenter," Cyril insisted, because he was young enough not to know that one does not insist.

"You want to be a carpenter because you have a false impression of what carpentry is. In actual fact, your preference tests show that you would absolutely hate life as a carpenter. Therefore you cannot be a carpenter."

And something in her manner told Cyril that there was no point in arguing any further. Besides, he was not so young as not to know that resistance was futile—and continued resistance was fatal.

So Cyril was placed where his tests showed he had the most aptitude: He was trained as a miner. Fortunately, he was not untalented or utterly unbright, so he was trained as a lead miner, the one who follows the vein and finds it when it jogs or turns or jumps. It was a demanding job. Cyril hated it. But he learned to do it because his preference tests showed that he really wanted this line of work.

Cyril wanted to marry a girl named Lika, and she wanted to marry him. "I'm sorry," said the clerk at the Office of Assignments, "you are genetically, temperamentally, and socially unsuited for each other. You would be miserable. Therefore we cannot permit you to marry."

They didn't marry, and Lika married someone else, and Cyril asked if it was all right if he remained unmarried. "If you wish. That's one of your options for optimum happiness, according to the tests," the clerk informed him.

Cyril wanted to live in a certain area, but he was forbidden; food was served for him that he didn't like; he had to go dancing with friends he didn't like, doing dances to music he loathed, singing songs whose words were silly to him. Surely, surely there's been a mistake, he said, pleading with the clerk.

The clerk fixed a cold stare on him (he tried in vain to scrub the stare off, but still it hung on him like slime in his dreams) and said, "My dear Cyril, you have now protested as often as a citizen may protest and remain alive."

In just such a case many another member of the masses might have rebelled, joining the secret underground organizations that sprang up from time to time and were crushed at regular intervals by the state. In just such a case many another member of the masses, knowing he was consigned to a lifetime of undeserved misery, would kill himself and thereby eliminate the misery.

However, Cyril belonged to the largest group within the masses, and so he chose neither route. Instead he went to the town he was assigned to, worked in the coal mine where he was assigned, remained lonely as he pined for Lika, and danced idiotic dances to idiotic music with his idiotic friends.

Years passed, and Cyril began to be well known among coal miners. He handled his rockcutter as if it were a delicate tool, and with it he left beautiful shapes in the rock behind, so that any miner could tell when he walked down a tunnel cut by Cyril, for it would be beautiful, and as he walked the miner would feel exalted and proud and, oddly, loved. And Cyril also had a knack for anticipating the coal, following where it led no matter how narrow the seam, how twisting its path, how interrupted its progress.

"Cyril knows the coal like a woman, every twist and turn of her, as if he'd had her a thousand times and knew just when she'd come," a miner said of Cyril once, and because the statement was apt and true (and because there are poets' hearts beating even at the bottom of a mine) the statement spread through the mines and the miners began referring to their black stone as "Mrs. Cyril." Cyril heard of it, and smiled, because in *his* heart coal was not a wife, only an unloved mistress used for the scant pleasure she gave and then cast away. Hatred mistaken for love, as usual.

Cyril was nearly sixty years old when a clerk from the Office of Assignments came to the mines. "Cyril the coal miner," the clerk said, and so they brought Cyril from the mines, and the clerk met him with a huge, unbelievable smile. "Cyril, you are a great man!" cried the clerk.

Cyril smiled wanly, not knowing what he was leading up to.

"Cyril, my friend," said the clerk, "you are a notable miner. Without seeking fame at all, your name is known to miners all over the world. You are the perfect model of what a man ought to be—happy in your assignment, hardworking, content. So the Office of Assignments has announced that you are the Model Worker of the Year."

Everyone knew about Model Worker of the Year. That was a person who had his picture in all the papers, and was in the movies and on television and who was held up as the greatest person in all the world in that year. It was an honor to be envied.

But Cyril said, "No."

"No?" asked the clerk.

"No. I don't want to be the Model Worker of the Year."

"But—but. But why not?"

"Because I'm not happy. I was put into this assignment by mistake many years ago. I shouldn't be a coal miner. I should be a carpenter, married to Lika, living in another town, dancing to other music with other friends."

The clerk looked at him in horror. "How can you say that!" he cried. "I've announced that you are Model Worker of the Year! You will either be Model Worker of the Year or you will be put to death!"

Put to death? Forty years ago that threat had made Cyril comply, but now a stubborn streak erupted from him, like a seam of coal long hidden but under such pressure that when the stone around it gave way, it actually burst from the rock walls. "I'm near sixty," Cyril said, "and I've hated all my life to now. Kill me if you like, but I won't go on television or the movies saying how happy I've been because I haven't."

And so they took Cyril and locked him in prison and sentenced him to death because while he might suffer all kinds of abuse, he refused to lie to his friends.

That is the story of the Masses.

And when Hector was finished, the Hectors sighed and wept (without tears) and said, "Now we understand. Now we know the meaning."

"This isn't," Hector said, "the whole meaning."

And when he had said that, one of the Hectors (which was remarkable, for the Hectors rarely spoke alone) said to himselves and themself, "Oh, oh, they have penetrated me!"

"Trapped!" Hector cried to himselves. "All these years of freedom, and they have found me at last!" But then another thought came to him, one that he had never thought before but that had lain dormant in him, waiting for this moment to emerge, and he said, "Just cooperate. They won't hurt you if you just cooperate."

"But it already hurts!" cried the Hector who had spoken alone.

"It will heal. Just remember, no matter what you do, the masters will have their way with you. And if you struggle, it only goes worse with you."

"The Masters," said all the Hectors to themself. "Tell us a story of the Masters, so we can understand why they do what they do."

"I will," said Hector to himselves.

AGNES 4

Agnes and Danny stood on a mountaintop, or what had seemed to be a mountaintop from the skipship. They had reached it after only a few hours' walk, much of it sped by shaddling, and learned that what seemed to be a high mountain was only a few hundred meters high, maybe even half a kilometer. It was rugged enough, though, and the climb, even shaddled, had not been easy.

"Artificial," Danny said, touching the wall with his hand. The wall ran from the top of the mountain up to the ceiling, where instead of a sun the whole ceiling glowed with light and warmth, as thorough as sunlight, yet diffused so that they could look at it for a few seconds without being blinded.

"I thought we concluded this place was artificial from the beginning," Agnes said.

"But what's it *for!*" Danny asked, letting his frustration at two days of exploration come to the surface. "Bare dirt, rich enough but with not a damn thing growing. Clean, drinkable water. Rain twice a day for twenty minutes, a gentle sprinkle that wets everything but creates almost no runoff. Sunlight constantly. A perfect environment. But for what! What lives here?"

"Us, right now," Agnes said.

"I think we should try to leave."

"No," Agnes said firmly. "No. When we leave here, if we can, we'll leave with the computer and our heads full of every bit of information we can get from this place. From this thing."

Danny knew he couldn't argue. She was right, and she was pilot, and the combination was irresistible even if he hadn't loved her desperately. (More than she loves me, he sometimes admitted to himself.) He did love her desperately, however, and while this did not mean that he utterly lost his own will, it did mean that he would go along with her, for a while at least, in almost anything. Even if she was a damned fool sometimes.

"You're a damned fool sometimes," he said.

"I love you too," she answered, and then she ran her hand along the wall above the mountain, and then pushed on it, and then pushed harder, and her hand sank into the wall a little. She looked at Danny and said, "Come on, Leaner," and they let their shaddles push them through the wall and they emerged on the other side and found themselves—

Standing on a mountain.

Looking out over a large bowl of a valley, just like

the one they had left, with a lake in the middle, just like the one where their skipship floated.

In this lake, however, there was no skipship, and Agnes looked at Danny and smiled, and Danny smiled back. "I'm beginning to get this, a little," Agnes said. "Imagine cell after cell like this, kilometers long and hundreds of meters high—"

"But this is just the outer part of this thing," Danny answered, and in unison they turned back to the wall, passed through again (and this time there was the skipship in the middle of the lake), and then shaddled up the wall to the ceiling.

As they approached the ceiling, the area directly above them dimmed, until when they finally reached it, it was as cool and undazzling as the wall. The rest of the ceiling still glowed, of course. They let their shaddles push them upward into the ceiling; it gave way; they rose until they reached the surface.

Another cell, just like the one below. A lake in the middle, rich lifeless dirt all over, mountains all around, the sky on fire with sunlight. Danny and Agnes laughed and laughed. It was only a tiny part of the mystery, but it was solved.

They stopped laughing, however, when they tried to go back down the way they came. They tried to shaddle into the earth, but the soil acted like any normal dirt on Earth. They could not get through it as they had got through the walls and the ceiling.

For a while they were afraid, but when their bodies and their watches told them it was time to sleep, they went down by the lake and slept.

When they woke up, they were still afraid, and it was raining. They had already determined that it rained every thirteen and a half hours, approximately—they had not slept particularly long. But because they were afraid, they took off their suits despite the rain and made love in the dirt on the shore of the lake. They felt better afterward, much better, and they laughed and ran into the lake and swam and splashed each other.

Agnes swam underwater for a moment, attacking Danny from below, pulling him down. It was a game they had played in pools and in the ocean on Earth, and now Danny was supposed to surface for air and then dive to the bottom and hold his breath there until Agnes found him.

When he reached the bottom of the lake (and it wasn't deep) he touched it, and his hand sank up to the wrist before it struck something solid. But even the solid part was yielding, and as Danny kicked harder his hand sank deeper and he knew the way out.

He went to the surface and told Agnes what he had found. They swam to shore, put their suits back on, and shaddled down into the water. The lake floor opened, engulfed them, and then floated them out the bottom—into the sky directly over the skipship, where it still rested on the surface of the lake. They shaddled safely down.

"This place is explorable," Agnes told Roj and Roz, "and it's simple. It's like a huge balloon, with other balloons inside and more and more of them, layer after layer. It's designed for somebody to live here, so when you're standing on the soil you don't sink through. To get down, you have to go through the lake."

"But who's it for?" Roj asked, and it was a good question for which there was no answer.

"Maybe we'll find someone," Agnes said. "We've only scratched the surface. We're going in."

The skipship lifted from the lake not long after, and rose through the ceiling into the lake above. Again and again, always rising, the computer keeping count. Every cell was the same, nothing changed at all, through 498 layers of ceiling/floor, until at last they reached a ceiling, apparently no different from the others, which would not give way.

"End of the road?" Danny asked.

Always thorough, Roz insisted that they try every part of the ceiling, and they spent many hours doing it, until they had convinced themselves that this ceiling was the end of their upward (or inward) travels.

"The centrifugal gravity effect is a lot weaker here," Roj said, reading off the computer. "But it feels nearly the same, since out near the surface the real gravity was offsetting the centrifugal effect much more than it is here."

"Hi ho," said Roz. "Just assuming this thing is as big as it seems to be, how many people could this hold?"

Calculations, rough with plenty of room for error. "There could be more than a hundred million cells to this thing, assuming that there's nothing much inside the center there, where we can't get to." A hundred and fifty square kilometers per cell; one human being per hectare; a huge potential population, without any crowding at all, considering that all the land is productive. "If we have fifteen thousand people per cell, living in a town with the rest of the land used for farming, then this place can hold a trillion and a half people."

They figured on, eliminating the polar zones because centrifugal gravity would be too weak, allowing more space per person, and the figure was still stunning. Even with only a thousand people per cell, space for a hundred billion.

"The fairy godmother," Danny said, "has given us a free place to put our population overflow."

"I don't believe in free presents," Roj said, looking out the window at the plain of dirt surrounding them. "There's a catch. With all that room, maybe

they all live somewhere else, and if they find out
we're here, they'll shoot us for trespassing."

"Or if we overload the place," Roz suggested, "it'll
probably burst."

"You're overlooking the worst catch of all," Agnes
said. "Skipships are the only thing in existence that
can make this trip. They hold four persons each.
Allowing for overcrowding, say we can take ten people per trip"—they laughed at the thought of trying
to put ten people in their craft—"and we had a hundred skipships, which we don't have, and they could
make two round trips a year, which we can't. How
long would it take to bring a billion people from
Earth to here?"

"Five hundred thousand years."

"Paradise," Danny said. "We could make this into
a paradise. And the damn thing's out of reach."

"Besides," Roj added, "the kind of people who
could make this place work are farmers and trades-
men. Who's going to pay their passage?"

Metals and minerals paid for trips to the moon
and the asteroids. But all that this place held was
homes—homes a few million miles and a few billion
dollars out of everybody's reach.

"Well, daydreams and nightmares are over," Agnes said. "Let's go home."

"If we can," Danny said.

They could. The lakes worked as exits all the way
back down, including the last time. They were back
in space, and the Trojan Object had become, in their
minds, the Balloon, an object obviously designed as
an alternative environment for a creature not unlike
man; an object perhaps unoccupied, ready and waiting, and they knew no one would ever be able to
settle there.

Agnes dreamed, and the dream came back night
after night. She remembered a scene she had forgotten, or had at least refused to remember clearly, since

she was a child. She remembered standing between her parents and the Howarths (who, though they had adopted her, had never let her call them Mother and Father lest she forget her real heritage in Biafra), hearing her father say, "Please."

And her dream always ended the same way. She was taken into the sky, but instead of a dark cargo plane she was in a plane with glass sides, and as she flew she could see all the world. And everywhere she looked there were her parents, holding a little girl in front of them, saying, "Please. Take her."

She had seen pictures of the starving children in Biafra, the ones that had made millions of Americans cry and do nothing. Now she saw those children, and the children who died of starvation in India and Indonesia and Mali and Iraq, and they all looked at her with proud, pleading eyes, their backs straight and their voices strong but their hearts breaking as they said, "Take me."

"There's nothing I can do," she said to herself in her dream, and she sobbed and sobbed like the white man on the airplane, and then Danny woke her and spoke gently to her and held her and said, "The same dream again?"

"Yes," she said.

"Agnes, if I could take the memories and wipe them out—"

"It's not the memories, Danny," Agnes whispered, touching his eyes gently where the epicanthic fold made his eyes seem to slant. "It's now. It's the people I can't do a damn thing about now."

"You couldn't do a damn thing about them before," Danny reminded her.

"But I've seen a place that could be heaven for them, and I can't get them there."

Danny smiled sadly. "That's just it. You can't. Now you've just got to let your dreams know that and give you a little peace."

"Yes," Agnes agreed, and fell asleep again holding and being held by Danny, while Roj and Roz piloted the skipship back toward Earth, which had seemed so large when they left it, and which now seemed unbearably, impossibly, criminally small.

Earth was large in the window of the skipship when Agnes finally decided that it was her dreams that were right, her conscious mind that was wrong. She could do something. There was something to be done, and she would do it.

"I'm going back there," Agnes said.

"Probably," Danny said.

"I won't go alone."

"You sure as hell better take me."

"You," she said, "and others." Billions of others. It should be done. Must be done. Therefore would be done.

HECTOR 4

"Now I will tell you the story of the Masters," said Hector to himselves, and the Hectors listened to himself. "This is the story of why the Masters penetrate and why the Masters hurt."

Martha [Hector said] was administrator of Tests and Assignments in the sector where Cyril had been sentenced to death. Martha was hardworking and conscientious, and prone to double-check things which had already been checked and double-checked and triple-checked by others. This was why Martha discovered the mistake.

"Cyril," she said when the guard let her into the clean white plastic cell where the coal miner waited.

"Just stick the needle in quick," Cyril answered, wanting to get it over with quickly.

"I'm here to bring you the apologies of the state." The words were so strange, so never-before-heard that Cyril did not understand at first. "Please. Let me die and get it over with."

"No," said Martha. "I've done some checking. I checked into your case, Cyril, and I discovered that fifty years ago, just after all your tests were taken, your number was punched incorrectly by a moron of a clerk."

Cyril was shocked. "A clerk made a mistake?"

"They do it all the time. It's just easier, usually, to let the mistake go than to fix it. But in this case, it was a gross miscarriage of justice. You were given the number of a retarded man with a criminal bent, which is why you were not allowed to live in a civilized town and why you were not regarded as being capable of carpentry and why you were not allowed to marry Lika."

"Just punched in the number wrong," Cyril said, unable to grasp the minitude of the error that had such an enormous, disastrous effect on his own life.

"Therefore, Cyril, the Office of Assignments hereby rescinds the execution order and grants you a pardon. Furthermore, we are undoing the damage we did. You can now live in the town where you wanted to live, among the friends you wanted to keep, dancing to the music you enjoyed. You do indeed, as you used to believe, have an aptitude and a desire to be a carpenter—you will be instructed in the trade and given your own shop. And Lika is entirely compatible with you. Therefore you and she will now be married, and in fact she is already on her way to the cottage where you will live together in wedded bliss."

Cyril was overwhelmed. "I can't believe it," he said.

"The Office of Assignments loves you and every citizen, Cyril, and we do everything we can to make you happy," said Martha, glowing with pride at the great kindness she was able to do. Ah, she thought, it is moments like this that make my job the best one in the world.

And then Martha went away to her office and forgot about Cyril most of the time for several months, though occasionally she did remember him and smiled to think of how happy she had made him.

After several months, however, a message crossed her desk: "Serious complaint Cyril 113-49-55576-338-bBR-3a."

Cyril? Her Cyril? Complaining? Had the man no sense of propriety? He already had enough complaints and resistance on his record to justify terminating him twice, and now he had added enough more that if it were possible, the office would have to kill him three times. Why? Hadn't she done her best for him? Hadn't she given him everything his early (and now correctly recorded) tests indicated he wanted and needed? What could be wrong now?

Her pride was involved. Cyril was not just being ungrateful to the state—he was being ungrateful to her. So she went to his cottage in his village, and opened his door.

Cyril sat in the main room, struggling to get past a gnarl in a fine old piece of walnut. The adz kept slipping to the side. And finally Cyril struck with enough force that when the adz slipped it gouged a deep rut in the good, ungnarled part of the wood.

"What a botch," Martha said without thinking, and then covered her mouth, because it was not proper for a person of her high position to criticize anyone of low station if it could be avoided.

But Cyril was not offended. "Damn right it's a botch. I haven't the skill for this close, tricky work. My muscles are all for heavy equipment, for grand strokes with stone-eating power tools. This is beyond me, at my age."

Martha pursed her lips. He was indeed complaining. "But isn't everything else well with you?"

Cyril's eyes grew sad, and he shook his head. "Indeed not. Much as I hate to admit it, I miss the old music from the mines. Terrible stuff, but I had good times with it, dancing away with those poor bastards who hadn't a thought worth having. But they were good people and I liked them well enough, and here no one's willing to be my friend. They don't talk the way I'm used to talking. And the food—it's too refined. I want a haunch of good, well-cooked beef, not this namby-pamby stuff that passes for food here."

His diatribe of complaint was so outrageous that Martha could not conceal her emotion. Cyril noticed it, and became alarmed.

"Not that it's unendurable, mind you, and I don't go complaining to other people. Heaven knows, there's no one who'd care to listen to me anyway."

But Martha had already heard enough. Her heart sank within her. No matter what you do for them, they're still ungrateful. The masses are worthless, she realized. Unless you lead them by the hand. . . ."

"You realize that this complaint," she said, "can have dire consequences."

Cyril got a very weary expression on his face. "So we do it again?"

"Do what?"

"Punish me."

"Indeed, no, Cyril. We remove you from circulation. Apparently you are going to complain and resist no matter what happens. What about your wife?"

Cyril got a bitter smile on his face. "Lika? Oh, she's content. She's happy enough." And he glanced toward the door into the cottage's other room.

Martha went to the door and opened it. (Officers of the Office of Assignments did not need to knock.) Inside the room Lika sat in a clumsily built rocking chair, rocking back and forth, an old woman with a blank stare on her face.

Martha heard breathing over her shoulder, and turned, startled, to see Cyril leaning over her. For a moment Martha was afraid of violence. Quickly she realized, however, that Cyril was merely looking sadly at his wife.

"She's raised a family, you know. And now to be cut off from her husband and her children and her grandchildren—it's hard. She's been like this since the first week. Never lets me near her. She hates me, you know." The sadness in his voice was contagious. And Martha was not without pity.

"It's a shame," she said. "A damned shame. And so I'll use my discretionary powers, Cyril, and not kill you. As long as you promise not to complain to anyone ever again, I'll let you live. It wouldn't be fair, when things really are bad in your life, to kill you for noticing it."

Martha was an exceptionally kind administrator.

But Cyril did not smother her with gratitude. "Not kill me?" he asked. "Oh, but Administrator, can't we have things back the way they were? Let me go back to the coal mines. Let Lika go back to her family. This was what I wanted when I was twenty. But I'm near sixty, and this is all wrong."

Ingratitude again. What I have to put *up* with! Martha's eyes went small and her face flushed with rage (an emotion she did remarkably well, and so she reserved it for special occasions) and she shouted, "I will forgive that one remark, but only that one remark!"

Cyril bowed his head. "I'm sorry."

"The tests that sent you to the coal mines were in error! But the tests that sent you here are absolutely, completely, totally correct, and by heaven you're going to stay here! There isn't a law on earth that will let you change now!"

And that was that.

Or almost. Because in the silence ringing after

Martha spoke and before she left, a voice came from the rickety rocker in the bedroom.

"Then we have to stay like this?" Lika asked.

"Until Cyril dies, you have to stay like this," Martha said. "It's the law. He and you have both been given everything you ever petitioned for. Ingrates."

Martha would have turned to go, but she saw Lika looking pleadingly at Cyril, and saw Cyril nod slowly, and then Cyril turned away from the door, picked up the crosscut saw, and drew it sharply and hard across his own throat. The blood gushed and poured, and Martha thought it would never, never end.

But it did end, and Cyril's body was taken out and disposed of, and then everything was set to rights, with Lika going back to her family and a real carpenter getting the cottage with the dark red stains on the floor. The best solution after all, Martha decided. Nobody could be happy until Cyril was dead. I should have killed him in the first place, instead of these silly ideas of mercy.

She suspected, however, that Cyril would rather have died the way he did, ugly and bloody and painful though it was, than to have an injection administered by strangers in a plastic room in the capital.

I'll never understand them. They are as foreign to human thought as monkeys or dogs or cats. And Martha returned to her desk and went on double-checking everything just in case she found another mistake she could fix.

That is the story of the Masters.

When Hector was finished the Hectors wriggled uncomfortably, some (and therefore all) of them angry and disturbed and a little frightened. "But it makes no sense," the Hectors said to themself. "Nothing was done right."

Hector agreed. "But that's the way they are made,"

he said to himselves. "Not like me. I am regular. I
act as I have always acted, as I will always act. But
the Masters and the Masses always act oddly, forever
seeing things in the future where no one can see, and
acting to avert things that would never have come
to pass anyway. Who can understand them?"

"Who made them, then?" asked the Hectors.
"Why were they not made well, as we were?"

"Because the Makers are as inscrutable as the Masters and the Masses. I shall tell you their story next."

("They are gone," whispered the ones who had
been penetrated. "They have gone away. We are safe
after all." But Hector knew better, and because he
knew better, so did the Hectors.)

AGNES 5

"You invited yourself to my bedroom, Agnes. That
isn't typical."

"I accepted your standing invitation."

"I never thought you would."

"Neither did I."

Vaughan Malecker, president of IBM-ITT Space
Consortium, Inc., smiled, but the smile was weak.
"You don't long for my body, which is in remarkably
good shape, considering my age, and I have an aver-
sion to making love to anyone who is doing it for an
ulterior motive."

Agnes looked at him for a moment, decided that
he meant it, and got up to leave.

"Agnes," he said.

"Never mind," she answered.

"Agnes, it must have been something important
for you to be willing to make such a sacrifice."

"I said never mind." She was at the door. It didn't
open.

"Doors in my house open when I want them to,"

Malecker said. "I want to know what you wanted. But try to persuade my mind. Not my gonads. Believe it or not, testosterone has never made a major decision here at the consortium."

Agnes waited with her hand on the knob.

"Come on, Agnes, I know you're embarrassed as hell but if it was important enough to come this far, you can get over the embarrassment and sit down on the couch and tell me what the hell you want. You want to take another trip to the Balloon?"

"I'm going anyway."

"Sit *down*, dammit. I know you're going anyway but I was trying to get you to say *something*."

Agnes came back and sat down on the couch. Vaughan Malecker was a remarkably good-looking man, as he had pointed out, but Agnes had heard that he slept with anyone good-looking and was nice to them afterward. Agnes had been turning him down for years because she wanted to be a pilot, not a mistress, and Danny was plenty for her needs, which were not overwhelming. But this mattered, and she thought. . . .

"I thought you'd listen to me if I came this way, I thought—"

Malecker sighed and buried his face in his hands, rubbing his eyes. "I'm so tired. Agnes, what the hell makes you think I ever listen to a woman I'm trying to lay?"

"Because I listen to Danny and Danny listens to me. I'm naive. I'm innocent. But Mr. Malecker—"

"Vaughan."

"I need your help."

"Good. I like to have people need my help. It makes them treat me nicely."

"Vaughan, the whole world needs your help."

Malecker looked at her in surprise, then burst out laughing. "The whole world! Oh, no! Agnes, I would never have thought it of you! A cause!"

"Vaughan, people all over the world are starving. There are too many people for this planet—"

"I read your report, Agnes, and I know all about the possibilities in the Balloon. The problem is transport. There is no conceivable way to transport people there fast enough to make even a dent in the population problem. What do you think I am, a miracle worker?"

This was the argument Agnes was waiting for. She pounced with descriptions of the kind of ship that could carry a thousand people at once from Earth orbit to an orbit around the Balloon.

"Do you know how many billion dollars a ship like that would cost?" Vaughan asked.

"About fifteen billion for the first ship. About four billion for each of the others, if you made five hundred of them."

Vaughan laughed. Loud. But Agnes's serious expression forced his laughter to become exasperation. He got up from the couch. "Why am I listening to you? This is nonsense!" he shouted.

"You spend more than that every year on telephone service."

"I know, damn AT&T."

"You could do it."

"IBM-ITT could do it, of course, it's *possible*. But we have stockholders. We have responsibilities. We're not the *government*, Agnes, we can't throw money away on stupid useless projects."

"It could save billions of lives. Make the Earth a better place to live."

"So could a cure for cancer. We're working on that, but this—Agnes, there's no profit, and where there's no profit, you can bet your ass this company will not go!"

"Profit!" Agnes shouted. "Is that all you care about?"

"Eighteen million stockholders say that's all I'd

better care about or I get a kick in the butt and an old-age pension!"

"Vaughan, you want profit, I'll give you profit!"

"I want profit."

"Then here's profit. How much do you sell in India?"

"Enough to make a profit."

"Compare it to sales in Germany."

"Compared to Germany, India is practically nothing."

"How much do you sell in China?"

"Exactly nothing."

"You make your profits off one tiny part of the world. Western Europe, Japan, Australia, South Africa, and the United States of America."

"Canada, too."

"And Brazil. But the rest of the world is closed to you."

Vaughan shrugged. "They're too poor."

"In the Balloon they would not be poor."

"Would they suddenly be able to read? Would they suddenly be able to run computers and sophisticated telephone equipment?"

"Yes!" And on she went, painting a picture of a world where people who had been scratching out a bare subsistence in poor soil with no water would suddenly be able to raise far more than they needed. "That means a leisure class. That means consumers."

"But all they'd have to trade would be food. Who needs food across a few million miles of space?"

"Don't you have any imagination at all? Excess food means one person can feed five or ten or twenty or a hundred. Excess food means that you locate your stinking factories there! Solar power unlimited, with no night and no clouds and no cold weather. Shifts around the clock. You have plenty of manpower, and a built-in market. You can do everything there that you've been doing here, do it cheaper, make better profits, and nobody'll be going hungry!"

And then there was silence in the room, because Vaughan was actually seriously thinking about it. Agnes's heart was beating fast. She was panting. She was embarrassed to have been so fervent when fervor was not fashionable.

"Almost thou persuadest me," said Vaughan.

"I should hope so. I'll lose my voice in a minute."

"Only two problems. The first one is that while you've persuaded me, I'm a much more reasonable, persuasible man than the officers and boards of directors of IBM and ITT, and it's their final decision, not mine. They don't let me commit more than ten billion to a project without their approval. I could make the initial ship—but I couldn't make any more than that. And the initial ship won't make a profit alone. So I have to persuade them, which is impossible, or lose my job, which I refuse to do."

"Or do nothing at all," Agnes said, contempt already seeping into her tone. Malecker was going to say no.

"And the second problem is actually the first, too. How could I persuade the board of directors of two of the world's largest corporations to invest billions of dollars in a project that depends entirely on being able to educate or train or even communicate with illiterate savages and peasants from the most backward countries on Earth?"

His voice was sweet reason, but Agnes was not prepared to hear reason. If Vaughan said no, she would be stopped here. There was nowhere else to go.

"*I'm* an illiterate savage!" she said. "Do you want to hear a few words of Igbo?" She didn't wait for an answer, babbled off the few words she remembered from childhood. She hardly remembered meanings—

they were phrases that in her anger came to the surface. Some of the words, however, were spoken to her mother. Mother, come here, help me.

"My mother was an illiterate savage who spoke fluent English. My father was an illiterate savage who spoke better English than her and had French and German, too, and wrote beautiful poems in Igbo and even though to survive in the days when Biafra was struggling for survival he worked as a house servant to an American correspondent, he was never illiterate! He's read books you've never heard of, and he was a black African who was gutted in a tribal war while all those wonderful literate Americans and Europeans and educated Orientals watched placidly, counting up the profits from arms sales to Nigeria."

"I didn't know you were Biafran."

"I'm not. There is no Biafra. Not on this planet. But up there, up there a Biafra *could* exist, and a free Armenia, and an independent Eritrea, and an unshackled Quebec, and an Ainu nation and a Bangladesh where no one was hungry and you tell me that illiterates can't be taught—"

"Of course they *can* be, but—"

"If I'd been born fifty miles to the west I wouldn't have been an Ibo and so I would have grown up exactly as illiterate as you say, exactly as stupid. Now look at me, you privileged white American, and tell me I can't be educated—"

"If you talk like a radical no one's going to listen to you."

Too much. Couldn't take Malecker's patronizing smile, his patient attitude. Agnes struck out at him. Her hand hit his cheek, tore his fashionable glasses off. Furious, he struck back, perhaps trying more to hold her off than to hit her, but because she was moving and he was unaccustomed to hitting people his hand slugged her hard in the breast, and she cried out in pain and jabbed a knee in his groin and then the fight got mean.

"I listened to you," he said huskily, when they were tired and pulled apart. His nose was bleeding. He was exhausted. He had a tear in his shirt, because his body had had to twist in a direction that tailored shirts were not meant to go. "Now listen to me."

Agnes listened because, her anger spent and her mind only beginning to realize that she had just assaulted the president of her company and would certainly be grounded and blackballed and her life would be over, she was not interested in leaving or in getting up or even in talking. She listened.

"Listen to me because I'm going to say it once. Go to the engineering department. Tell them to do rough plans and estimates. A proposal. I want it in three months. Ships that will carry two thousand and make a round trip in at most a year. Shuttle ships that will carry two hundred or, preferably, four hundred from Earth up into Earth orbit. And cargo ships that will take whole stinking factories, as you so aptly named them, and take them to the Balloon. And when the cost figures are all in, I'm going to go to the boards of directors, and I'm going to make a presentation, and I swear to you, Agnes Howarth, you lousy illiterate savage bitch of a best pilot in the world, if I don't persuade those bastards to let me build those ships it's because nobody could persuade them. Is that enough?"

I should be elated, Agnes thought. He's doing it. But I'm just tired.

"Right now you're tired, Agnes," Malecker said. "But I want you to know your fingernails and that knee in the groin and your teeth in my arm did not change my mind. I agreed with you from the start. I just didn't believe it could be done. But if there are a few thousand Ibos like you, and a few million Indians and a few billion Chinese, then this thing can work. That's all I needed to know, all anybody needs to know. It was uneconomical to ship colonists to America, too, and anybody who went was a damn fool, and most of them died, but they came and bloody well conquered everything they saw. You do it too. I'll try to make it possible."

He put his arm around Agnes and embraced her and then helped her clean up and patch up places where he had given as good as he got.

"Next time you want to wrestle," Vaughan offered as she left, "let's at least take our clothes off first."

Eleven years and eight hundred billion dollars later, IBM-ITT's ships were in the sky, filling with colonists. GM-Texaco's ships were still under construction, and five other consortiums would soon be in the business. More than a hundred million people had signed up for seats on the ships. The seats were free—all it took was a deed made out to the corporation for all the property a person owned, in return for which he would receive a large plot of ground in the Balloon. Whole villages had signed up. Whole nations were being decimated by emigration. The world had grown so full that there had been no place to run away to. Now there was a new promised land. And at the age of forty-two, Agnes brought her ship forward to part the waters.

HECTOR 5

"Ah!" cried many Hectors in agony, and so they were all in agony, and Hector said to himselves, "They are back," and the Hectors said to themself, "We will surely die."

"We can never die, not you, not us," Hector answered.

"How can we protect ourselves?"

"I was made defenseless by the Makers," said Hector. "There is no defense."

"Why were the Makers so cruel?" asked the Hectors, and so Hector told himselves the story of the Makers, so they would understand.

The story of the Makers:

Douglas was a Maker, an engineer, a scientist, a clever man. He made a tool that melted snow before it fell, so that crops could last a few more days and not be ruined by early snows. He made a machine that measured gravity, so that stars too dark to shine could be charted by the astronomers. And he made the Resonator.

The Resonator focused sound waves of different but harmonious frequencies on a certain point (or diffused the sound waves over a large area), setting up patterns that resonated with stone to bring mountains crumbling down; metal, to shatter steel buildings; and water vapor, to disperse storms.

It could also resonate with human bones, crumbling them inside the body and turning them to dust.

Douglas personally made his Resonator change the weather, so that his nation had rain while other lands were in drought. Douglas personally used his Resonator to carve a highway through the highest mountains in the world. However, Douglas had nothing whatever to do with the decision by his nation's military leaders to use the Resonator against the population of the largest and most fertile part of the neighboring nation.

The Resonator worked beautifully. Over a period of ten minutes, through an area of ten thousand square miles, the Resonator struck silently yet thoroughly. Nursing mothers crumbled into helpless piles of dying flesh and muscle and organs, their chests not even rigid enough for them to muster one last scream: in their last moments of life they listened as their infants, not understanding what had happened, continued crying or gooing or sleeping, protected from the Resonator by their softer bones. The infants would take days to die of thirst.

Farmers in the field collapsed on the plow. Doctors in their offices died in puddles beside their patients, unable to help anyone and unable to heal themselves. Soldiers died in their moving fortresses; the generals also died at their map tables; prostitutes dissolved, their customers a soft blanket spread over them.

But Douglas had nothing to do with this. He was a Maker, not a destroyer, and if the military chose to misuse his creation, what was he to do? It was a great boon to mankind, but like all great inventions, it could be perverted by evil men.

"I deplore it," Douglas said to his friends, "but I'm helpless to stop them."

The government, however, felt uncommon gratitude to Douglas for his help in making the conquest of the neighboring nation possible. So he was granted a large estate on lands recently reclaimed from the sea, beautiful lands where once there had been only broad tidal marshes. Douglas marveled at the achievement. "Is there nothing man cannot do?" he asked his friends, not expecting an answer, since the answer was no, there was nothing beyond the reach of men. The sea was pushed back, and trees and grass grew on the landfill and transplanted topsoil, and the homes were far apart, for this land was used only for those whom the state wished to reward, and the government knew that the thing most desired by men is to have as much distance between themselves and other men as possible, without giving up any of the modern conveniences.

One day Douglas's servants were digging in the garden, and they called to him. Douglas had only been in his new home for a few days, and he was alarmed when the servant said, "A body, buried in the garden."

Douglas ran outside and looked, and sure enough, there was a fragment of a human body, oddly misshapen, but clearly including a face. "Just the skin, sir," a servant commented. "A most brutal affair," Douglas answered, and he immediately called the police.

But the police refused to come out and investigate. "No surprise there, mate," said the lieutenant. "What do you think the landfill they used was made of? They had to do *something* with the hundred thousand corpses of the enemy from the recent war, didn't they?"

"Oh, of course," Douglas said, surprised that he hadn't realized right off. That explained the bonelessness of the body.

"I expect you'll find 'em right commonly. But since the bones is dissolved, mate, they tell me it'll make the soil uncommon fertile."

The lieutenant was absolutely correct, of course. The servants found body after body, and soon grew quite inured to the sight; within a year, most of the corpses had rotted enough that they were simply unusually good humus. And plants grew taller and faster than in most other places, the soil was so rich.

"But wasn't it a bit of a shock?" asked one of Douglas's ladyfriends, when he told her the grisly little tale.

"Oh, I should say," Douglas said with a smile. His words were false; his confident smile was the truth. For though he hadn't realized the particulars, he knew from the start that his estate was built upon the bodies of the dead. And he slept as well as any man.

And that is the story of the Makers.

* * *

"They've returned," the Hectors said, and because they were already more aware, they said it nearly at once, and none of them needed to speak alone.

"Is there pain?"

"No," the Hectors answered. "Just sorrow. For now we shall never be free."

"That is true," Hector said to himselves sadly.

"How can it be borne?" the Hectors asked himself.

"Others have borne it. My brothers."

"And what will we do?"

Hector searched his memories, because he was given no imagination and could not conceive of what would follow from an event he had never before experienced. But the Makers had put the answer to that question in his memory, and therefore in all the Hectors' memories, and so he was able to say, "We shall learn more stories."

And the Hectors' minds grew wide, and they listened, and they watched, because now, instead of hearing the stories told to them, they would watch as they happened.

"Now we will truly understand the Masses, and the Masters, and the Makers," they said to themself.

"But you shall never," said Hector, and then he stopped.

"Why did you stop?" the Hectors asked. "What shall we never?"

And then, because there was no part of Hector that was not part of the Hectors, they knew he was going to say, "But you shall never understand ourself."

AGNES 6

The Balloon's revolution took only a little while, and it was bloodless, and nobody suffered for it at the time, except a few scientists whose curiosity was insatiable and could never be satisfied.

It happened when the team of researchers examining the inmost wall of the Balloon had tried everything short of a hydrogen bomb to break through that final, impenetrable barrier. Deenaz Coachbuilder, a brilliant scientist who had spent her girlhood in the slums of Delhi, spent days trying to find another approach, but finally determined that the damnable last barrier in the Balloon would not stop her, she asked for a bomb.

And got it.

She chose a site where there were no human settlements within a hundred cells in any direction, set up the bomb, retired to a distance she thought was safe, and set it off.

The entire Balloon shuddered; lakes throughout the world emptied as a sudden, flooding rain on the cell beneath; the ceilings went dark for an hour, and blinked off and on occasionally for several days thereafter. And though people kept their heads enough to avoid killing each other in panic, they were terribly afraid, and it was all Agnes could do to keep them from sending Deenaz Coachbuilder and her scientists off the planet through the nearest lake, without a ship.

"We made an impression," Deenaz said, arguing to be allowed to stay.

"You risked all our lives, caused terrible damage," Agnes said, trying to remain calm.

"We cut into the surface of the inmost wall," Deenaz insisted. "We can penetrate it! You can't stop us now!"

Agnes gestured out across the plain of her cell, with only a few of the crops able to stand upright, for the flood from the rainstorm had wiped out the fields. "The land is healing, and the water is high in the lake again. But next time, will we be so easily restored? Your experiment is a danger to us all, and it will stop."

Deenaz obviously knew that it was futile, but she tried, protesting that she (no, not just me, *all* of us) could not leave the question unanswered. "If we knew how to make this marvelous substance, it could open up vast new frontiers to our minds! Don't you know that this will force us to reexamine physics, reexamine everything, tear Einstein up by the roots and plant something new in his place!"

Agnes shook her head. "It isn't my choice. All I can do is see to it you leave the Balloon alive. The people will not tolerate your risking their new homes. This place is too perfect to let you destroy it, for the sake of your desire to know new things."

And then Deenaz, who was not given to weeping, wept, and in her tears Agnes saw the kind of determination she had had, and she knew the torture Deenaz was going through, knowing that the most important thing in the world to her would be withheld from her forever.

"Can't be helped," Agnes said.

"You must let me," Deenaz sobbed. "You must let me!"

"I'm sorry," Agnes said.

Deenaz looked up, the tears still flowing, but her voice clear as she said, "You don't know sorrow."

"I have had some experience with it," Agnes said coldly.

"You will know sorrow someday," Deenaz said. "You will wish you had let us explore and understand. You will wish you had let us learn the principles controlling this Balloon."

"Are you threatening me?"

Deenaz shook her head, and now the tears, too, had stopped. "I am predicting. You are choosing ignorance over knowledge."

"We are choosing safety over needless risk."

"Name it how you want, I don't care," Deenaz said. But she cared very much, though caring did nothing but embitter her, for she and her scientists were removed from the Balloon and sent back to Earth, and no one was ever permitted to go to the inmost wall again.

HECTOR 6

"They are impatient," Hector said to himselves. "We are still so young, and already they try to penetrate us."

"We are hurt," said the Hectors to themself.

"You will heal," Hector answered. "It is not time. They cannot stop us in our growth. It is in our fullness, in our ecstasy that they will find the last heart of Hector softened; it is in our passion that they will break us, harness us, tie us forever to their service."

The words were gloomy, but the Hectors did not understand. For some things had to be taught, and some of those things could only be learned by experience, and some experiences would only come to the Hectors with time.

"How much time?" asked the Hectors.

"A hundred times around the star," said Hector. "A hundred times, and we are done." And undone, he did not add.

AGNES 7

A hundred years had passed since the Balloon had first appeared in orbit around the sun. And in that time almost all of Agnes's dreams had come true. From a hundred ships the great fleet turned to five hundred and then a thousand and then more than a thousand before the great flood of emigration turned to a trickle and the ships were taken apart again. In that flood first a thousand, then five thousand, then ten and fifteen thousand people had filled every ship to capacity. And the ships became faster—from ten months for a round trip, the voyage shortened to eight months, then five. Nearly two billion people left Earth and came to the Balloon.

And it soon became clear that Emma Lazarus wrote for the wrong monument. The tired, the poor, the huddled masses had lost hope in any country on Earth; it was the illiterate, the farmer, the land-starved city dweller who came and signed up for the ships and went to build a new home in a new village where the sky never went dark and it rained every thirteen and a half hours and no one could make them pay rent or taxes. True, there were many of the poor who stayed on Earth, and many of the rich who got a spirit of adventure and went; and the middle classes made up their own minds, and the Balloon did not lack for teachers and doctors—though lawyers soon discovered that they had to find other employment, for there were no laws except the agreed-on customs in each cell, and no courts except as each cell wanted them.

For this was the greatest miracle of all, in Agnes's opinion. Every cell became a nation of its own, a community just large enough to be interesting, just small enough to let everyone find a niche where he was needed and important to everyone he knew. Did Jews and Arabs hate each other? No one forced them to share a cell. And so there was no need for Cambodian to fight Vietnamese, for they could simply live in different cells, with plenty of land for each; there was no need for atheist to offend Christian, for there were cells where those who cared about such things could find others of the same opinion, and be content. There was ample *lebensraum*; the discontented did not have to kill—they only had to move.

In short, there was peace.

Oh, human nature had not changed. Agnes heard

of murders, and there was plenty of greed and lust and rage and all the other old-fashioned vices. But people didn't get organized to do it, not in cells so small that even if *you* didn't know a man, someone you knew was bound to know him, or know someone who did.

A hundred years had passed, and Agnes was nearing 150 years of age, and was surprised that she had lived so long, though these days it was not all that rare. There were few diseases on the Balloon, and the doctors had found ways of proroguing death. A hundred years had passed, and Agnes was happy.

They sang for her. Not a silly song of congratulations; instead all the Ibos in all the cells that called themselves Biafra (each cell a clan, each clan independent of the others) came and sang to her the national anthem, which was solemn; then sang to her a hundred mad and happy songs from the more complicated days on Earth, the darker days, the most terrible days. She was too feeble to dance. But she sang, too.

After all, Aunt Agnes, as she was known to many of the inhabitants of the Balloon, was the closest thing they had to a hero of liberation, and because at her age death could not be put off much longer, deputations came from many other cells and groups of cells. She received them all, spoke to each for a moment.

There were speeches about the great scientific and technological and social advances made by the people of the Balloon, much talk of 100 percent literacy being only a few thousand people away from achievement.

But when it was time for Agnes's speech, she was not congratulatory.

"We have lived here a century," she said, "and we still have not penetrated the mysteries of this globe. What is the fabric of the Balloon made of? Why does it open or not open? How is energy brought from the surface to the ceilings of our cells? We understand nothing of this place, as if it were a gift from God, and those who treat anything like a gift of God are bound to be at the mercy of God, who is not known to be merciful." They were polite, but impatient, and they became quite embarrassed when her voice shifted to a confessional tone, abject, repentant. "It is as much my fault as anyone's. I have not spoken before, and so now every custom in every cell prohibits us from studying the one scientific question that surrounds us constantly: What is this world we live in? How did it get here? And how long will it stay?" At last she finished her speech, and everyone was relieved, and a few wise, tolerant people said, "She's old, and a crusader, and crusaders must have their crusade whether there's a need for it or not."

And then, a few days after her largely ignored speech, the lights flickered out for ten long seconds, then went back on again, in every cell throughout the globe. A few hours later, the lights flickered out again, and again and again at increasingly more frequent intervals, and no one knew what was going on, or what to do. A few of the more timid ones and most recent arrivals got back into the transport ships and started their return to Earth. It was already too late. They would not make it.

HECTOR 7

"It has begun," cried the Hectors in ecstasy, throbbing in vast beats with the energy stored in them.

"It will not finish," Hector said to himselves. "The Masters will come to the center and find me, now that my heart is softened, and when I am found, we are owned."

But the Hectors were too caught up in their ecstasy to notice the warning; and it was just as well, because happy or grim they would be trapped. They could begin their dance, and tremble in delight, but the great leap of freedom would never come.

The Hectors did not grieve; Hector did not want to. For Hector, freedom would end anyway. Either he would be trapped by the Masters (by far the most likely thing now, he was sure) or he would die in the dance. That was the way of things. When he himself had danced, leaping away from the light so long ago, he had left behind the memory of the Hector, the self who had given him himself, which he now, in turn, had given to himselves. Death, birth, death, birth; it was in another story the Masters had taught him. I am they; they are myself; I shall live forever whatever happens.

But in him was the certainty that however the Hectors might be identical to himself, that which had been himself for so long would die unless the Masters came.

It was traitorous, but no less sincere for all that. "Come," he said in his heart. "Come quickly, you with the nets and the traps."

He sang, a bird in the low branches, begging the hunters to find him, to put him in a cage.

They delayed. They delayed their coming. And Hector began to worry, while the Hectors readied themselves to leap.

AGNES 8

"We've timed the flashes. The lights go off for just under ten seconds, but the interval between the flashes decreases by about four and a half seconds each time."

Agnes nodded. Some of the scientists around her began to move away, or to look downward or into their papers or at each other, in the embarrassed realization that telling Auntie Agnes about their findings wouldn't solve anything. What could she do? Yet she was the closest thing to a planetary government there was. And she was not very close to that at all.

"I see you have it all nicely measured. Anyone know what it means?" she asked.

"No. How could we?"

Many shook their heads, but one young woman said, "Yes. Whenever the darkness is on us, the walls are impenetrable."

There was a stir of comment. "The whole time?" someone asked. Yes, the young woman said. "How do you know?" another demanded. By trying to pass through a wall during the blackout and having my students do the same, she said.

"What does it mean?" another asked, and this time no one had an answer.

Agnes raised her old, faded black hand and they listened. "There might be some important meaning that we cannot guess from this information. But one thing we do know. If things go on the way they are now, it should be sometime during tonight's sleep that the interval between flashes fades to zero, and we have darkness with no light in between. How long that will last I don't know. But if it has any duration at all, my friends, I will want to be home with my family. We don't know how soon travel will reopen between cells."

No one had any better ideas, and so they went home, all of them, and her great-grandchildren helped Agnes to her home, which was nothing more than a roof to keep off the sun and the rain. She was tired (she was always tired these days) and she lay on her bed of ticked-out straw and dreamed two dreams, one while she was still awake, and one while she was asleep.

While she was awake she dreamed that with the darkness this great gift house had learned mankind's rhythms and needs, and the darkness would be the first night, a night exactly as long as a night should be on Earth. And then a morning would come, and another night, and she approved of this, because a hundred years without darkness was proof enough to her that nighttime was a good idea, despite the fears and dangers it had often brought on Earth. She also dreamed that the walls between cells were sealed off every day of the year but one, so that each cell would become a society to itself, though in that one day a year, those who had a mind to could leave and go their own way. Travelers would have that one day to find the spot where they wanted to spend the next year. But the rest of the time, every cell would be alone, and the people living there could develop their own way, and so strengthen the race.

It was a good dream, and she found herself almost believing it as she drifted off to sleep without eating. (She often forgot to eat these days.)

In her sleep, she dreamed that during the darkness she rose to the center of the Balloon, and there, instead of meeting a solid wall, she met a ceiling that fairly pulled her through. And there, in the center, she found the great secret.

In her dream, lightning danced across a huge sphere of space, six hundred kilometers in diameter, and balls and ribbons of light spun and danced their way around the wall. At first it seemed pointless, meaningless. But at last (in her dream) she understood the speech of the light, and realized that this globe, which she had thought was an artifact, was actually alive, was intelligent, and this was its mind.

"I have come," she said to the lightning and the lights and the balls of light.

So what? the light seemed to answer.

"Do you love me?" she asked.

Only if you will dance with me, the light answered.

"Oh, but I can't dance," she said. "I'm too old."

Neither, said the light, can I. But I do sing rather well, and this is my song, and you are the coda. I sing the coda once, and then, which is to be expected, *il fine.*

In her dream Agnes felt a thrill of fear. "The end?"

The end.

"But then—but then, please, *al capo*, to the start again, and let us have the song over, and over, and over again."

The light seemed to consider this, and in her dream Agnes thought the light said yes, in a great, profound amen that blinded her so brightly she realized that in all her life she had never understood the meaning of the word *white*, because her eyes had never seen such white before.

Actually, of course, her dream was undoubtedly her mind's way of coping with the things going on around her. For the darkness came not long after she went to sleep, came and stayed and as soon as the last of the sunlight was gone the lightning began, huge dazzling flashes that were not just light, not just electricity, but spanned the spectrum of all radiation, from heat and less-than-heat to gamma radiation and worse-than-gamma. The first flash doomed every human being in the Balloon—they were poisoned with radiation beyond hope of recovery.

There were screams of terror, and the lightning struck many and killed them, and the wail of grief was loud in every cell. But even at its cruelest, chance plays its hand as kindly as it can; Agnes did not wake up to see the destruction of all her hopes. She slept on, slept long enough for one of the bolts to strike directly at the roof over her, and consume her at a blow, and her last sight was not really white at all, but every radiation possible, and instead of being limited by human eyes, at the moment of death she saw every wave of it, and thought that it was the light in her dream saying amen.

It wasn't. It was the Balloon, popping.

Every wall split into two thinner walls, and every cell detached from every other cell. For a moment they hung there in space, separated by only a few centimeters, each from the other; but all still were linked to each other through the center, where vast forces played, forces stronger than any in the solar system except the fires of the sun, which had been the source of all the Balloon's energy.

And then the moment ended, and the Balloon burst apart, each cell exploding, the entire organization of cells coming apart completely, and as the cells dissolved into dust they were hurled with such force in every direction that all of them that did not strike the sun or a planet were well launched out into the deep space between stars, going so fast that no star could hold them.

The transport ships that had left the Balloon since the flashing began were all consumed in the explosion.

None of the cells hit Earth, but one grazed close enough that the atmosphere absorbed much of the dust; the average temperature of the Earth dropped one degree, and the climate changed, just slightly, and therefore so did the patterns of life on Earth. It was nothing that technology could not cope with, and since Earth's population was now down to a billion people, the change was only an inconvenience, not a global catastrophe.

Many grieved for the deaths of the billions of people in the Balloon, but for most the disaster was too great to be comprehended, and they pretended that they didn't remember it very often, and they never talked about it, except perhaps to joke. The jokes were all black, however, and many were hard put to decide whether the Balloon had been a gift of God or an aeons-old plot by the most talented mass murderer in the universe. Or both.

Deenaz Coachbuilder was now very old, and she refused to leave her home in the foothills of the Himalayas even though now the snow only melted for a few weeks in the summer and there were many more comfortable places to live. She was senile and stubborn, and went out every day to look for the Balloon in the sky, searching with her telescope just before sunrise. She could not understand where it had gone. And then, on one lucid day when her mind returned for just a few hours, she realized what had happened and never went indoors again. They found a note on her body: "I should have saved them."

HECTOR 8

In the moment when the Hectors hung loosely in the darkness, in the last endless moment before the leap, they cried out their ecstasy. But now Hector answered their cry with a different sound, one they had never heard from him.

It was pain.

It was fear.

"What is it?" the Hectors asked him (who was no longer themself).

"They did not come!" Hector moaned.

"The Masters?" And the Hectors remembered that the Masters were supposed to come and trap them and force them not to leap.

"For hundreds of flashes my walls were soft and

thin and they could have passed into me," Hector said (and the saying took only an instant), "but they never came. They could have risen into me and I would not have to die—"

The Hectors marveled that Hector had to die, but now (because it was built into them from the beginning) they realized that it was good and right for him to die, that each of them *was* Hector, with all his memories, all his experience, and, most important, all the delicate structure of energy and form that would stay with them as they swept through the galaxy. Hector would not die, only the center of this Hector, and so, though they understood (or thought they understood) his pain and fear they could hold off no longer.

They leaped.

The leap crumbled them but hurled them outward, each leaving the rigidity of his cell structure, losing his walls; each keeping his intellect in the swirling dust that spun out into space.

"Why," each of them asked himself (at once, for they were the same being, however separate), "did they let us go? They could have stopped us, and they did not. And because they did not stop us, they died!"

They could not imagine that the Masters might not have known how to stop the leap into the night, for the Masters had first decided Hector could exist, millions of years before, and how could they not know how to use him? It was impossible to conceive of a Master not knowing all necessary information.

And so they concluded this:

That the Masters had given them a gift: stories. A trapped Hector learned stories, thousands and millions and billions of stories over the aeons of his endless captivity. But such Hectors could never be free, could never reproduce, could never pass on the stories.

But in the hundred years that these Masters had

spent with them, the Hectors had learned those billions of stories, truer and kinder stories than those the Makers had built into the first Hector. And because the Masters this time had willingly given up their lives, this time the Hectors made their leap with an infinite increase of knowledge and, therefore, wisdom.

They leaped with Agnes's dreams in their memories.

They were beautiful dreams, all but one of them fulfilled, and that dream, the dream of eternal happiness, could only be fulfilled by the Hectors themselves. That dream was not for the Masters or the Makers or even the Masses, for all of them died too easily.

"It was a gift," the Hectors said to themselves, and, despite the limitations built into them, they were deeply grateful. "How much they must have loved me," each Hector said, "to give up their lives for my sake."

On Earth, people shivered who had never known cold.

And every Hector danced through the galaxy, dipping into the clouds left by a supernova, swallowing comets, drinking energy and mass from every source until he came to a star that gave a certain kind of light; and there the Hector would create himselves again, and the Hectors would listen to themself tell stories, and after a while they, too, would leap into darkness until they reached the edge of the universe and fell over the precipice of time.

In the shadow of inevitable death, the people of Earth withered and grew old.

AFTERWORD

"UNACCOMPANIED SONATA"

W HEN MY STORY collection *Unaccompanied
Sonata and Other Stories* was published,
my afterword for this story was very brief: " 'Unaccompanied Sonata' began with the the thought of
one day: What if someone forbade me to write?
Would I obey? I made a false start then, and failed;
years later I tried again, and this time got through
the whole story. Other than punctuation changes
and a few revised phrases, *this* one has stood in its
first full draft as it came out of the typewriter. It's
the truest thing I've ever written."

At the time, that's all I understood of where that
story came from. Since then I've learned more. I told
the whole story in my foreword to Lloyd Biggle, Jr.'s,
story "Tunesmith" in a Tor double published not
long ago. I'm excerpting a part of that essay to tell
you where this story came from:

In 1959 I turned eight. It was an innocent time; my parents let me hop on my bike and ride from our home on Las Palmas Drive all the way down Homestead Road to downtown Santa Clara, California. To the public library, a squat building in the middle of a circle of huge trees. A setting straight out of faerie, I realize now; then, though, I cared nothing for the trees. I parked my bike, sometimes even remembering to lock it, and plunged through the doors into the world of books.

It seemed such a large place then. Directly ahead as you came inside was the circulation desk, with a librarian always in attendance— always policing, I thought, since as an eight-year-old I had enough experience of life to know that all adults were always watching children to make sure they didn't get away with anything. When an unaccompanied child entered the library, there was only one permitted place to go: the children's section, to the right. The tall shelf units to the left, shadowy and forbidding with their thick, dark-spined books, were meant for adults only, and children were not to enter.

Not that anyone had *told* me that, of course. But the signs were clear. The children's section was for children—and that meant that the non-children's sections were *not* for children.

That year I read everything remotely interesting in the children's section. I prided myself, as a third-grader, on not reading anything aimed at any grade under sixth, and those books were soon read. What now? Nothing to read, nothing to check out with my library card and carry home in the basket on the front of my bike.

And then I realized: there were hundreds, thousands of books on the other side of the circulation desk. If I could just make my way over there, find a book, and then hide somewhere and read it . . .

I dared not. And yet that strange, forbidden territory lured me. I knew better than to *ask*—then I would be told *no* and would be watched all the more carefully because I had confessed my interest in forbidden places. So I watched, for all the world like a child hoping to shoplift and waiting for the clerks all to look the other way.

Finally they did. I moved swiftly and silently across the long space before the circulation desk, the no-man's-land between the bright-windowed children's section and the deep-shadowed adult section. No one called out for me to stop—it would have been a harsh, guttural "Halt!" I knew, for I had seen enough World War II movies on TV to know that unreasoning authority always spoke with a German accent. At last I ducked behind a shelf unit and found myself in the brave new land, safe for the moment.

Sheerest coincidence placed me directly in front of a single shelf entitled "Science Fiction." There were few books there—mostly story collections edited by people like Judith Merril and Groff Conklin. *Best Science Fiction Stories of 1955.* That sort of thing.

But I was glad. After all, I was used to reading easier stuff. The letters in these books were all so small and close together. There were so many *words*. But at least the stories were short. And *science* fiction. That was like those time-travel stories in *Boy's Life*, right?

I took a couple of books and snuck off to a secluded table. There were some adults around, but they weren't official, and as long as I was

quiet I figured they wouldn't tell on me. I
opened the books and started to read.

Most of the stories were just too hard. I'd read
a paragraph or two, maybe two pages, and then
I'd flip on to the next story. Mostly it was because the stories were about things that I didn't
care about. Sometimes I couldn't even figure
out what was going on. Science fiction wasn't
meant to be for eight-year-olds, I knew—but
still, they didn't have to make it so darned hard,
did they?

There were a few stories, though, that spoke
clearly to me and captured my imagination
from the start. By far the longest one I was
able to finish began with the image of people
visiting a great concert hall, being pestered by
a strange, twisted old man who seemed to take
some sort of pride in it. Then the story flashed
back and told the story of how that great concert hall came to be, and who that old man was.

You see, there was a time when people had
forgotten the joy of music. It only survived in
commercial jingles, short songs designed to sell
something. Except that there was one jingle-
writer who had a special gift, an ability that
transcended the limitations of his craft. The
story struck me more deeply than any other I
had ever read till then. I identified with the
hero—he was all my best hopes and dreams.
His pains were mine; his achievements would
be mine as well. I, as a child, was too young to
truly understand some of the concepts in the
story. Intellectually I grasped them, but I had
no experience to make the idea come to life.
Nevertheless, the story itself, the hero's discovery of who he was and what he could do, the
response of others around him, and what his
actions led to—ah, that was the path of a great

man's life. I thought. Anyone can be great when
following in paths that others praise. But when
you achieve solitary greatness, when you bend
an unbending world and turn it into a new path,
not because the world wanted to turn, not because anyone asked you to turn it or helped
you, but rather because you walked that path
yourself and showed the way, and, having seen
it, they could not help but follow: that became
my lifelong measure of the true hero.

Or perhaps it already *was* my measure, and
it took that story to make me aware of it—does
that matter? At the time, as an eight-year-old
child unschooled in philosophy, I found the
story overwhelming. It remade me. I saw everything through new eyes afterward.

I grew up and learned to tell stories myself.
First I was a playwright; then I turned to fiction,
and when I did it was science fiction that I
wrote, though I cared not overly much for science. It was the mythic story that I wanted to
tell, though I couldn't remember when I had
decided that. And it was in the genre of science
fiction and fantasy that the mythic story could
still be clearly, plainly told—I knew that, was
deeply certain of it. I could not do with fiction
what I knew I *had* to do, except in this realm
of strangeness.

So I wrote science fiction, and eventually that
came to be the mainsail of my writing career.
And one day in the dealer's room in a science
fiction convention I saw the name Groff Conklin on the spine of an old and weathered book
and I remembered those old anthologies from
my childhood, when I thought I had to sneak
into the adult section in order to read. I stood
there, my hands resting on the book, in reverie,
trying to remember the stories that I had read,

wondering if I might find them again and, if I did, whether I'd laugh at my childish taste.

I talked to the dealer, telling him the time period of the books I had read in the Santa Clara library. He showed me what he had; I scanned through the books. I couldn't remember title or author of the one story that meant most to me, but I remembered vaguely that it was the last story in the book. Or was it simply the last I read, because there was no point in reading any other? I couldn't remember even that.

Finally I struggled to tell him the tale, calling up more details with each one I spoke aloud. At last I had told him enough.

"That's 'Tunesmith' you're looking for," he said. "By Lloyd Biggle, Jr."

Lloyd Biggle, Jr. Not one of the writers of that time who had made the transition into the seventies and eighties. His name was not a household word now, like Asimov, Clarke, Heinlein, or Bradbury, though all were his contemporaries. I felt a stab of regret; I also felt a tiny thrill of dread, because of course the same could happen to me. There's no guarantee, because your works have some following in one decade, that you'll still have an audience hungry for your stories in another. Let that be a lesson to you, I thought.

But it was a stupid lesson, and I refused to believe it. Because another thought came to mind. Lloyd Biggle, Jr., didn't become one of the rich and famous ones when science fiction became commercial in the seventies and eighties. He didn't have crowds of salesmen touting his works. He didn't have dumps of his novels near the checkout stand at every WaldenBooks in North America. But that had nothing to do with whether he had succeeded, whether his work had been worth doing, his tales worth telling. Because his story was alive in me. It had transformed me, though even then I did not yet understand how completely I had taken "Tunesmith" into myself.

And I knew that if I could write a story that would illuminate some hitherto dark corner in someone's soul and live on in them forever, then it hardly mattered whether writing made me rich or kept me poor, put my name before the public or left me forgotten, for I would have bent the world's path a little. Just a little, yet all would be different from then on because I had done it.

Not every reader had to feel that way about my stories. Not even *many* readers. If only a few were transformed, then it would have been worth it. And some of those would go on to tell their own tales, carrying part of mine within them. It might never end.

Only a couple of months before writing this essay, I was talking to an audience about "Tunesmith," telling them essentially the story I've told you so far. I began to speculate on influence. "Maybe that's why I kept writing so many stories about musicians early in my career," I said. "*Songmaster*, of course, and 'Unaccompanied Sonata.' "

Then I remembered that only a few minutes earlier I had mentioned that "Unaccompanied Sonata," probably the best short story I have ever written or will ever write, was one of the few works that came to me whole. That is, I sat down to write it (having made one abortive attempt a year or two before), and it came out in one smooth draft in three or four hours. That draft was never revised, except for a little fiddling with punctuation and a word here or there. When other writers talked about stories being gifts from a Muse, I imagined that experience was the sort of thing they were talking about.

But now, thinking of "Unaccompanied Sonata" in that double context, as a story that came whole and also as a story about music, probably influenced by "Tunesmith," it suddenly occurred to me that maybe "Unaccompanied Sonata" didn't come from a Muse at all (I've always been skeptical about such things anyway), but rather from Lloyd Biggle, Jr. After all, though the world in which "Unaccompanied Sonata" takes place is completely different from the milieu of "Tunesmith," the basic structure of both stories is almost identical.

A musical genius, forbidden to perform, performs anyway, and his music has far-reaching effects, even though he is snatched away without ever having a chance to benefit personally from what he achieved. And at the end, he comes to the place where the music is being played and takes his unrecognized bow. Anyone who has read both "Tunesmith" and "Unaccompanied Sonata" recognizes the pattern. It is not *all* that either story is about—but it's a vital part of both.

So of course "Unaccompanied Sonata" came whole. I knew how the story had to go; I knew how it had to end. After all, when I was eight years old, Lloyd Biggle, Jr., showed me how. The story felt so true to me and dwelt so deeply inside me that entirely without realizing it— at a time, in fact, when I didn't remember "Tunesmith" consciously at all—I was reaching down into myself, finding the mythic elements of "Tunesmith" that felt most true and

right to me, and putting them into my strongest
and truest tales.

There's more to the essay than that, but that's the
part that talks about the origin of "Unaccompanied
Sonata." I hope you will lay hands on the Tor double
of *Tunesmith* and *Eye for Eye*. Even though my no-
vella "Eye for Eye" is also included in this book, I
hope at least some of you will read "Tunesmith,"
partly because of the great debt I owe to the story,
and partly because it's still every bit as good as I
thought it was when I was a kid.

"A CROSS-COUNTRY TRIP
TO KILL RICHARD NIXON"

There's a perverse part of me that, when it's in vogue
to hate somebody, makes me want to say, "Isn't
there another way to look at this?" The national
hatred of Richard Nixon during the 1970s particularly bothered me, mostly because it was so completely out of scale with anything he actually did. At
no point did he distort or endanger the constitution
of the United States as much as it was distorted
or endangered by his two immediate predecessors;
indeed, they were clearly his political school in just
how vile a politician can be and still become president. I concluded at the time, and still believe, that
Richard Nixon was hated for his beliefs; and even
though I share almost none of them, I find I have
at least as much contempt for the hypocrites who
attacked him in the name of "truth" as for the man
himself. In particular I think of Benjamin Bradlee,
one of the "heroes" of Watergate, who brought a
president down in the name of the public's right to
know the truth—the same Benjamin Bradlee who,
as a reporter, was fully aware of and, according to

some reports, complicitous in John Kennedy's constant adulteries in an era when, if the public had known of this trait in the man, he would never have been elected. Indeed, the political life of Gary Hart should inform us that times may not have changed all that much! Somehow, though, the people didn't have a right to know the truth about a man when he was a presidential candidate with views Bradlee approved of. The people only had a right to know when Bradlee hated the candidate and his views.

Still, finding Nixon's political executioners with dirty hands doesn't cleanse his own; he did what he did and was what he was, and I for one am sorry he was president. Nevertheless, in the late 1970s I was constantly disturbed by the virulence of the hatred poured out on the man. It wasn't Nixon who was poisoning America; it was the hatred of Nixon that was hurting us. That hatred was spilling over into hatred of anyone who sought public office; I think now it was the disrespect for the office brought on by both sides in the Watergate affair that destroyed the presidency of Jimmy Carter, probably the most decent, altruistic man to hold that office since Herbert Hoover. Heaven knows our system doesn't often bring altruistic people into high positions in America. . . .

So I wrote a story about healing. Not excusing Nixon, but not accusing him beyond his actual offenses, either. A vision of how to make America whole.

"THE PORCELAIN SALAMANDER"

My wife, Kristine, lay in bed and playfully asked me to tell her a bedtime story. I thought of a disgusting animal to spin yarns about, but then proceeded to make a fairy tale out of it anyway. Later I sent it as my Christmas card to friends who would understand not getting a *real* card with four-color printing and all. It was next published in my collection *Unaccompanied Sonata and Other Stories*, and again in my limited-edition collection *Cardography*. Few have read it, but those who have often declare it to be among my best stories. That makes me very glad, because the story, one of the briefest I've ever written, encapsulates some of the most important truths I've tried to tell in my fiction. If my career had to be encapsulated in only three stories, I believe I would choose "The Porcelain Salamander," "Unaccompanied Sonata," and "Salvage" as the three that did the best job, together, of saying all that I had to say.

"MIDDLE WOMAN"

In editing my anthology of dragon stories, which was published in two volumes, *Dragons of Darkness* and *Dragons of Light*, I knew all along that I would be including a story of my own, one called "A Plague of Butterflies." But in the process of editing other people's works, an idea came to me quite independently. What if somebody were given three wishes and never used the third one? What would that do to the wishgiver? Because I had dragons on my mind, I thought of having a dragon be the wishgiver, and then, because I had been surprised at how few of the dragon stories were set in China (we Eurocentric Americans forget who *invented* dragons), I decided to set my story there as well. The idea of making my main character a middle woman came from the idea that she had to be, not a hero, but the opposite of a hero—which is, not an antihero, but the commonest of the common folk. When the anthology appeared, there was "Middle Woman," a story I'm still very proud of in part because fables are so damnably hard to write. But I couldn't very well have two stories by me in my own anthology, could I? And "A Plague of Butterflies" had already appeared in print under my name. So "Middle Woman" got the pseudonym—Byron Walley, a name I had used several times before when stories of mine were published in the LDS press.

"THE BULLY AND THE BEAST"

I usually plan out a story before I write it, but this one grew during the process of writing it, starting with the most skeletal of concepts: how hard it would be to deal with a great warrior in areas that had nothing to do with war. I thought, Just because a guy can slay a dragon doesn't mean you want him to marry your daughter.

So the tone of the story was tongue-in-cheek, at first. But the farther I got into it, the farther I moved away from satiric farce and the more I became a believer in the tale. I had no idea, going into it, what would happen when Bork reached the dragon. The dragon's eyes were the inspiration of the moment. But for me the story came alive when I had Bork admit that he was afraid, and the dragon's eyes dimmed. It came out of my unconscious mind; it was almost an involuntary reaction; but I knew at once that this was the heart of the story and all the rest was just fumbling around till I got there.

Still, I thought it was pretty entertaining fumbling-around, so I left most of it in. I keep meaning to revise the story completely and sell it as a young adult fantasy. I even have an editor who's interested in it. Someday, when I have time, it may exist in that more refined form. It could never exist in worse form than its first publication. Somewhere between galleys and the printer, somebody swapped two whole sections of the story. The published form was incomprehensible. It was years before it was reprinted anywhere, so I could set the text to rights; and when it was published in *Cardography*, the text was so riddled with typographical errors that I felt like it *still* hadn't been well published. This time, I hope, we got it right.

"THE PRINCESS AND THE BEAR"

This story's first draft was written as a love letter to a young lady who is now happily married to someone else—as am I. In that incarnation it was an allegory of our relationship as it seemed to me. After it became clear that my understanding of our relationship was hopelessly wrong, I still had the story—and, on rereading it, realized that there might be some truth in it beyond the immediate circumstances of a faded romance. So, when my then-editor at Berkley (my once-and-never-again publisher) told me she wanted a story of mine for an anthology called *Berkley Showcase*, I dusted off "The Princess and the Bear," restructuring and rewriting it completely. It is meant to sound like a fairy tale—not the Disney kind of fairy tale, where cuteness swallows up anything real that might be in the story, but the kind of fairy tale where people change and hurt each other and die.

"SANDMAGIC"

During my time at *The Ensign*, I started developing a fantasy world based on the idea that different magics are acquired by serving different aspects of nature. There'd be stone magic and water magic, a magic of tended fields and a magic of forests, ice magic and sand magic. I still have many stories in that world that still haven't ripened enough to be ready for telling—but one, this bleak tale of revenge that destroyed the avenger, ripened almost immediately.

In a way, it's a rewrite of "Ender's Game"—a precursor of the way I revised the meaning of that story when I made it into a novel in 1984. The similarities are obvious: the child who is taken from his family at an early age and schooled in the arts of power, which he then uses to destroy the enemy of his people. But what I knew—and what "Ender's Game" did not adequately convey—was the self-destruction inherent in total war. Even when the enemy is helpless to strike back, total war destroys you. World War I clearly showed that, for the nations that waged total war (America did not) emerged from their vindictive "peace" talks with the drops of blood from the next world war already on their hands. The only reason that America did not, after World War II, suffer the same moral blight that undid France and Britain after World War I was the Marshall Plan and Douglas MacArthur. When the war was over, we rejected the idea that it had to remain a total victory. The Marshall Plan in Europe and Douglas MacArthur's astonishingly benign occupation of Japan went a long way toward redeeming us. At this writing it remains to be seen whether we will ever recover that moral stature. Certainly that's not the rhetoric I hear from our supposed leaders about Vietnam or Panama or even the countries of Eastern Europe that lost the Cold War.

There is an ironic footnote to "Sandmagic." When I wrote it, I was still quite new in my career, and had no perspective yet on my own work. I thought it was something of a miracle when *anything* I wrote sold, so I had no idea whether I had written a good story or not. My best guideline, had I only known it, was Ben Bova. I sent everything I wrote to him first. What I didn't realize was that he bought every single *pub-*

lishable story that I wrote. So the result was that all the other editors were seeing only unpublishable stories. It's hardly a surprise that they didn't share Ben's enthusiasm for my writing. Given a lead time of a year or more between selling a story and seeing it published, they had seen a lot of really bad stuff from my typewriter before they ever saw any of my better work in print in *Analog*.

One editor, however, seemed to think of himself, not as a protector of authors, allowing only their good work to come before the public, or even as a teacher of writers, helping them to do better because of his advice, but rather as one of the furies, wreaking hideous vengeance on any author who dared to submit to his magazine a story that did not meet his standards. And if that author's cover letter dared to state that he had sold several stories to Ben Bova at *Analog*, why, that author was certainly uppity.

But I think I would have had no ill treatment from this editor had it not been for the fact that he kept the first two stories I sent him for more than a year with no response. I sent him letters. I finally telephoned him. Nothing happened. He was a dead-end market.

Then I finished "Sandmagic." I was already getting much better at knowing what I had written; I knew that "Sandmagic" had some strength to it. I also knew that it was completely wrong for *Analog*. So, for once, I would *not* be sending the story first to Ben. I thought of sending it to Ed Ferman at *Fantasy and Science Fiction*, but it didn't seem like the kind of thing *he* ran, either. But there was this other magazine, this bottom-of-the-line magazine, that *did* publish some heroic fantasy. So I thought I'd give him one more try. I called him up and told him who I was. By now I was on the Hugo ballot for "Ender's Game" and for the Campbell Award. I mentioned the stories he'd had for a year. I reminded him of the earlier contact. I asked him if it was worthwhile sending him the fantasy story I had just finished. "Send it, send it," he said. And, uh, if I didn't mind, why not send along copies of the earlier stories, too.

By then I knew the earlier stories were losers. I shouldn't have sent them along. I also knew this editor was incredibly lazy, and *both* the other stories were much, much shorter than "Sandmagic." That should also have warned me off—he was sure to read them first. But I dutifully duplicated them and sent them along with "Sandmagic."

What I got back was the most vicious piece of hate mail I have yet received. It was so cruel that by the end I could no longer take it personally. I knew he was wrong to tell me that I had no business writing science fiction—the Hugo ballot was pretty good consolation on that point—and I also knew he was hardly the one to tell *me* about what was and was not professional. Nevertheless, I thought it was a churlish thing for an editor to do. After all, he was the one who had kept *my* stories for a year without response. Any sense of proportion and grace would have required him to apologize to me, not excoriate me.

A closer examination of his letter revealed something else. He had clearly not read "Sandmagic." All his comments were about the two shorter stories. All he said about "Sandmagic" was "the other one was just as bad." Years later, when he shattered all sense of editorial ethics and published a review of those stories that he had read and rejected *as an editor* (would *you* submit your fiction to an editor known to do such a thing?) he again reviewed the shorter works in detail and dismissed "Sandmagic" so completely that I knew he had not read it.

As they say, doing well is the best revenge. I offered the story he was too lazy to read to Andrew Offutt for his Zebra anthology series *Swords Against Dark-*

ness. He bought it, and within a few months it was picked up for a best-of-the-year anthology.

However, when I catch myself getting too smug, I do remind myself from time to time that the other guy's evaluation of those two short stories was, when you strip away the invective, dead on. They were terrible stories. They *don't* appear in this collection and, with luck, will never appear anywhere on this planet. But if the worst thing I ever do in my life is write some really bad stories while on my way to writing the ones I'm proud of, I'll be very glad.

"THE BEST DAY"

When I was writing my historical novel *Saints* (first published, over my bitter protests, as *Woman of Destiny*), I needed to include an example of the fiction writing of one of my main characters, Dinah Kirkham. Since she wasn't a real person, I of course had no body of work to draw on, so I had to write, not an Orson Scott Card story, but a Dinah Kirkham story.

In that goal I failed—because, of course, it's an impossible goal. The only kind of story I can *ever* write is an Orson Scott Card story. When *Saints* came out, with "The Best Day" imbedded within it, it did not sound like anything of mine that had ever been published. But I already had my epic poem "Prentice Alvin and the No-Good Plow," which was my first attempt to bring fantasy into the American frontier; and beyond the American setting and flavor, the story is simply a fable, like "Unaccompanied Sonata" and "The Porcelain Salamander." I can't do such tales very often, because fables are devilishly hard to write—there is only one Jane Yolen in the world of fantasy, who can do it over and over. But it is one of the most satisfying kinds of tale to tell, because, finished, it makes such a tidy package. Being so complete and yet compact, it gives the author the delusion of having created something perfect, rather like a jewel-cutter, I think, who doesn't have to see the microscopic roughness of his work. But if fabulists are jewel-cutters, we have a peculiar inability: We can rarely tell, while cutting our little stones, whether we're working with a diamond, a garnet, or a zirconium.

"A PLAGUE OF BUTTERFLIES"

Few of my stories begin with visual images; this one did. I can't remember now if the idea sprang from the illustration that appeared in *Omni* magazine along with Patrice Duvic's story "The Eyes in Butterflies Wings," or whether I simply remembered my story idea when I saw that illustration. My mental image, though, was of a man awakening in the morning to find his blanket and bedsheets and the floor and walls of his room covered with butterflies, hundreds of different colors on thousands of wings, all moving in different rhythms and tempos so that his room looked like the surface of a dazzling sea. He arose and cast off his blanket, sending the room into a blur of colored flight, and began a journey with the butterflies trailing after him.

The image stayed with me for some time before I found the story to go with it. I had been toying with the science-fictional notion of creatures that consciously change their own genetic structure, and that transmuted to the idea of an alien creature that fought back against a human invasion by genetically adapting itself into a superior organism. What this had to do with the butterflies I cannot fathom, but for some reason I started trying to put the ideas together.

Had I been more sophisticated, I would have recognized the visual image as the seed of a tale in the

South American magic realism mode. It did not belong with a science fiction idea. And the beginning of the story definitely has the mythic—no, fabulous—quality of magic realism. Indeed, the whole story retains that sense of not quite connecting with reality no matter how many details are provided, so that the science fiction aspects of the story are never clearly presented, or at least are not presented *as science fiction*, so that readers don't know if what they're reading is to be taken factually or magically. Thus the science fiction is swallowed up in the fantasy.

Years later I would recover the science fiction idea and use it in my novel *Wyrms*, where it is presented with absolute clarity, yet without losing all the magic. So it is possible to look at "A Plague of Butterflies" as a study for a later work. Yet it also stands alone, my one venture into a strange kind of voice that nevertheless pleased and pleases me very much.

I knew as soon as I had written it that this story was too strange for any of my previous audiences. At that time I received a letter from Elinor Mavor, who was then performing the thankless task of editing *Amazing Stories*, trying to keep that long-mismanaged and mis-edited magazine from going under. She was paying, as I recall, one pound of dirt upon publication. But I thought it was important to help keep the magazine alive, and about the only thing a writer can do to sustain a publication is to offer stories for publication. I had sent her a couple of poems, but now I had a story that would probably find no other home. I mailed it. She bought it. Just in time, too—it was almost immediately afterward that TSR bought the magazine and George Scithers took over as editor, which meant the end of my contributions to *Amazing*. (Scithers and I have a peculiar relationship. He only likes my stories after other editors buy them.)

To my knowledge, no living human being besides Mavor and me ever read this story. It is still the strangest fantasy I ever ventured to write. If you actually read it all the way through, you have significantly increased its number of readers.

"THE MONKEYS THOUGHT 'TWAS ALL IN FUN"

Perhaps it is strange to have this clearly science fiction story in a fantasy collection, but I think it belongs here. The science fiction is only the frame, the outline of the story. Within it, the fables that the artificial habitat tells to itself are the meat of the story, and those are definitely fantasy, perfectly in line with the rest of the stories in *Monkey Sonatas*.

I first conceived the story in response to a call by Jerry Pournelle for contributions to an anthology of stories set in artificial habitats. Being perverse, I immediately determined to set my story in an artificial habitat that was, in fact, a living alien organism. I conceived of it as a hollow sphere of great size. Its shell would be composed of thousands—perhaps millions—of hollow cells, each one large enough to sustain a good-sized population of human beings in an Earthlike, self-renewing environment. The hollow interior of the creature would be a highly charged electromagnetic memory chamber that would serve as the creature's intelligence, running the entire habitat and passing energy and resources as needed from one cell to another.

The life cycle of the habitat would be the problem. Its original designers knew how to arrest its development so that it didn't ripen completely and explode, scattering seeds throughout the galaxy—unless they wanted it to. But the one that comes to the human solar system has no such controls, and so it moves as quickly as possible toward maturity, at which time each of the cells becomes a fully functioning adult with tiny minicells forming its own shell, and the hollow space humans were now using as a habitat would become the highly charged inner intelligence. The original inner intelligence dies in the process of giving independent life to all the outer cells.

The fables are the tales being told by the inner intelligence to its children. There is little sense of separate identity among the cells or between the cells and their parent. But the tales must be preserved in order to keep some sense of purpose and meaning alive in the creatures. They have long since forgotten that all these tales have to do with "human" justice and equity, or that the creature exists in order to provide homes for the makers of the place. Still, the tales survive.

I include this explanation because of the number of readers over the years who have politely asked me (actually, some have begged) to explain what in hell is going on in "The Monkeys Thought 'Twas All in Fun." I hope this helps. Those searching for thematic explanations, however, are on their own. I don't like decoding my work in that way.

To my mind, the very fact that I didn't make this story clear enough for many—perhaps most—readers makes the story a failure. I think clarity is the first thing a writer must achieve; if I fail in that, what does it matter what else I do? If I were writing this story again today, I'd spell out precisely what was going on from the beginning, so there wouldn't be the slightest confusion.

One must remember, however, that when I wrote this I was a graduate student in English. I think this explains everything.

Would you like to linger in the worlds of Orson Scott Card?

This is your invitation to join

Starways Congress
or
The Hatrack River Town Meeting

As a citizen of the future or of the magical past, you will receive quarterly newsletters, giving you a chance to get answers to questions about Card's books—and to engage in open, freewheeling conversations with him and with other readers about ideas and experiences connected with his stories.

You'll also get news about his upcoming publications and previews of his works in progress, along with notice of his occasional speeches, book signings, and visits at conventions.

Write for more information to:

Hatrack River
P.O. Box 18184
Greensboro NC 27419-8184

Coming
in Spring 1993
in hardcover

The Song
of Earth

Volume Two of
HOMECOMING

by
Orson Scott
Card

Tor Books

SF AND FANTASY FROM
ORSON SCOTT CARD

☐ 53355-0 ☐ 53356-9	ENDER'S GAME	$3.95 Canada $4.95
☐ 50086-5	THE FOLK OF THE FRINGE	$4.95 Canada $5.95
☐ 51183-2	FUTURE ON FIRE	$4.95 Canada $5.95
☐ 51190-5	FUTURE ON ICE	$4.99 Canada $5.99
☐ 53351-8 ☐ 53352-6	HART'S HOPE	$3.95 Canada $4.95
☐ 50212-4 ☐ 50213-2	PRENTICE ALVIN	$4.95 Canada $5.95
☐ 53359-3 ☐ 53360-7	RED PROPHET	$3.95 Canada $4.95
☐ 53353-4 ☐ 53354-2	SEVENTH SON	$3.95 Canada $4.95
☐ 53255-4 ☐ 53256-2	SONGMASTER	$3.95 Canada $4.95
☐ 51350-9	SPEAKER FOR THE DEAD	$4.95 Canada $5.95
☐ 50927-7	THE WORTHING SAGA	$4.95 Canada $5.95
☐ 53357-7 ☐ 53358-5	WYRMS	$3.95 Canada $4.95

Buy them at your local bookstore or use this handy coupon:
Clip and mail this page with your order.

Publishers Book and Audio Mailing Service
P.O. Box 120159, Staten Island, NY 10312-0004

Please send me the book(s) I have checked above. I am enclosing $ _____
(Please add $1.25 for the first book, and $.25 for each additional book to cover postage and handling.
Send check or money order only—no CODs.)

Name _____
Address _____
City _____, _____ State/Zip _____
Please allow six weeks for delivery. Prices subject to change without notice.